DAY OF RECKONING

a novel by

LEON DIAMOND

Strategic Book Publishing and Rights Co.

Strategic Book Publishing and Rights Co.
12620 FM 1960, Suite A4-507
Houston, TX 77065
www.sbpra.com

For information about special discounts for bulk purchases, please contact Strategic Book Publishing and Rights Co. Special Sales, at bookorder@sbpra.net.

ISBN: 978-1-63135-008-5

AUTHOR'S NOTE

"Day of Reckoning" is a tribute to Truman Khumalo and the many intrepid people who presided over the fall of apartheid.

The book is written against the background of the political climate that existed in South Africa during the years 1979–1981.

In reality Truman Khumalo spent 27 long years on the island, which deprived the country of his undoubted leadership talents.

The government were not prepared to give him up. The only option left to the forces of freedom was to plan his escape. The risk factor was very high. 'Day of Reckoning' tells the tale.

As fact and fiction intermingle, the names of individuals and organizations have had to be changed.

ACKNOWLEDGMENTS

First and foremost, I would like to thank my wife, Carol, for her enduring patience in teaching me to type and comforting me when the computer had ideas of its own.

To Vice Admiral Woody Woodburne, retired SA Navy, sadly recently deceased: The day spent with you at the Cape Town Waterfront turned me into an avowed sub-mariner. Your knowledge of submarines and its complexities is truly amazing, as was your genuine enthusiasm for the project. This contributed materially to the successful resolution of the storyline. Rest well, old friend.

To Gabriel Athiros, editor at *Cape Odyssey*: Your detailed knowledge of the Cape and its mountain climbs is unmatched.

Special thanks also to father and son, Vladimir and Andrey Chechen (Rainbow Aircraft), for their specialized knowledge of microlites. How well I remember the Chechens dragging me kicking and screaming into their newly made microlite aircraft for a short giddy flight over Springs.

I am also especially indebted to the following people, who gave so generously of their time and knowledge:

Chris Roelofse	warden, Robben Island
Tesseyman Peters	Radar and Sonar expert
Trygve Skorge	Aquila Microlite Club
Mike Blythe	Rainbow Aircraft, Springs
Colonel Gerry Broberg	SA Civil Aviation
Captain Mike Joyce	ex-SA Police Service.

It was wonderful having you all aboard.

SOUTHERN AFRICA

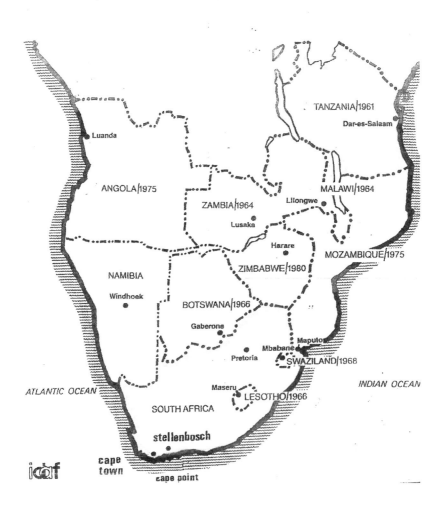

TANZANIA/1961

Dar-es-Salaam

Luanda

ANGOLA/1975

MALAWI/1964

ZAMBIA/1964

Lilongwe

Lusaka

Harare

MOZAMBIQUE/1975

ZIMBABWE/1980

NAMIBIA

Windhoek

BOTSWANA/1966

Gaberone

Maputo

Mbabane

Pretoria

SWAZILAND/1968

ATLANTIC OCEAN

INDIAN OCEAN

Maseru

LESOTHO/1966

SOUTH AFRICA

stellenbosch

idaf

cape
town

cape point

TABLE OF CONTENTS

INTRODUCTION

Situated on the southern tip of Africa, South Africa enjoys a warm and sunny climate. Its beaches compare with the best in the world. It is by far the most highly developed and richest country in Africa. The mineral reserves alone are the world's envy. In 1980, the president of the Chamber of Mines was able to report that the country was the largest producer of gold, platinum chromium, and vanadium in the world. The only strategic mineral not available in reasonable quantities was crude oil.

The sale of coal exceeded one billion rand for the first time, and the value of South Africa's total mineral reserves increased by 42 percent over the previous year to 9,768 billion rand. There was a growing demand for the country's mineral products, and South Africa was enjoying an export-led boom.

Yet all this mattered little as the dreaded policy of Apartheid tightened its sinister grip on every feature of the country's life. With each successive stroke of the legislative pen, the country lurched from crisis to crisis, seemingly being drawn deeper and deeper into the political quagmire. What began as an honest experiment in social engineering, referred to as "separate development" or Apartheid, dually escalated out of control and became identified by the rest of the world with White domination, repressive race laws, and the denial of human rights on a large scale.

Some would say the seeds of Apartheid began soon after the Dutch stepped ashore in 1652.

Prior to 1910, a number of vocal but largely ineffectual Black associations existed in South Africa. These combined in 1912 to form one unit—the United African Congress (UAC).

Millions of Blacks were uprooted and forced to live in rural slums.

On March 21, 1960, in the township of Sharpeville, in the Transvaal, stones were thrown at the police, who retaliated. In the ensuing melee, sixty-seven Blacks were killed, and 200 were wounded. It was bloodshed; the massacre was international news. Before the shootings, South Africa, in spite of its racial policies and widespread condemnation, was still an accepted member of the international community. After 1961, it slid slowly into isolation. Black leaders now realized that non-violent tactics were not enough. By 1961, the UAC had changed tactics—it had gone underground.

The government declared a state of emergency immediately after the Sharpeville Massacre, outlawing the UAC and other Black organizations. Many Black leaders went into exile. A few, like Truman Khumalo, remained to carry on a different kind of struggle. He was smuggled out of the country to study revolutionary tactics and to raise finances for the "struggle." For decades, the disenfranchised majority had tried to resolve the central issues by peaceful means, and gained only oppression. However, in June 1961, on Khumalo's initiative, it decided on a policy of violent subversion and, to this end, formed a military wing.

The government responded in June 1962 by introducing the Sabotage Act, and hundreds of suspected subversives were placed under house arrest. Khumalo, now a legend, returned to go underground. His ability to elude the police embarrassed the government. He took elaborate precautions by frequently changing disguises and using various alibis. He had truly become a creature of the night.

On August 5, 1962, Truman Khumalo, or "the Black Pimpernel" as he was dubbed by the press, was on his way from Durban to Johannesburg to see his family. At the small town of Howick near Pietermaritzburg, he was cornered by three cars and ordered to stop. The police had known precisely where to set up the roadblock that ensnared him. He realized that his eighteen months on the run were over. A tall, slender man with a stern expression, came over to him, introduced himself as a police office, and produced a warrant of arrest. It was obvious from the police officer's dishevelled appearance that he and his men had been lying in wait for him for several days. Someone had tipped off the police about Khumalo's whereabouts, and it was painfully obvious that the *Movement* had been infiltrated. The case made headline news in the press.

The so-called Black Pimpernel was no more. The government was taking no chances. On the outskirts of Johannesburg they were met by a sizeable police escort. Khumalo was handcuffed and spent the night in jail. The next day he appeared in court where he was formally remanded.

From the Court, Khumalo was taken to Johannesburg Fort where he was placed in an area with impregnable walls. Access to the inside could only be gained through four massive locked gates. Khumalo only spent a few days in the fort before being transferred to Pretoria, where he was found guilty of the relatively mild crime of "inciting people to strike" and "leaving the country without a passport." He was sentenced to five years in prison.

On the afternoon of July 11, 1963, a dry cleaner's van entered the driveway of Lillieslief Farm on the outskirts of Johannesburg—the headquarters of the UAC. No one at Lillieslief Farm was expecting a delivery. The vehicle was stopped

by a young African guard who became overwhelmed when dozens of armed policemen and several police dogs sprang from the vehicle. The police searched the entire farm and confiscated hundreds of highly incriminating documents and papers. In one swell swoop, the police had captured the entire "high command." The raid was a major coup for the regime. On the first day in court, the accused were brought before a magistrate on a charge of treason. He fought against racial discrimination and supported a free society. Courageous words indeed, but for the time being, the liberal movement had been shattered. The case lasted nine months, and the accused were all sentenced to life imprisonment.

Robben Island. Early July 1964

From Pretoria prison, they were taken to a small military airport, where a Dakota transport plane, which had seen better days, flew them to Cape Town. They landed on an airstrip on one side of the island. Robben Island, situated in Table Bay off the coast of Cape Town, is the South African equivalent of Alcatraz. It is the state's maximum-security prison, and no ships are allowed within 1.6 kilometres of its coast. Escape was considered impossible. The island has a checkered history, being at one time a leper colony, a lunatic asylum, and a naval base before becoming a maximum-security prison. From a distance, it looks green and beautiful, more like a resort than a prison.

On the fourth morning there, they were handcuffed and taken to a prison within a prison. This new structure was a one-story, rectangular, stone fortress forming a courtyard. It had cells on three sides and on the fourth side was a six-metre high wall with a catwalk patrolled by guards and vicious dogs. Each cell had one small window covered with iron bars. The general prison contained about 750 common-law prisoners. In a few days, more prominent activists would arrive, and they would eventually become a core group of about twenty of the most wanted political prisoners. As befits a top-security prison, there were as many guards as prisoners. There were no Black wardens and no White prisoners. It was a world of its own. By 1996, Apartheid was in full cry. So was the counter-revolutionary movement. It is against this background that this novel is written.

CHAPTER 1

REFLECTIONS

February 11, 2008. 9:00 a.m.

The Dining Room of the House of Parliament, Cape Town.

"Mr. Khumalo, thank you, sir, for granting me and my newspaper the privilege of interviewing you on this special day, the twenty-eighth anniversary of your escape from Robben Island. I believe the house has invited you to lunch to mark the occasion."

"Yes, and to make it even more special, they have made this day a public holiday for all time to come. Isn't that something? I also thought it a nice touch to name it 'The Day of Reckoning' in reference to a speech I made way back in 1954, when I was 36 years old. Let me see if I can still recall it," Khumalo said sinking back into his chair, and he rattled off the speech without fault.

"Good heavens, sir, what a remarkable memory you have."

"I may be in my nineties, but I can recall events as if they were yesterday. In the last few years, we have made great strides in developing our young democracy, but the year of my escape, 1980, were indeed dark days for our country."

"Wasn't it risky mounting an escape for you, sir?" asked the reporter timorously, in awe of his subject's undoubted reputation.

"I was only ten years old at the time, but from what I can recall, Robben Island was an impregnable fortress."

"It certainly was. The escape had to be meticulously planned and executed," replied the elder statesman, warming up to his task. "Members of the task force had to be carefully assembled and screened, as the regime had infiltrated many of our cells. It was a brilliant idea to conscript a person from Stellenbosch University onto the task force, since at the time, the university was staunchly loyal to the government, and no one would suspect a Stellenbosch University student of acts against the state."

"You could have been killed, sir."

"Yes, it was touch and go at times, but the situation in the country was deteriorating rapidly. People were being hauled in for almost nothing to be tried under the most vicious of acts, the Terrorism Act. Township life was becoming unbearable. The UAC obviously felt that risks had to be taken."

"I would be fascinated to learn more about the escape from you personally, sir, especially as we have a new generation of readers who would be intrigued by your story," the reporter reflected.

There was a pause while the nonagenarian collected his thoughts.

"Well, we have a few hours before lunch. Let me see what I can recall. The story really began in Stellenbosch on a sunny morning in 1979 . . ."

CHAPTER 2

STELLENBOSCH, SOUTH AFRICA

Saturday, May 5, 1979

It was a glorious day in the Western Cape. Yet there was a bite in the air, signalling the early onset of winter. The abundant flora took on an altogether greyer look, and the mighty oaks had begun to shed their leaves. The mountains framed the town in a seemingly continuous backdrop, providing a comforting sense of enclosure.

Colder days were on the way. Stellenbosch, the second oldest European settlement in the country, is one of its most picturesque. Being the centre of the wine industry, it boasts a multitude of wine estates and cellars. The vineyards are invariably heavy with fruit.

Its unique Cape Dutch architecture is characterized by thick, white-washed walls, thatched roofs, and elegant gables. After the Great Fire of 1875, the thatch roof—so suitable to the climate and so pleasant to the eye—had all but vanished. The remnants of this wonderful heritage of Cape Dutch architecture now sit quite happily with splendid examples of Victorian and Georgian architecture.

There are at least eighty state-declared monuments in the town, making it the best preserved *locus* in the country. Huge, spreading oak trees planted centuries ago line the streets, and the city fathers have been zealous in maintaining the relaxed atmosphere of this quaint, little university town.

This laid-back atmosphere contrasts sharply with the frenetic atmosphere of Cape Town, the mother city, a forty-minute drive to the west. The town is predominantly Afrikaans-speaking, as is the medium of instruction at the university. The local university is an icon of the Afrikaner establishment, having produced no fewer than six presidents or prime ministers.

The fairways at the Stellenbosch Golf Course glistened in the early morning dew. Philip Watermeyer and his friend, Jannie De Beer, had become firm friends ever since they met at university and were allocated adjacent rooms at Res house. Although they held opposing views and philosophies on just about every topic, they had agreed to differ in the interests of their special friendship.

"How far to the green?" enquired Jannie, who played off a handy seven handicap.

"About 160 metres," replied Philip.

Taking a six-iron from his bag, Jannie sent the ball unerringly into the heart of the green. Philip's shot was less successful.

"If you'd remember to keep your left arm straight, you wouldn't duff so many shots," observed Jannie, going through the motions for the umpteenth time.

Philip was preoccupied. "Did you see the news on TV last night?" he inquired, his brow creased with concern.

"No, I did not," replied Jannie dismissively. "Actually, I find the news boring. Anyway, what was the main story?"

"There was another clash between the police and Blacks in the township of Diepkloof yesterday," said Philip. "Fifteen Blacks were killed, and twenty-five were injured. It appears from the pictures that the Black community was unarmed, and the cops were actually using live ammunition. What sort of image of our country do you think this will portray overseas?"

"You know, Philip," countered Jannie, "you are always seeing things from a blinkered point of view. Apartheid gives everyone a fair chance. The Blacks are quite happy with their lot. There are good jobs to be had. Just look at other countries in African-poverty. Wars and civil commotion are the order of the day. Here in the southern tip of Africa, we live in relative peace and tranquillity. So, we have the occasional clash. I think we can live with that."

"You overlook one thing," said Philip, pressing home the point. "Apartheid regulates every aspect of a Black person's life— where they can live, where they can work, who they can marry, and even with whom they can have sex. Twenty-five million people out of a total population of thirty million are totally disfranchised. How much longer will they put up with this state of affairs?"

"Really, Philip," replied Jannie, "you are beginning to sound more and more like a communist every day. What has got into you? My father says 'thank God we have a strong government who can put the Black troublemakers in their place.' Besides, if you give them the vote, we'll be swamped, and what'll happen to our cherished culture and standard of living? If things get really hot here, the English can always go back to England, the Dutch to Holland, and the Germans to Germany. We Afrikaners have nowhere to go. We are here to stay."

They had reached the par-3 short hole.

"I think I'll take another six-iron," Jannie said, reaching for his club.

The game continued and the conversation gave way to lighter topics.

The above discussion encapsulated the great debate in South African politics at the time. You were either for government policy or against it; there was no middle road.

CHAPTER 3

THE EARLY DAYS

Philip Watermeyer was born to Hendrik and Hendrina Watermeyer on a farm in the North West Province. The farm, "Goede Hoop" (Good Hope), was situated a few kilometres south of the town of Vryburg, on the main road to Kimberley. Vryburg derived its name from the *Free Settlers* who received 416 farms of 100 hectares each for services rendered to the Tswane Chiefs. Vryburg is cattle-breeding country, well-known for its hot, dry climate.

The town has a colourful history. In the nineteenth century, it was rumoured to be the haunt of Scotty Smith, the notorious, illicit diamond buyer, horse rustler, and gun-runner.

The homestead could be seen from the main road and was designed in a vernacular typical of the time. All the floors were of wooden boards, as was the ceiling. The furniture was that of a bygone era, later to become prized antiques. The lamps resembled gas lights, but were not gas, as they were fortunate in being able to tap into the passing national-electric grid.

It had a corrugated, iron roof painted bright blue and a spacious veranda encircling three sides of the house, which kept it cool even during the sweltering heat of summer. Often on hot nights, the family would dine on the veranda and gaze out into the flat, semi-barren veld, which seemed to stretch forever.

Existence in arid Vryburg had been a struggle with life-giving water in short supply. To conserve water, all rainwater running off the steep roofs was collected in gutters and deposited into two, large, corrugated iron-tanks, each controlled by a tap at its base. In addition, a nice sized dam had been built and later extended, which was to serve them well during the long, dry months of summer.

Philip had been taught the rudiments of mechanics by his father, so he could repair the tractor when it broke down, which was quite often. From this, he had developed a passion for things mechanical.

His parents were poor, but religious, and they had imbued him with a strong feeling of fair-play and the necessity to show respect and tolerance for others. This legacy was to influence his life in ways he couldn't then imagine. All meals began with a prayer of thanksgiving, as, being religious, they firmly believed that the Lord would provide.

Being semi-isolated on the farm had its advantages. As with so many rural families, luxuries were few and far between, but Philip, nevertheless, had a happy upbringing. His untroubled upbringing, however, was shattered by one notable event: His bachelor uncle had been caught by the police in a compromising position with a coloured person, and Philip had been incessantly teased by his school mates, which left an indelible scar on his young mind that would not easily heal.

The Prohibition of Mixed Marriages Act of 1949 had made it illegal for Whites to marry Blacks, and The Immorality Act of 1950 widened the racial definition of immorality by declaring sex across the colour line strictly illegal.

To enforce the act, police raided homes and broke into bedrooms to photograph couples breaking the law. Such was the stigma attached to having sex with coloured people that the shame of being caught under this act was unimaginable, not only for the culprit himself, but also for his family. The newspapers played their nefarious part, too, by publishing incidents under the act. It was, unfortunately, newsworthy!

Philip was expected to help out on the farm during his out-of-school hours. This exercise had given him a firm, fit body and his face was continuously bronzed. His close friend during his school days was Simon Radebe, the son of his father's Black foreman. He had grown up with Simon and in an odd kind of way, he was the brother Philip never had.

Although Simon attended the farm school and Philip the nearby Vryburg High School, a great deal of their spare time was spent doing all the carefree things that boys do when not helping out with chores.

The dam was stocked with bass. One of Philip's favourite pastimes was to go with Simon to the dam with their homemade fishing rods and catch a fish or two. They would then take their catch back to the homestead, where Philip's mother would cook it for them. The catch would then be their supper, which would somehow have a special taste, as it was their fish.

Mindful of the impoverished conditions of his father's employees, Philip used to collect tid-bits from the dining room table, wrap them in a paper serviette, and take them to Simon's shack, about a kilometre from the main homestead, down the dust road. As he was an only child and one year older than Simon, Philip would pass down his clothes to him, when had positively outgrown them.

Attending school in nearby Vryburg meant a daily two-kilometre trudge for Philip, usually in the scorching sun. A large straw hat, which covered his sleek black hair, and a good pair of running shoes were his constant companions. Often he would jog all the way to school and back, and this exercise kept him super fit.

The Vryburg High School was a large co-educational school for about 1,150 pupils, with boys slightly in the majority. The layout and design came straight out of the department of public works manual for co-ed schools of this size. At the entrance, two rusty flagpoles proudly supported the South African and school flags and bolted to the lower end of the poles, was a board indicating the school's name.

This was a "Whites only" school in terms of government policy and, like many rural schools at the time, it was no model of racial tolerance.

Once when Philip was about to enter the grounds, he observed a fracas. Three of his school mates, each about fifteen years old, were punching a young Black boy, who was lying prone on the ground offering no resistance. The Black boy was wearing a jacket, a torn shirt, and was barefoot.

Resentment welled up in Philip, and, against his better judgement, he rushed in to intervene.

"What is going on here?" he shouted.

"Well, we caught this blighter wearing our school blazer," said the taller of the boys irately. We cannot allow that. He probably stole it."

Turning to the boy on the ground, who was bleeding from cuts, Philip enquired how he had acquired the jacket. He responded that his mother's employer in town had given it to her, as it was very old and they had no further use for it.

The boy's answer had the ring of truth about it. It did not occur to the assailants that this was probably the only jacket the poor boy owned.

The boys were adamant that he was not entitled to wear the school blazer.

Philip, with a wisdom beyond his years, ordered the prostrate figure to hand the jacket over and promised that if he would rendezvous with him at the same time and place the next day, he would replace it with one of his own. The following day he kept his promise, but the incident left a bitter taste in his mouth.

The prospect of attending a university would have been bleak had he not been fortunate in obtaining a bursary from Stellenbosch University and a rather generous loan from his uncle in Vryburg. In addition, being a good swimmer, he had decided to spend a year as a swimming instructor before entering university. He had wisely saved the income.

His friend Jannie had had a completely different up-bringing.

The De Beers lived in one of Bloemfontein's finer suburbs in a more than comfortable seven-room house, including two maids' rooms, as well as outbuildings containing three garages.

Born to Pieter and Sannie De Beer some twenty years before, it was ordained that he would follow his father's footsteps into law, like his father's father before him. Pieter De Beer happened to be the senior partner in the prestigious Bloemfontein law practice of De Beer, Louw, and Hanekom. It was a given that Jannie would, on graduation, enter the family law practice. His future had long been mapped out for him.

As a youngster at Grey College, one of the country's best schools, Jannie had excelled at sport. Of medium height and blessed with a strong, stocky build, he was the apple of his father's eye. His father never missed a rugby match in which he was playing, even if this meant having to slip out of the office mid-week. Jannie had two sisters who were equally good at sport, but it was he who enjoyed the limelight.

Although a perfectly good university existed in Bloemfontein, Jannie was destined for Stellenbosch University, a trend set by previous generations of De Beers. When the time came to enter university, his father travelled down to Stellenbosch with him to help him settle in. He had bought him a serviceable, second-hand Volkswagen Beetle. The car, in a vivid yellow colour, became quite a landmark around the campus.

CHAPTER 4

UNIVERSITY DAYS

At university, Philip was conscious of the privileged position in which he found himself. The university was steeped in history and tradition. He had decided to enroll for a mechanical engineering course and realized he would have to concentrate on his studies to the exclusion of most other social and extramural activities. It was imperative that he use his money sparingly. There would be plenty of time for socializing once he had obtained his degree.

He would confine his activities to the debating society, a religious study group, and swimming. He had always taken a keen interest in religion and thought, rather naively, that the Debating Society might give him a forum for his views, which arguably were atypical of the prevailing attitudes. In private discussions with fellow students, he often found himself subconsciously in the role of devil's advocate, championing the rights of the under-privileged and down-trodden Black community.

For this and other reasons, he had begun to make a name for himself as something of a liberal. In South Africa, the word liberal held sinister connotations, even to the point of being equated with communism—and South Africans were fiercely anti-communistic. How he would react to this challenge was still uncertain.

By contrast, Jannie had a pleasant, outgoing personality which made him instantly popular with his fellows and members of the opposite sex. He revelled in the exciting inter-action and experiences of campus life. His political outlook was to the far right.

Philip was fortunate in that his friendship with Jannie had raised his acceptability level. One of his indulgencies (if one can call it that) was an occasional game of golf at student rates, using an odd collection of clubs given to him by his uncle. Jannie had taught him the rudiments of the game, which he had not quite mastered. He tried his hand at rugby, but it was not his cup of tea. He did not fit the profile of a typical Stellenbosch University student.

To supplement his income, Philip had obtained a part-time job as a waiter at the local Golden Fig Restaurant on Bird Street. The restaurant had an attractive Victorian facade painted in a distinctive green colour, which contrasted with the delicate white, wrought-iron work bolted between the columns.

Internally, floors and walls were in a rich terracotta colour, which contrasted with the white table cloths and serviettes. *Objet d'art* hung from the ceiling creating a cosy old-world atmosphere. The restaurant was popular with the townsfolk, and while the waiter's pay was modest, the tips more than made up for this. Philip was fortunate that the restaurant was only a twenty-five minute walk from Res House on campus, as he had no transport.

At the restaurant, Philip made the acquaintance of an Indian waiter, Faizil Khan, who lived with his parents on the outskirts of Cape Town in the suburb of Rylands Estate. The estate was reserved exclusively for Indians under Apartheid's Group Areas Act. Faizil commuted the thirty-minute distance to Stellenbosch every day in his beat-up Toyota. The car was kept on the road with spit and polish, and when a mechanical break-down occurred, there were innumerable little back-street garages one could take it to for temporary repairs, which would keep it going again for a couple of months. He needed the job at the Golden Fig, as good jobs for Indians were hard to obtain.

Philip's upbringing had allowed him to mix more freely with other racial groups than was the case with other boys who had grown up under the government's strict separation laws.

CHAPTER 5

THE DEBATE AND THE INTER-VARSITY

May 11, 1979. The Debate

One evening after returning to the residence halls, Philip found a note under his door. It said tersely that he had been chosen to be one of the main speakers at the next meeting of the university debating society to be held on Friday, May 18, 1979. This did not surprise him, as he was an enrolled member of the debating society. What did surprise him was the topic chosen: "Should the church support Apartheid?" This was a touchy subject. Anything to do with the church in South Africa was touchy.

He would be opposing the church's support of Apartheid, and a fellow student, Ernie De Vos from the law faculty, would represent the other side. He was quite excited, as this would afford him the opportunity of espousing his views in public, which he had so often and fearlessly done in private. Although he realized that his viewpoints might not be popular at a conservative university, it was only a debate and a feather in his cap to have been chosen to be one of the main speakers.

He decided to wait up for Jannie to tell him the news. At about 1:00 a.m., there was a slight commotion in the corridor, followed by a jangling of keys in the door. Jannie had returned home from a night of socialising.

"Jannie," Philip said excitedly, "guess what? I have been chosen to be one of the main speakers at next month's meeting of the debating society to which the public is invited."

Jannie congratulated him and said he too had good news. He had been selected to play fly-half for the First XV, in the forthcoming inter-varsity rugby match.

May 18, 1979

The university debating society had purposely chosen Friday, May 18, as the date for their next meeting. This was the night before the annual inter-varsity rugby clash between the two rival Western Cape universities: Stellenbosch and the University of Cape Town.

With so many visitors in town for the rugby match, they were assured of a good turn-out. The debate would be open to the public and posters advertising it had been affixed to hundreds of trees around the town. The society had shrewdly chosen a controversial topic, guaranteed to ensure a lively debate.

Philip was on tenterhooks all day. He would certainly be in the limelight. He mentally rehearsed his arguments over and over. He was always a nervous starter. Supposing there were newspaper reporters present, he decided to play it safe and dress formally.

At exactly 8:00 p.m., the chairman rose to welcome the large audience present and to introduce the topic and speakers. He said this was the biggest debating-society turn-out he could ever recall, due, no doubt, to the public interest in the special subject matter. He announced that each speaker would address the audience, which would be followed by audience participation.

He then introduced the two speakers and said that Ernie De Vos, a third-year law student, would speak in favour of the church's support of Apartheid, and Philip Watermeyer, a first-year engineering student, would oppose the motion. He called on Ernie to open the debate.

In the ensuing debate, both Ernie and Philip gave good accounts of themselves, having spoken from inner conviction. The debate drew passionate responses from the floor, and the speakers faced some tricky questions.

At 10:30 p.m., the chairman rose to close the meeting. He said the standard of debate had been very high, and it had been a stimulating evening. He tactfully declared the debate a draw, which evoked large heckling from a large segment of the audience. The topic had invoked such interest, that even after the meeting had officially closed, both Ernie and Philip were still engaged in conversation with little groups in the audience.

May 21, 1979

On the Monday after the debate, Philip was approached by many students on campus, a few praising him for his courageous stand, others berating him for so stoutly defending unreasonable black aspirations. Some even said that he had won.

Anything to do with the church always elicited strong feelings. However, he had noticed a change. Where previously he had walked about the campus largely unnoticed, suddenly he had come out of the shadows. He had even achieved a certain notoriety, however temporary.

On the way to the first lecture of the day, he was approached by a theology student who handed him an envelope. Before opening it, he noticed an inscription at the back of the envelope which read FROM THE DEAN OF THE FACULTY OF THEOLOGY. *What would the dean of the faculty of theology be writing to me about?* he wondered.

Feverishly he opened the envelope, which said tersely that the dean wanted to see him at his office at 1:15 p.m. that day. He was on time, knocked on the door, and a strong voice from inside bade him enter.

Professor Johan Bekker was a tall, bespectacled man, with hunched shoulders. He was well-liked by the students.

"Please sit down, Philip," said the professor. Philip sat down expectantly. "Are you enjoying your course?"

"Very much so," replied Philip, waiting for the professor to get to the nub of the matter.

"Well," said the professor, "I wanted to talk to you about last Friday's debate."

Oh, oh, thought Philip, *perhaps I overstepped the mark.*

"You know I was in the audience."

"Yes, I caught a glimpse of you, sir."

"Well," said the professor, "you may not be aware of this, but I was approached by the debating society to nominate two speakers for the evening. You were not my first choice for the church's opposition to Apartheid. My first two nominations turned me down, as they considered the subject to be too contentious. You were actually my third choice. However, I was pleased you accepted.

"Many people have the misconception that our university is inflexible in its views. This is not exactly true. Although most of us consider Apartheid to be a fair policy, we like to air all viewpoints, as the recent debate confirms. And in this connection, it was a good move to open it to the public, especially as our liberal counterparts from the University of Cape Town would be present.

"I, for one, am all in favour of fresh thinking and new initiatives. In fact, I have noticed that many young Afrikaner students are starting to wrestle with some of the fundamental issues affecting

South African society and showing a real concern for improved race relations. Congratulations, I thought you gave a good account of yourself the other night." He handed Philip his hand.

On his way out, Philip thought, *So I wasn't the dean's first choice speaker, but he actually congratulated me.* Perhaps the university was not as monolithic as he had imagined. There was evidence of fresh thinking. He felt a renewed sense of hope.

May 19, 1979. Office of the South African Communist Party.

First Operative: "Well, comrade, what did you think of Watermeyer's performance last night?"

Second Operative: "I felt he gave a good account of himself, but remember, it was only a debate."

First Operative: "Our contacts on the campus have informed us that he has strong anti-apartheid views, and he took his uncle's humiliation under the Immorality Act very badly last year."

Second Operative: "He may be just the man our partners in the UAC are looking for, but we have to be sure. I believe he moonlights at night at The Golden Fig on Bird Street. By some stroke of luck, Faizil Khan works there and is a member of Arthur Norman's group. If there is something phony about Watermeyer, Faizil will find out. He is a shrewd judge of character."

First Operative: "Well, then, our next step is to contact Faizil Khan and get him to file a report on Watermeyer directly to Comrade Arthur Norman."

May 19, 1979. The Inter-Varsity.

Geographically, they may have been seventy kilometres apart, but politically they were light years away. The English-speaking

University of Cape Town (UCT) nestled on the slopes of Table Mountain, was dedicated to the establishment of a non-racial university, although it must be said that, while the Students Representative Council of Cape Town insisted on student facilities being open to all racial groups, it did not always have the support of its own university council. Their arch rivals at Stellenbosch steadfastly toed the government's racial separation line.

The climax of the day was the annual clash of the First XV Rugby teams. This year it was Stellenbosch's turn to host the event, and the University of Cape Town supporters descended on Stellenbosch in droves. They came in cars, trucks, and even bikes. It was always a festive occasion with flags, ribbons, and even some bodies hanging out of the windows. For one day, at least, the calm and tranquillity of this peaceful little town was shattered.

In the history of the event, Stellenbosch had won thirty times, Cape Town twenty times, and there had been nine draws. This was to be the sixtieth official inter-varsity rugby match.

The previous year at Newlands, Cape Town, only a late try by the visitors enabled Stellenbosch to scrape home by 15-13 in a thriller. Jannie had been the regular second XV fly-half all season. Due to an injury to the regular first XV fly-half, he had been called up to take his place. His proudest moment was donning the famous first XV maroon jersey and running onto the field to the cheers of the 17,520-capacity crowd.

It was a typical abrasive game with no quarter asked or given. With a dominant pack of forwards, Stellenbosch eventually ran out winners by 20-6. Jannie felt he had performed adequately. After the game, the restaurants and pubs did a roaring trade.

CHAPTER 6

FIRST CONTACTS

July 26, 1979

One evening after the Golden Fig had closed, Faizil got into a casual conversation with Philip. Little did Philip realize where this meeting would lead and the fateful consequences which would engulf both of them. The odd passerby looked askance at these two in animated conversation but strolled on.

"So, tell me about your background," asked Faizil. "I have often seen you serving in the restaurant, but know so little about you. Where do you come from, what course are you embarked on at university, and do you have any brothers and sisters?" The questions seemed to tumble out. Conversation came easy, and it was clear that a rapport was developing between the two.

They parted in the early hours of the morning.

The following morning, July 27, 1979, the *Cape Times* screamed moral support to defy race laws. Helen Suzman, chief opposition spokesman for law and order, said she gave church leaders her wholehearted support.

A few days passed, and in a spare moment in the restaurant, Faizil asked Philip if he had seen anything of the famous wine lands that surrounded Stellenbosch. Philip responded that, through lack of transport, he had not seen much.

"If you are free on Saturday," said Faizil enthusiastically, "perhaps we can go for a spin in my car, and I will show you around. After all, I grew up around here."

Philip accepted and arrangements were duly made.

The wine lands are some of the finest in the world. Estates, such as Spier, Delheim, Simonsig, Neetlingshof, and others, have achieved world-wide recognition for their distinctive blends of wine. The area surrounding the town is intensely cultivated with some vineyards extending well up the gentle slopes of the surrounding Pappagaaiberg (Parrot Mountain). To many, this is the red-wine producing area of South Africa, and yet, many of its white wines, such as bubblies and fortifieds, also featured in the South African premier league.

For a while there was silence, as the two new friends took in the visual beauty and ageless grace of the surrounding countryside. Being July, the vines had already lost their leaves.

Philip was the first to speak. He had something on his mind, which had to come out. "I see in this morning's *Cape Times* that they can now detain people without trial," he said concernedly. "And to ban organizations just because they don't toe the government line is a travesty of justice. Helen Suzman, chief opposition spokeswoman, was right when she said that the bill was a major assault on people's liberties. I can't understand why people are generally so complacent?"

Faizil remained silent for a while, waiting for the right moment to play his cards. Then he responded. "Yes, I'm afraid things are going from bad to worse. Every year new laws are introduced that further restrict the movement of people of colour. The situation is like a pressure cooker—the lid must surely come off."

"We have all grown up with it," Philip said, "but it has become completely out of hand." He recalled the embarrassing incident with his uncle under the Immorality Act. "I wish I could play a more positive role in opposing Apartheid," he said, "but one feels so helpless. It is almost as if the security forces must report something to their masters to justify their employment."

Faizil did not answer, but he was becoming more and more convinced of Philip's sincerity and commitment to the cause. Besides, he had implicit faith in his own judgement, which had never let him down before. *Yes*, he thought, *Philip can be trusted.*

A week or two passed. Philip was studying one afternoon when he received a message to phone Faizil. There was a public phone off one of the lobbies at Res. He dialed. Faizil answered.

"You phoned me?" Philip asked.

"Yes," answered Faizil. "My parents would like you to do us the honour of coming to dinner on a night when we are both off duty. I will fetch you," he said. "You can spend the night at my place, and I will drive you back the next day. Will you come?"

"Yes," Philip said. "I would be glad to. I am free on Thursday evening."

"Thursday will be fine," countered Faizil. "Then it's settled. I will pick you up on the street outside Res at 5:30 p.m. on Thursday."

They drove out of town on the 310 and took a right onto the National Road, west to Cape Town. They had left the wine lands behind with its softly undulating hills and the topography suddenly flattened. A sidewise view of majestic Table Mountain in the distance came into view and gradually grew larger. Soon they turned off to Rylands Estate, the suburb where Faizil lived with his parents.

Turning on to his street, they passed rows of neat little houses on under-sized stands, with the occasional luxury home built on a double stand. Likewise, the mode of transport varied from modest cars to luxury vehicles, indicative of an area where rich and poor are required to live, cheek-by-jowl, in terms of the Group Areas Act.

Faizil parked his car in the driveway, as they had only one garage. His parents had been planning to build a carport for Faizil's car for some time, but had never got around to it. The boys were met at the door by Faizil's father, Riz Khan, a dapper little man in his early sixties, who sported a grey, goatee beard.

Riz Khan welcomed Philip effusively. Soon Faizil's mom, Zakkiya, appeared fresh out of the kitchen still wearing her apron and, with a big smile on her face, said, "You are most welcome," and disappeared back into the kitchen to add the final touches to the evening meal.

Philip and Faizil were ushered into the living room, which tradition has it should face the street, as it was a pastime to observe the comings and goings of people outside.

"What would you like to drink?" inquired Rjz Kahn. "We don't drink ourselves, but always keep a supply of whiskey and brandy in our cupboard for visitors."

Philip settled for a coke. Soon dinner was ready. Piping hot curry was served, as only the Indian community know how, complete with sambals and condiments. Philip was thankful there was a jug of iced water on the table.

Dinner completed, Riz Kahn suggested they retire to the living room.

"So, Philip, Faizil tells me that you are studying mechanical engineering at university," remarked the senior Khan, his deep voice resonating around the room.

"Yes," answered Philip. "Actually, I am in my first year of a four-year course."

"Will you be going back to Vryburg to settle, once you have your degree?" he asked.

"No," answered Philip. "Vryburg is a very small town. I intend to seek a position in Cape Town as I am quite familiar with the city, and opportunities are available there.

As the evening wore on, the conversation became more spontaneous, with the dialogue being dominated by Philip and Riz Khan. At times Philip got the distinct impression he was being interrogated, but instantly dismissed the idea.

At about 10:00 p.m., Zakkiya served tea and more sweetmeats, after which she retired, leaving the men with their *small talk*, as she put it. Suddenly at about 10:30 p.m., Khan senior became more serious, and the conversation veered toward politics, as it often does.

"Did you see they have now passed the internal security bill?" Riz Khan asked excitedly. "Now they have the right to ban any organization. Soon we will have no civil liberties at all."

Philip agreed saying that the present system could no longer be sustained. Although his views were expressed in a less forceful manner, he had nevertheless made it clear where his sympathies lie.

Faizil remained silent during the political part of the discussion. He was, however, studying every nuance and utterance delivered by his new friend for signs of any betrayal.

Later in bed, Riz Khan turned to Zakkiya and said, "I like that boy. I think we can trust him."

The following morning, Zakkiya served breakfast on the veranda at the back of the house, after which Faizil drove Philip back to Stellenbosch.

CHAPTER 7

UNDER SURVEILLANCE

August 31, 1979

It was about 5:45 p.m. a week later, when Philip was walking to the Golden Fig for his evening stint. The streets were comparatively quiet, yet he had the distinct impression of being followed. He looked around—there was nothing out there, neither human nor animal. A branch on a tree stirred in the wind. Nothing else!

He instinctively raised his collar as if to shield himself, stood up straight, and walked on. *Only the wind*, he told himself, but why was he feeling so jumpy? The restaurant was particularly busy that evening, and any feelings of unease he had earlier felt were soon forgotten. In any case, it had been a particularly good night for tips.

Some time later

It must have been 4:00 p.m. when Philip donned his running shoes and vest for his customary jog. He asked Jannie to join him, but he declined, so he set off on his own, which didn't exactly displease him. He was not unhappy in his own company. He had a well-known route he traversed many times.

It began by covering a few blocks which took him out of town, then up a gentle slope, followed by a steeper slope that ended in a plantation where the forests grew thicker. This was his turning point, some five kilometres out of town. He had just entered the tall plantation with its eerie shafts of light and dark, when he became aware of a sound: a faint crackling not his own. It sounded very much like footsteps crunching onto beds of dry leaves. He knew there were no animals in this part of the woods. He lessened his stride so as to cut out his own noise. He carried on for a few more paces.

There it was again! Was he being stalked?

He stopped abruptly. Turning to the source of the sound, he peered into the darkness. The branches took on more ominous shapes. He was alone, and a feeling of alarm gripped him. He imagined he heard deep breathing. Was that a figure? It was too dark to see clearly. Instinctively he called out, "Anyone there?" No one answered. He knew it was a stupid thing to say. Fresh beads of perspiration began to form on his forehead. He thought he had better get the hell out of there. He turned and ran. First he trotted, then sprinted, and only stopped once he had reached the safety of town.

Looking around for the first time, everything looked so peaceful. *What was that all about?* he wondered. Then he remembered a similar feeling of foreboding the night he had walked to the restaurant. Strange. He had always felt so safe.

CHAPTER 8

FURTHER CONTACT

October 8, 1979

It was a particularly busy evening at the Golden Fig. To attract patrons at what was normally the quietest night of the week, management had decided to sell pizzas at half price on Monday nights. A large banner on the veranda outside proclaimed this fact. Many students took advantage of this bonanza, particularly as the larger pizzas could be cut in half and shared by two people. Philip found himself on the move all night and was light-heartedly ragged by some of his classmates who had turned up.

At about 9:00 p.m., a group of Black American tourists arrived. They had come for a meal and were turned away by management, with the comment that the restaurant was reserved for whites only. An embarrassing scene ensued, as visiting Black groups from overseas were laughably given honorary white status while in South Africa.

Philip felt his stomach churn. When was this nightmare going to end? He felt himself sharing in their shame. *Honorary status*, Philip thought, *what rubbish*. After the restaurant had closed for the evening, Faizil and Philip once again engaged in casual conversation, this time in Faizil's car.

"When we were driving around the wine lands the other day, you remarked that you wished you could do more to fight the yoke of Apartheid. Did you mean that?" asked Faizil.

"Yes, absolutely."

"Well, could you come to our house for a light lunch on Sunday?" asked Faizil. "Some interesting people will be there, and I would like you to meet them."

Philip agreed and arrangements were duly made.

On the road to Rylands Estate, he wondered if this was not to be a determining factor in his life. He had chosen a course from which there may be no retreat.

The UAC military machine was broken into cells, which, of necessity, were situated in black areas, because of the group-areas act. Each cell was responsible for terrorist activity within a designated area. Recruits to the *cause* from any race group were welcomed, but were extensively scrutinized before acceptance. Since the Liliesleaf episode, they were only too aware of the threat posed by government infiltration.

Sunday, October 14, 1979

Arriving at Number 19, Faizil ushered Philip directly into a back room, which was used as an office. Seated around the table was a White gentleman named Arthur Norman and two Black gentlemen named Vincent Malopo and Sipho Nkosi. Philip was introduced to each in turn. Firm handshakes were exchanged.

Arthur Norman studied at the University of the Witwatersrand, during which time he met and was influenced by prominent Black activists. They all had distinctly liberal tendencies and were prominent members of the National Union of South African Students (NUSAS). After obtaining his master's degree in politics, Norman spent some time in London before joining the Communist Party. He then returned to South Africa to take a leading part in the struggle.

Norman was first to speak. He appeared to be in his early fifties and had a large physique with flowing blonde hair, greying at the temples. He had a commanding presence and spoke in a well-modulated English voice.

"A special welcome to you, Philip," he said. "Faizil has told us much about you. I am the head of this cell. We are committed to fighting the scourge of Apartheid and feel strongly that the system is an affront to human dignity and has to go. The majority of South Africans feel as we do, but are powerless to do anything about it. That is the function our cell has been entrusted with.

"Faizil tells us that you would like to be of service to us. Before I go any further, please inform us if we can place our trust in you."

Philip nodded.

Arthur continued. "That was a rhetorical question, as we actually know a great deal more about you than you think. By the way, we heard that you gave a good account of yourself at the university debating-society meeting recently."

In a flash Philip recalled his uneasy feelings and remarked without thinking, "Has anybody been following me?"

"Well," said Vincent with a half-smile, "We had to make sure of you. After all, you could have been a member of the special branch, posing as a sympathizer. You must understand that in this business we simply cannot take any chances."

Philip remained silent. There was obviously a point to all this.

"May I continue?" asked Arthur, addressing Philip.

"Please do."

"As you know, our leader, Truman Khumalo, has been imprisoned on Robben Island for the past fifteen years. To overthrow the present regime, we need our leader to be released.

Besides concerns for his health there is the all-important invitation from the Apartheid Committee of the United Nations for Truman to address them. Should this eventuate, it will be a great victory for our side and give our struggle the world-wide exposure it needs.

"As the government will never give him up, we have to plan his escape. Our cell has been entrusted with this great responsibility. We believe you could be especially useful to us in the task that lies ahead."

"Why me?" responded Philip. "Surely there are better qualified and more deserving people than me in your organization."

"Actually, you fit the bill perfectly," interjected Vincent. "As you know, the movements of Black people are restricted by having to carry passbooks everywhere. Whites do not have to carry passbooks, so a White recruit in our cell would be of immense value."

"You are fit, intelligent, and committed to our cause," chipped in Sipho, "but most important of all, as a Stellenbosch University student you would have the perfect cover. As the regime has files on some of us, your obscurity could prove extremely valuable."

"I might also mention," interjected Arthur, "that because of the importance of the mission, it is going to receive special overseas funding. We will be well paid for our efforts, but it is worth emphasizing that the regime is ruthless and well-armed. There are harrowing tales of police atrocities, and many of our people have died in custody. They have a pathological hatred of Blacks and have many ways of extracting information. One method is to attach wires to a captive's hand and feet and use a generator to send electric shocks through his body. Another is to hold a person's hands down, while placing a plastic bag over his head, in order to deny him air. The idea is to inflict as much pain as possible. In these circumstances only the strongest resist. Many people, too, are on the death list as compiled by the government's hit squads. I imagine you have a host of questions to ask."

Philip thought for a while, then replied. "Robben Island must be a fortress, and I imagine that security is tight. After all, in the eyes of the government, Khumalo is public enemy number one. Does anybody on this task force have any specialized knowledge or training in guerrilla tactics?"

"I do," interjected Arthur. "I have served in the British Army 2nd Intelligence Division for a number of years. Also, I have been to the Soviet Union a number of times. The UAC Headquarters in Dar-es-Salaam has arranged for me to go back to the Soviet Union for a month of intensive briefing. They have all the facilities at their Institute of Strategic Studies in Moscow. On my return, I will thoroughly brief the task force. I believe the Soviets are masters at this sort of thing, and I will be coming back with a detailed plan of action. Does that answer your question?"

"Yes," said Philip, with a slight hint of apprehension.

"I won't go into further detail right now," concluded Arthur. In fact, I don't expect an answer from you straight away. It is an important decision to make, so please take some time to think things over and phone me at this number." He handed Philip a scrap of paper. "I suggest you commit the number to memory and destroy the paper. It goes without saying that matters discussed here are highly confidential."

Philip looked at the scrap of paper on which was written (021) 410-1762. He thought for a minute, memorized the number, and tore the paper into little pieces, before throwing it into a rubbish bin under the table.

"I will be in touch with you," Philip said.

A light lunch was served, and nothing more about the meeting was said. Philip asked Faizil if he could drive him back to Stellenbosch. On the way back, he was deep in thought. Arthur intrigued him. Why was a White person—especially one with Russian connections—chairing such an important meeting of the UAC?

Maybe he was a communist. He had never come face to face with a communist before. Then he recalled reading somewhere that, although the communist alliance did not enjoy universal approval with Black groups, membership of the UAC was open to anyone who shared their ideals of a democratic society.

He was still deep in thought as they reached the outskirts of Stellenbosch.

CHAPTER 9

THE AWAKENING

October 23, 1979, 9:30 a.m.

Jannie and Philip met in the corridor of Res house. "I have seen so little of you lately. Where have you been?" asked Jannie.

"I have been swotting for the exams with a colleague," answered Philip. "And how is your swotting going?"

Jannie merely answered "Okay."

Philip knew full well of Jannie's habit of leaving things to the last minute. Nevertheless, he always managed to scrape through.

"By the way, Philip," asked Jannie," will you be going home to Vryburg at the end of the year?"

"Yes," replied Philip. "I intend to see my parents and help out on the farm. I expect the tractor will need fixing again. In fact, I have already made arrangements for someone to take my place at the Golden Fig during my absence."

"Well, Philip," replied Jannie, "I am going to Bloemfontein straight after the exams and can take you most of the way. Why not come with me? I have an empty car and would welcome the company."

"That is very kind of you," replied Philip. "I accept, but on the proviso that we share all expenses."

"That won't be necessary, as I am going home anyway," said Jannie, conscious of Philip's financial position.

Jannie has his heart in the right place, thought Philip.

November 5, 1979

The end-of-year exams had begun and all efforts were focused on studying and getting through. Socializing was over for the time being, and an unusual hush had descended over the campus. Philip had six subjects to prepare for, which was occupying all his time. He felt he had prepared adequately for the exams and was fairly confident, but one never knew. The examiners could slip in a *stinke*r.

As it turned out, the exams went well, and he was optimistic of getting a good mark. Jannie, too, with far less preparation, was reasonably happy with his efforts. Finally, the results were announced, and both boys were thrilled to have passed—Philip with a 75-percent pass rate and Jannie with 58-percent. After obtaining his results, Philip went straight to the public phone on the second floor and phoned his dad.

"Dad," he said excitedly. "I have passed!"

"Wonderful," his dad said. "When do we see you?"

"Jannie is giving me a lift, and I hope to back on December 1," Philip said.

"We look forward to seeing you," replied his dad. "Drive safely."

The year-end exams being over, both Philip and Jannie were on an emotional high.

Jannie turned to Philip and said, "We must celebrate. In fact, I have been thinking of you. You lead too monastic a life. Well, it is high time you let your hair down, and I have just the answer. Remember I was telling you about those pretty hostesses at the

Royal Hotel? I find them most agreeable, and I am going to arrange a double date, if that's okay with you. It won't cost an arm and a leg either. Their names are Lauren and Marie, and they share an apartment in a block called Protea Mansions, in Protea Street. If we make an arrangement for a Monday evening, we can buy take-away pizzas at half-price at the Golden Fig and celebrate our success over a bottle of wine at their apartment. It should be fun."

Philip had had a slightly Calvinistic, even puritanical upbringing. His attitude, inculcated by his mother, was to save himself for the *right girl*, one with whom he was in love. This was a trifle old-fashioned in this day and age, but there it was. Casual sex, for the sole purpose of gratification, was wrong. In any case, gratification could be obtained in other ways, well-known to thousands of boys. Fantasizing about sex would suffice until the real thing came along.

At the same time, he couldn't help wondering what the real thing was like. He had many times, both at school and at university, heard his peers discussing, even boasting, about their sexual exploits. He always was aroused by sex talk, but had so far managed to suppress his feelings. Secretly though, he envied those of his peers who had achieved sexual freedom and gratification.

Also, he believed there was an imbalance to his education and upbringing. He felt he was politically mature and had unilaterally condemned the direction in which the present government was taking the country. In this connection, he was on firm ground. He had always taken a keen interest in politics. On the other hand, he was sexually immature and still a virgin at twenty years of age. He had begun to question his standards. Besides, Jannie was subconsciously opening the door for him, and he had secretly yearned for more experience in these matters.

"Yes," he said nervously. "It seems like a fun idea." No sooner had he said that than he began to feel ambivalent about his response, but he had to start somewhere. Perhaps he had misconstrued the situation. Jannie's next statement, however, removed any lingering doubts.

"We had better take condoms with us in case we get lucky," said Jannie. "Leave the arrangements to me."

Mid-November 1979

The date assumed some significance for him. He fussed about his clothes for the occasion, trying on and discarding items of clothing until he felt reasonably comfortable. He had never been this fussy before. His final choice eventually fell on a pair of tight fitting blue jeans and a royal blue tee shirt which outlined his finely chiselled physique.

On the other hand, Jannie seemed quite cavalier in his approach to the evening. He had done this many times before, as if it were the most natural thing in the world. *This is not my first date*, Philip thought, *so why do I have this nervous tingling in my stomach? If things get out of hand, I could always bale out.*

Before leaving Res, Jannie had packed two bottles of chardonnay in a cooler bag and, on the way to Protea Mansions, had stopped off at the Golden Fig for the pizzas. It was agreed that Lauren would partner with Philip and Marie would be Jannie's date for the evening.

They knocked on the door of the apartment and Philip was pleasantly surprised to find both girls attractive, even sexy. *The early exit is no longer an option*, he thought.

Jannie introduced the girls to Philip, after which Marie disappeared into the kitchen to place the pizzas in the warmer. Jannie placed one bottle of chardonnay on ice and opened the other. Four glasses were filled. A few strategically placed candles provided lighting, a Bee Gees tape played in the background, and the curtains were drawn.

Simple, but effective, thought Philip.

"So, Jannie tells me you are an expert swimmer," said Lauren, as an ice-breaker. "Which event do you specialize in?"

"The freestyle," answered Philip, "in particular the 200 metres."

"What is your best time for the event?" countered Lauren, trying her best to sound knowledgeable about swimming.

"Two minutes, five seconds," answered Philip.

"What is the university record for the 200 metres?" inquired Lauren, knowing she was on safe ground.

"One minute, fifty-nine seconds," replied Philip.

"Well, that is not far off the record," Lauren responded.

Philip nodded. They had got off to a good start, and he was suitably impressed.

At about 9:00 p.m., both girls disappeared into the kitchen to prepare the food. "What do you think of him?" inquired Marie.

"I think he is kind of cute," answered Lauren.

Food was served, and Jannie opened the second bottle of chardonnay, by which time the conversation had become more spontaneous, even a little boisterous. After dinner, Jannie suggested they dance. The music was turned up a notch, and the furniture cleared from the centre of the room. The candles were blown out, and both couples started smooching on the floor. The music had become less important and was now barely audible.

Jannie steered Marie toward the bedroom, and the door clicked shut behind them. Philip felt awkward. He was not at all confident of himself. Besides, Lauren seemed like a nice girl, and he hardly knew her. To move too fast could invite a rebuff. On the other hand, maybe he was expected to perform. He was not sure what to do. He would take his cue from her. He pressed himself ever closer to her so that she could feel his enlarging manhood. She was not resisting. He thought, *Could this be it?* She was definitely aroused, too.

Suddenly, he felt her hands undoing his trouser buttons, one by one. His trousers dropped to his ankles. He pulled off his tee shirt and deftly she pulled his briefs down. Hastily he kicked off both trouser legs and briefs in two shakes of each leg. He was naked and hugely aroused. There was no turning back now.

He lifted her off the floor and walked to her bedroom. She managed to open the door with her free hand. Then he feverishly undressed her. Her young breasts stood firm and erect in the dim light. He laid her out on the bed and for a moment, he gazed on this god-given form—so pink, so lithe, so supple.

She had shut her eyes. He reached for the condom which he had rescued from his trousers' pocket and hurriedly slipped it on. Then he positioned himself astride the prone figure and gently lowered himself into her until he was fully received. He began to move up and down, slowly at first, then faster and faster, evoking periodic moans of delight from the prone figure below.

His heart was beginning to beat furiously. Then suddenly, with the fury of an uncontrolled volcano, he climaxed. For a second, all time seemed to stand still. A few more strokes, and then peace. She had managed to climax with him. *God*, he thought, why had he waited so long? He rolled off her, and they both fell into a deep sleep.

At 3:30 a.m., he awoke with a start. Realizing where he was, he dressed quietly and left the apartment. He would phone Lauren later to thank her for a special evening. In the quiet of the night, he walked back to Res. Jannie was not home yet. He flopped into bed fully clothed.

When he awoke at 9:30 a.m., his eyelids were heavy, and his mind unclear. But one thing was clear: he has passed his own private Rubicon. He imagined he would feel differently, but he did not. Suddenly, he realised with a shock that he had missed the first lecture of the day. In all his time at university, he had never missed a lecture. He hurriedly spruced himself up and ran off in time for the second lecture.

At 5:00 p.m. that afternoon, he met up with Jannie, who said simply, "Well?"

"I made home base," replied Philip proudly.

"Put it there, pal," said Jannie with a wide grin.

CHAPTER 10

HOMECOMING

The exams were over and all thoughts were now on the holidays. It was arranged that they would head for Kimberley, from which point Philip could take a short train ride to Vryburg and Jannie would carry on to Bloemfontein.

December 1, 1979

They rose at 6:30 a.m. to pack the car. Jannie was taking his golf clubs with him, but golf was the furthest thing from Philip's mind. He offered to pay his share of the petrol, but was again politely refused. The warm sunshine gave a hint of the scorching day to come. Fortunately, the car was fitted with air conditioning.

They reminisced about the past year, which made the journey seem so much shorter. *Jannie is such good company*, Philip thought, *and so easy to get along with. Pity he holds such racist views.*

Although it had been a pleasant journey, pervading his mind and dominating his every thought was the fact that he had yet to answer Arthur about the mission. However, he had already made up his mind.

They reached Kimberley by late afternoon. "Did you know, Philip," said Jannie, "that Kimberley was the first town in the southern hemisphere to install electric street lights?"

"No, I did not. Isn't that interesting?" responded Philip.

Jannie drove straight to the railway station. "I'll park here while you check the train schedules. If you've missed the last train, you can spend the night at my place, and I will bring you back here in the morning. Philip agreed and disappeared into the bowels of the station.

As soon as he was inside, he rushed to a phone booth and dialed Arthur's number, the number he had memorized.

"Hello," the voice on the other side said.

"Arthur, it's me. Philip Watermeyer. Arthur, I have thought about your proposition and have decided to turn it down." Realizing how vulnerable he was, being the possessor of such vital information, he added hastily and rather defensively, "However, I won't breathe a word about this to anyone. Trust me"

The voice on the other side said simply, "Thank you." There was an audible click.

Philip left the phone booth with a sinking feeling. Emerging from the station, he sought out the yellow Volkswagen, which stood out in a sea of cars and, turning to Jannie, he said, "Jannie, I have missed the train for today. Thanks for the offer of accommodation, but I have a feeling I should be getting home. Tell you what. Drop me off on the road to Vryburg, and I will hitch a ride home."

"Okay," said Jannie, "but phone me if you get stuck."

Jannie dropped Philip off on the side of the road and, on parting, said, "If I don't hear from you, have a good vacation. See you next term."

He was in luck's way as no sooner had he hit the road, when a passing panel van stopped and the driver offered him a lift to his destination. From the road, he saw the familiar homestead, with its bright blue roof a short walk along the dust road he knew so well. There didn't seem to be much activity on the farm, he mused.

As he approached the homestead, he was overtaken by an ambulance with sirens wailing and heading straight for the house. He sprinted the remaining distance, suitcase in hand. The ambulance screeched to a halt and two paramedics emerged carrying a stretcher. He and the ambulance men arrived at the front door at the same time. He was met by a tearful mother who hugged him and announced that his father had had a heart attack and was being taken to the Medi-Clinic, a private hospital in Kimberley. The ambulance departed with his father on board.

Seeing the perplexed look on his face, his mother said, "Let's follow the ambulance in the bakkie, and I'll fill you in on all the details." They walked to the vehicle and got in and headed down the drive. "Dad hasn't been feeling well lately, but this morning he complained of severe chest pains, had a sweating brow, and numbness down his left side. I recognized the symptoms and phoned Dr. Marais, who came within minutes, having already phoned for an ambulance. I am very worried about dad. He has never had heart trouble before."

Driving behind the ambulance, the 200-kilometre journey to Kimberley seemed to take an eternity. At the Medi-Clinic, they filled in all the necessary forms, while the specialist examined his father. While they waited in reception, they were impressed by the smart décor, a far cry from the spartan look of the provincial hospital to which they were accustomed. *This is going to be very expensive*, Philip thought.

Soon a doctor arrived and asked them to accompany him to a private interview room. The doctor was a tall dignified man who seemed to be in his fifties.

"I am Dr. Grant Nicol," he said, "head of the cardiac unit here." Turning to Mrs. Watermeyer, he said, "Your husband has a heart condition that will require bypass surgery. There is nothing to be worried about, as it is quite a common procedure these days. In America alone, as many as half a million people have coronary bypass surgery every year to relieve these very symptoms. Mr. Watermeyer has been stabilized now, and the operation is scheduled for tomorrow morning at 8:30 a.m. After the operation, he will need to spend seven to ten days in hospital, followed by complete rest. I suggest you both get a good night's sleep. You will be able to see him tomorrow, after the operation."

The previous year's drought had devastated the family's finances, and it was apparent that the bills for his father's treatment were going to stretch their financial resources to the limit.

"I will leave varsity," said Philip on the drive back, "and come home and run the farm."

This drew a strong reaction from his mother, who said in no uncertain terms, that that was out of the question. She recalled the sacrifices they had made in getting him to university in the first place. She knew his father would feel the same. "We will find the money somehow," she said unconvincingly.

The next day, when he was certain that he would not be overheard, he dialed Cape Town.

"Hello? Arthur, is that you?"

"Yes," came the response.

"Philip speaking. Is that position still open?"

"Yes," said Arthur.

"I have reconsidered. Count me in," replied Philip, oblivious of the perils that lie ahead. All he could think about was his father's complete recovery.

"Are you sure?" came the response. "This will be no walk in the park."

"Yes, quite sure," said Philip.

Arthur's voice had assumed a pseudo-military tone. "Meet us at 2030 on Saturday, December 8 at the usual place. Bye."

After the phone call, Philip sought out his old pal Simon and found him under the tractor. He recalled this had been his job in the old days.

Hearing his voice, Simon shot out from below the tractor and gave his friend a big bear hug. "Wonderful to see you again, Philip. How is your dad?"

"He is recovering," answered Philip. "Let's go fishing. When are you free?"

"At about 4:00 p.m.," answered Simon.

"Fine," said Philip, "Let's meet at the dam at 4:00 p.m."

At the dam, Philip was less than his usual self, a mood instantly picked up by his friend. Sensing something pressing on his mind, he inquired. "Why don't you tell me what's bothering you?"

"Well," said Philip, "I have something important to tell you, but before I do, I must have your solemn promise not to reveal this information to anyone. If you do, you will be risking my life."

Appreciating the gravity of his mood, Simon responded, "You know you can count on me," a phrase he had used many times before, but was no less sincere for its repetition.

Philip did not question that reply. "Well," said Philip after a pause, "you know my feelings about politics in this country and the way the Black people are being treated."

Simon nodded.

"Well, I won't go into detail, except to tell you that I have volunteered to join a special task force that is going to launch a major strike on Apartheid. I do not need to emphasize that this is a very dangerous mission, and there is a chance I could be arrested, or even worse, get shot."

Simon recoiled, but stayed silent. He had learned from his father the wisdom of silence.

Philip continued. "My father's heart condition requires that he spend a long period convalescing. I offered to leave varsity and run the farm, but my folks won't hear of it. I will be extremely well paid for my involvement in the mission, which will help pay for my dad's medical expenses. Do you think that between you and your father you could hold the fort until my dad regains his strength? I will arrange for my uncle in Vryburg to pop in from time to time to keep an eye on things."

Simon nodded and said simply, "You can count on us."

"I know I can," said Philip. "I won't be telling my parents about my plans, as I know they will worry, and worry is the last thing dad needs right now. You won't be seeing me for a while, as I am due to start the mission soon. Here is a sealed letter which explains everything. Keep it in a safe place, and only hand it to my parents in the event that something serious happens to me. Can I trust you with this?"

"Yes," his friend said and slipped the letter into his inner pocket.

The next few days were exhausting. Philip and his mom paid daily visits to Kimberley and were pleased that his dad was making progress. He had contacted his uncle in Vryburg and received the necessary promise of support. The most awkward job of all still lay ahead. He had to leave for Cape Town and needed to explain his hasty departure to his parents at such a critical time. He chose the night before his departure to broach the subject.

Addressing his father first he said, "Dad, as you know I have offered to leave varsity and help run the farm, but mom has turned me down flat."

His father interjected, "I support your mother entirely on that point. You must continue with your studies. The farm can take care of itself."

47

Addressing them both, he said, "I have established from Dr. Marais that the medical expenses in connection with your condition will be about 15,000 rand. Please be frank with me. Do you have the funds available?"

The shocked look on their faces provided the answer. They obviously had not had a chance to consider costs during the trauma of the past few days.

Perhaps he could kill two birds with one stone, Philip thought. "I have some good news," he said. "The Golden Fig restaurant has offered me a full-time job during the varsity recess. Being the tourist season, the tips are excellent, and I can do some swimming coaching on the side. I have been offered free accommodation with a friend of mine, Gunther Schultz, in Fresnaye, a suburb of Cape Town. Working during the holidays will bring in some money, which I will transfer to dad's account. Please don't argue with me as my mind is made up. The only drawback is that I have to start straight away and must leave for Cape Town tomorrow."

Although he did not like lying to his parents, the end justified the means, he thought. "Dad," he said, "I am pleased to see you making such good progress. I'll be in touch with you as soon as possible"

His dad was misty-eyed when the time came for him to say goodbye.

The next day he bade a tearful farewell to his mom and left for Cape Town.

CHAPTER 11

OPERATION KHULULA

Saturday, December 8, 1979

Philip had hitched a ride back to Kimberley, from where he had taken the train to Cape Town. From the Cape Town station, he caught a bus to Riz Kahn's house in Rylands Estate and arrived there with fifteen minutes to spare for the 20:00 p.m. meeting.

Riz welcomed him in his usual effusive manner. They went straight to the back office, where Arthur, Vincent, Sipho, and Faizil were already seated, waiting for his arrival. The first thing he noticed was a crutch hanging over the side of Arthur's chair. Before he could say anything, Arthur spoke in his usual concise and well-modulated manner.

"First, I would like to welcome everyone here today and to wish everyone much success for this important mission. The secret code name of the mission will be Operation Khulula, which is the Xosa word for liberate."

Turning to Philip he said, "Philip, I am particularly pleased that you have decided to come aboard. I need not emphasize how important it is that we succeed. The future of our country is at stake, and we have the support of millions of people. It would be remiss of me not to mention again that the mission is a dangerous one. The government can be ruthless, and we have to plan carefully."

"As you can see, Philip, I had a fall while hiking on Table Mountain and badly sprained an ankle. It has swollen up like a balloon, and I can hardly walk. This is most unfortunate, as in my condition, I can now hardly go to the Soviet Union for the necessary training. Sprains, as you know, take months to heal. So the first and most important item on the agenda today is the choice of someone to take my place to the Soviet Union. Do I have any nominations?"

Vincent was the first to speak. "With our notorious pass laws, a person of colour can easily be picked up at night. Apart from you, Arthur, Philip is the only White person on our committee and as you are out of action, that leaves Philip. The overseas training is going to be very strenuous, and Philip has the necessary level of fitness. Also he is studying engineering, which may come in very handy. My vote goes to Philip," said Vincent.

"Can we not choose someone from outside the group?" asked Faizil, noting Philip's obvious discomfort. "Someone with more experience in these matters,"

"I know someone outside this group who might be suitable," volunteered Sipho.

"I believe the fewer people who know about this venture the better," said Arthur in his usual emphatic manner. "Philip's relative obscurity could actually be an asset. I also think Philip would be perfect."

There were murmurs of assent.

Addressing Philip, Arthur said, "How do you feel about it? This will be a rare adventure for you and an opportunity to make a real difference to the lives of millions of people. All we are asking you to do is to go to the Soviet Union, obtain the necessary training and instruction, and come back and brief us.

You will have all the back-up you need on your return. I will still be in charge."

Philip had turned pale. The suddenness of events had taken him by surprise. He did not answer immediately. His mind started racing. He recalled the nasty incident at school when a little Black boy was knocked semi-conscious because of his blazer; he recalled the embarrassing scene at the Golden Fig when overseas visitors were turned away because of the colour of their skin. He recalled the shame brought on his family by his uncle's prosecution under the Immorality Act. Most importantly, however, he desperately needed funds for his father's medical bills for which he had already committed himself. After all, Arthur did say he would still be in charge on his return. All this passed through his mind in a flash.

"Yes," he answered. "I will accept." He knew full well that those three words might change the course of his life.

Congratulations echoed all round.

"Wonderful," said Arthur. "We must get you ready for the Soviet Union."

"But on one condition," Philip remarked to a stunned audience. "On condition that when I have successfully liaised with your contacts in the Soviet Union, you will immediately deposit fifteen thousand rand into this bank account. My dad is very ill, and the money is needed for his medical expenses. I don't think this is asking too much, considering the dangers to which I will be exposing myself." He handed Arthur a piece of paper, containing the details of his father's bank account. "Is it a deal?"

"It's a deal," replied Arthur. "Do you have a passport?"

"No," replied Philip, "I have never been out of the country."

"Please take a minute to fill in these forms, and we will arrange the necessary documentation for you. Please let me know where I can contact you in the next few days."

Philip said he was staying with a friend, Gunther Schultz, and wrote down his phone number and address. After the meeting, Faizil offered Philip a lift back to his friend's house in Fresnaye.

Philip and Gunther had met at Stellenbosch University when Gunther was in his final year and Philip in his first. Both held strong feelings about the political situation and through this shared belief had become firm friends. They had spent hours discussing the deteriorating political situation. When he had needed accommodation in Cape Town while waiting for his orders, he knew he could count on Gunther. Gunther knew nothing of the mission.

CHAPTER 12

HAMBURG, WEST GERMANY

December 24, 1978

Frau Hula Schtiller was enjoying a cosy evening at home with her two daughters, Greta, age seventeen and Claudia, age fifteen. There was a roaring fire in the fireplace, which contrasted sharply with the icy weather outside.

Hamburg, Germany's largest port, only 110 kilometres upstream from the North Sea, was experiencing a particularly bitter winter. The temperature outside had dropped to negative eight degrees Celsius, and the sky had taken on a consistently grey colour. All over Europe it was the same story, with over-flowing rivers and large scale flooding being reported from many places. Scientists had speculated that the particularly atrocious weather was caused by global warming, which, in turn, was responsible for irregular weather patterns. They said the weather could even get worse.

In and around Hamburg, the trees had long since shed their leaves, and the roads were covered in slush. Driving had to be undertaken with great care. Its two principle lakes, the Alster and the Aussenalster, and the river Elbe that crosses the city, had frozen over, making it impossible for fishermen to ply their trade.

Frau Schtiller was pleased that she and her family did not have to go out that night. She was expecting two couples for Christmas Eve dinner, and she and the girls were completing final decorations to the large Christmas tree, which occupied a prominent corner of their spacious lounge. A servant was preparing the dining table, and the cook was feverishly putting the final touches to the traditional turkey dinner. Both servants had been in their employ for decades and were accepted as virtual members of the family.

The two couples expected the Mannheims and the Kretzmanns, old friends of the family, and Frau Schtiller was looking forward to some easy-going, relaxing company. She was aware of her guest's wine preference and had laid in a reasonable stock of Auslese and Liebfraumilch. She had phoned the Mannheims and the Kretzmanns to inform them that they could park their cars under cover in her garage next to the BMW 325 and the Volkswagen Kombi, which she used to transport the girls to school. For the first time since she could remember, there would be space in her four-car garage.

Sharing Christmas Eve with good friends would be idyllic, except for one missing element: Herr Otto Schtiller. Herr Schtiller was twenty-three years old when he obtained his chemistry degree with honours at Hamburg University. That was twenty-eight years ago. His first and only job was with B.A.S.E. Pharmaceuticals, a German multi-national company, where he had, through a combination of sheer ability and hard work, clawed himself up the executive ladder. When the chief executive had prematurely retired through ill health some five years ago, Otto had been hand-picked by the retiring chief executive and leap-frogged over two senior candidates. He found himself rather prematurely in the driver's seat.

He had, however, long-coveted this position. B.A.S.E. had a work force of some 8,000 people, operating in five different countries and was Europe's third-largest chemical maker. With the job came awesome responsibilities, sweetened by a huge salary, share-option schemes, a chauffeur-driven Mercedes SLC 500, and other perks. He was a natty dresser and able to indulge himself in one of his favourite pastimes—purchasing clothes at some of Europe's trendiest boutiques.

Otto was on top, but for one thing: his relationship with his wife had deteriorated due to his penchant for young, lusty brunettes. He had at first steadfastly denied these liaisons, but after mounting pressure from his wife, had apologized and promised to turn over a new leaf. But like a moth to a flame, he continued philandering. Argument followed argument. The situation had become intolerable.

Acknowledging the inevitable, Frau Schtiller had reluctantly decided to consult Henry Weiskopff and Partners, a well-known firm of divorce attorneys in Hamburg. In her emotional state, she had asked Henry Weiskopff to settle the proceedings as soon as possible. However, Henry had advised her that if her marriage had irretrievably broken down, it was necessary to obtain irrefutable proof of her husband's infidelity to achieve the best possible settlement. The attorney had recommended hiring a well-known detective agency specializing in obtaining video or photographic material for use as evidence at a divorce hearing.

Frau Schtiller, within a month or two, had obtained the irrefutable evidence the attorney sought. The report indeed had confirmed the fact that Otto was indulging in more than one liaison and contained the surprising fact that he had a penchant for off-beat sexual adventures. Psychologists would attest to the fact that many of the highest achievers in life have credited their superior accomplishments to the power of their abnormal sex drives.

The divorce was messy, but Frau Schtiller had obtained their luxury house, the Kombi, and a large cash settlement and support for the girls' upbringing and education. In return, Otto had obtained the BMW plus visitation rights with the girls.

After the divorce, Otto had bought a luxury apartment for himself. The settlement, although generous to his former wife, had made only a small dent in his personal wealth.

Being Christmas Eve, he had given instructions that his staff be allowed to leave early and he, too, had left early. It was to be his quietest Christmas in years, enlivened only by a colleague who had come over to have a drink with him.

He had phoned Greta and Claudia to wish them a happy Christmas and promised to drop off Christmas gifts the next day. No sooner had he concluded his phone conversation with his daughters, when the phone rang. It was Gunther Schultz, the young, dynamic director of his South African operations on the line. The South African operation was a small, but growing part of B.A.S.E. and served as a springboard to service the burgeoning African market.

Gunther Schultz and his parents had emigrated to South Africa from Germany in 1975 and Gunther, then twenty-six years old, had decided on a bachelor of science degree. His English was not good, but he spoke German and Dutch fluently. His parents had settled in Cape Town, and he had decided to enroll at the nearby Stellenbosch University, an Afrikaans Medium University as Afrikaans was derived from Dutch. He majored in chemistry, physics, and mathematics.

Within four years, he had graduated with honours. After graduation, he saw an advert in the *Cape Times* that a large

German pharmaceutical company was offering a top position. He had successfully applied for the position and within eighteen months was appointed managing director. It was the practice of B.A.S.E. Pharmaceuticals to employ bright young men and promote them to senior positions, offering them share-option schemes as part of their income package. On the whole, this was a successful policy to prevent rival companies from poaching their staff.

"Herr Schtiller," said the voice on the other side, "It is Gunther Schultz here. How are you?"

"I have been better," replied Schtiller, "and please call me Otto. You are a director now, you know. To answer your question, Gunther, my recent divorce has left me terribly depressed. This is the first Christmas I am spending away from my family, and even the weather is lousy."

Gunther paused and, sensing an opportunity to ingratiate himself with his chief, said, "Herr Schtiller, I mean Otto, I have a great idea. Why not come and spend a few days in Cape Town? The weather is marvellous right now, and the sunshine will really lift your spirits. It's just what you need. At the same time, you can review our operations and comment on the changes I have made. You are most welcome to stay with me, as I have two spare rooms."

"You know, Gunther, I might just take you up on that," said Otto.

"Why not come?" asked Gunther eagerly. Let me know what flight you decide on, and I will meet you at the airport."

The chief executive had indeed taken the bait. Within a day or two, Gunther was informed by headquarters that Herr Schtiller would be arriving on Friday, January 5 to review his operations.

CHAPTER 13

THE AUCTION SALE

January 5, 1979

Gunther fetched his chief executive at Cape Town International Airport and drove him back to his house in the suburb of Fresnaye.

Fresnaye is situated on what is called the Atlantic Seaboard and popular with young executives, many of whom had renovated their homes and given them a trendy look. In common with other homes in the suburb, there were superb sea views to be had. Gunther had added a bathroom and sitting room to the second bedroom, creating a self-contained suite. It was this suite which was earmarked for the chief executive.

"This place is a tonic," observed Otto on the way back from the airport. "I had almost forgotten just how beautiful it is. I'm already feeling better."

"If I may say so, Otto, you are looking very pale. May I respectfully recommend that we begin your visit by going to the beach tomorrow? As it is the holiday season, the beaches will be crowded, especially in this hot weather, so we should get there early. Clifton Beach is renowned for its beautiful girls, many of whom walk around topless."

Pretty girls had always interested Otto. "Sounds good to me," he replied. "I have brought my swimming trunks with me."

Bright and early the following morning they drove to the beach, parked the car on Victoria Road, and descended the long, winding steps to Clifton's First Beach, which was well below road level. They found a nice spot on the beach, hired some beach chairs, covered themselves with sun-block, and awaited the tanning process of the warming sun.

"I must say, this is a spectacular beach," said Otto. "Just look at those apartment blocks cascading down the cliff side. And many of those houses higher up the mountainside have a distinctly Mediterranean look about them. In fact, for a moment, I imagined I was on France's *Cote d'Azur.*"

Having adjusted his deck chair into a horizontal position so that his back was fully exposed to the sun, Otto, with his face buried in the canvas and in a slightly muffled voice said, "You know, Gunther, I simply can't believe I was sitting in frozen Hamburg only a few days ago. One has a strong urge to own a piece of this place."

"Well," replied his subordinate, "hundreds of our countrymen have already done just that. You are not the first to fall under its spell. In fact, the locals are complaining that the German, British, and American tourists are spoiling the market for them. Many of them live here permanently, while others simply come over to escape the harsh, northern-hemisphere winters."

"You know, Otto, you could do a lot worse for yourself than buy a holiday home here. A person with a heavy workload like you needs a break from time to time. Our branch here is growing, and the house could even be bought in the company's name."

There was silence, and it was obvious to the junior executive that his words had found fertile ground.

"That is not such a bad idea," said the senior executive. "Our best customers could be rewarded with a holiday in the sun at our guest house, instead of going to some inhospitable hotel. It would be good for business. One thing that bothers me, though, is the bad press this country is getting overseas because of its Apartheid policies. You know, we Hamburgians are a tolerant and open-minded lot, and, in fact, my own political outlook is to the left. From what I can make out, the Black people are very badly treated in this country. My fellow directors may not be so keen to invest further money here."

"I share your views about the political situation here, but under the new prime minister, Peet Bothma, things have eased a lot, and people of colour are even being considered for parliament. In my opinion, it is only a matter of time before Apartheid is abolished altogether, and then the country will really take off. One should get in on the ground floor."

"Is that so?" remarked Otto. "I didn't know that. Obviously you are well-informed about the political situation here. Anyhow, what's available on the property market?"

"It just so happens that I have brought the *Weekend Argus* with me, and being Saturday, today's edition contains the property supplement. Let's have a look."

Gunther retrieved the newspaper from his rucksack and paged nonchalantly through the property pages. It was a bumper edition, as the tourist season was a good time to advertise.

"Good heavens," he exclaimed. "I see Sid Kaplan's estate is being sold at public auction on Tuesday. Sid Kaplan is a hugely successful hotel magnate, who heads a large and dynamic hotel group in Southern Africa. He owns an estate on a mountain slope in a beautiful part of the peninsula called Hout Bay. I have heard that he has ambitions of entering the American and Caribbean markets. Obviously he is moving into the international scene.

Anything that Sid Kaplan builds is special. There is a picture of the house in the paper."

Pricking up his ears and lifting his seedy, white body off the deck chair, Otto inquired, "May I have a look?"

"If you are serious about buying property here," said Gunther," this is a rare opportunity to acquire something special. As he is leaving the country, he probably will sell all the furnishings, which will save you the hassle of furnishing. It probably won't go cheaply, but it can only escalate in value over time. A property like this comes onto the market once in a lifetime and will enhance the image of our company enormously."

"You certainly have aroused my interest. Maybe we should go to the auction," said the senior executive. "If the price is reasonable, perhaps we can make a bid."

"They have a policy here," countered Gunther, "that you have to obtain a number before you can bid and should you be successful, you have to produce a bank-guaranteed cheque for 15 percent of the purchase price as a deposit. The purpose of this policy is to keep out non-genuine buyers."

"Let's see," said Otto, "the time now is 10:30 a.m., and in Germany it must be 9:30 a.m. I would like to get my bank manager on the line."

"Well, I have a friend who owns a beach house here in Clifton," observed Gunther. "I am sure he won't mind our using his phone. Come with me. We can leave our things here. It is quite safe."

The two men went back up the long winding steps and, at a point three quarters of the way up, took a left and went down a short path to Gunther's friend's beach house.

"The Clifton beach houses are very popular among the younger set," said Gunther, "as they make great venues for beach parties."

Luckily his friend was at home, and after having been introduced to the senior executive, he readily agreed to the use of his phone.

Otto dialed Hamburg, and when the switchboard operator answered, he gave his name and asked to be put through to the manager.

"Hello, Otto," said the manager. "Nice to hear from you. How can I be of service?"

"Well," replied Otto, "I am in Cape Town, South Africa, right now. In fact, my local director and I are speaking to you from the beach—"

"Lucky devil," interrupted the manager. "It's bitterly cold here."

"I'm considering purchasing a rather large property here to serve as a guest house for our company's clients. The auction is next Tuesday, and I'll need a bank-guaranteed cheque." Turning to Gunther he said, "Please give me the details of our bank account here," which Gunther swiftly wrote down and passed on to the bank manager. "They need a deposit as a guarantee, which should be the equivalent of 180,000 rand in South African currency," said Otto. "I won't bid beyond that point."

"You'll have the guarantee by Monday," concluded the manager. "Enjoy the rest of your holiday."

Property had always excited Otto, and armed with the guarantee, he and Gunther set off to attend the Tuesday auction sale. He decided to slip on one of his designer suits for the occasion, since he always was conscious of his appearance in public. He would far rather be over-dressed than under-dressed.

From Fresnaye, they took a short cut over Kloof Road and emerged at Camps Bay Beach, a popular beach known for its stately palms. They had left early, as Gunther knew the traffic would be heavy.

At this time of the year, the city was swollen with up-country holidaymakers abuzz with fashionable cars and noisy motor bikes and youngsters on their roller blades. It reminded Otto of Miami in season.

Victoria Road, winding along the coast, was not unlike the famous Amalfi Drive off the Tyrrhenian Sea, where legend has it that the Greek gods came to play. The colour of the sea varied from deep blue in the bay to azure blue on the coastline, where large boulders, smoothed by the ravages of time, lapped the shoreline far, far below.

They drove past the Twelve Apostles on the left, a mountain formation that formed the western rampart to Table Mountain, then Llundudno, a fashionable hamlet on the seaside, before ascending the rise that led to the quaint little village of Hout Bay.

"I don't suppose it can get any better than this," said Otto, admiring the view from different perspectives, as the road twisted and turned toward its final destination. He was to be proved wrong.

As they reached the crest of the rise, a picture-perfect vista of Hout Bay came into view: a placid little bay, colourful fishing boats, and blue-grey mountains. *An artist could not have composed a better picture*, he thought. They had just started the descent to the village, when a large auctioneer's sign board beckoned them off to the right toward an area called Little Lions Head. It was obvious that the Kaplan Estate was to share that extraordinary view he had witnessed on the crest of the hill. He was so overcome by a sense of rising expectation, that he had not noticed a long queue of cars forming, all going to the auction. Gunther noticed, however, that his company-owned Mercedes 200D was in sharp contrast to the more fashionable Mercedes, Porches, and BMWs present. This was obviously the auction sale of the year.

About 200 metres off the road, they came to a pair of gilded, ornamental entrance gates, which were separated by a guard house on which a brass sign read VILLA CASTELLO. As they drew alongside the left-hand gate, a smartly dressed guard with the words VILLA CASTELLO embroidered on his tunic gave them a formal salute.

A cobbled, winding driveway led them up a slight incline to the crest of the hill where the buildings were situated. There were four buildings in the complex, comprising the main villa, caretaker's flat, glazed pool house, and servants' quarters. The buildings formed a courtyard with an ornamental fountain as the central focus. The fountain, designed in perfect scale to the buildings, was in the form of three prancing horses supported by a large, scalloped-edged mosaic bowl.

The complex was designed in the Italian Tuscan Style, so fashionable in South Africa at the time. South Africans were very fond of imitating overseas styles in a vain attempt to establish an architectural identity of their own.

Villa Castello was a perfect example of the Italian style it was imitating. Otto had been to Italy many times on holiday with his family. For him, Tuscany had always had a timeless quality as the land of wine, wheat, and olives. He instinctively conjured up images of palatial, classical villas set among rolling hills or on the side of lakes. With its finely proportioned Roman arches, beautiful classical columns, and the delightful courtyard, Villa Castello could compete with the best he had seen abroad. A little bit of Italy, he mused. How magical! He found himself forming an immediate attachment to the property.

Because of the volume of cars, they were forced to park about 100 metres from the house and walk the remaining distance. Gunther was glad they had arrived early so they could get a good look at the property.

"We must be very close to Sandy Bay," observed Gunther. "That's South Africa's premier nudist beach."

Otto did not respond, but intuitively stored that information in the back of his mind for future use.

On entering the auction room, Otto requested a bidding number at the auctioneer's desk and sat down to study the brochure. In keeping with the grandeur of the property, the brochure was produced on the highest quality gloss paper.

The villa contained five reception rooms, plus seven bedrooms with attached bathrooms, or *en suites*. Imported marble was used in liberal quantities. It was plain that the original owner had spared nothing in the attainment of perfection.

Otto did not feel out of place in his blue designer suit, as the people present were all fashionably dressed for the occasion.

At exactly 10:00 a.m., the auctioneer stood up to welcome the public and, as is customary, read the conditions of sale. He announced that the buyer would have to pay transfer duty, as the property had to be bought out of the company. He also announced that the estate was being sold *voetstoets*, which meant "as is," complete with all furniture and fixtures. He added that occupation would be given on October 1, when the present owner would be vacating.

The audience settled down, and the auctioneer began the bidding. "Who will start off at 7 million rand?" he asked. Someone put up his finger and the bidding went up briskly in half-million rand increments to 11 million rand, where it began to falter.

"Any advance on 11 million rand?" he barked. "This is a real bargain. Going for the first time, going for the second time, and—"

At the penultimate moment, Otto raised his finger and bid 11.5 million rand. The audience quieted down, as they often do, when the bidding reaches a climax.

"Gone to number thirty-six, the man in the blue suit," said the auctioneer.

The audience clapped. Strangers came up to Otto to congratulate him. Some even said he had bought a bargain.

Otto remained on to complete the paper formalities and was then taken on a conducted tour of the property by the auctioneer. There were features he had not noticed on his earlier, brief examination. For example, the pool had a patented invisible edge design, a function which removed the harsh edges and allowed the water to merge with the sea when viewed from certain angles. He hadn't seen this idea before nor had he fully examined the impressive pool house with the large, heated, spa bath. The latter could seat ten people comfortably.

Otto was excited as he and Gunther drove home. *It's not every day*, he thought, *that one buys a house of such splendour.* Even the trials and tribulations of his recent divorce were all but forgotten—temporarily at any rate. But, as so often happens when one buys a property, buyer's remorse began to set in, and he started to wrestle with his mind. *Had he perhaps not overpaid in the heat of the moment? And what about his fellow directors in Hamburg, would they not perhaps raise objections?*

No! he thought finally. He had always had an unerring touch, which is why his fellow directors always rubber-stamped his decisions. It would be different if the company were not doing well, but the share price had more than doubled on the Hamburg bourse during his control period.

"You certainly were impressive at the auction today," interjected Gunther.

Even this gratuitously flattering remark failed to disturb his reverie. He would take some photographs back for his fellow directors. He felt sure they would applaud his purchase. A little bit of Italy in Africa—what a concept!

He wasn't to know that events would take a different course.

On the Monday before the auction, he had accompanied his junior executive to the Cape Town plant to review some figures and to honour the promise made to him to inspect the improvements. He was pleased to note that sales were up from the previous year, particularly from the neighbouring countries of Zimbabwe, Malawi, and Mozambique. He had read somewhere that there were 200 million people living in Sub-Saharan Africa. *What a potential customer base*, he thought.

On Wednesday following the auction, he was called for by an old friend and dined with him and his wife.

As he was heading back to Hamburg, he had instructed Gunther to take possession of the villa when it became available on October 1 and to renegotiate the re-employment of the resident caretaker. He said he would be back in December, having enjoyed his few days in Cape Town immensely. He admitted that the break had done him the world of good. He left on Thursday, January 11, for Hamburg.

CHAPTER 14

THE REPORT BACK

Friday, January 12, 1979

Otto Schtiller was met at Flughafen Fuhlsbuttel at 7:30 a.m. by his chauffeur and driven the ten kilometres to B.A.S.E. Headquarters on the Jungfernstieg, a wide, attractive promenade overlooking the Alster Lake.

It was still bitterly cold, and he was pleased that he had changed to warm clothing before landing. Being a workaholic, he wasted no time heading back to the office and getting stuck into his backlog of paperwork.

The first director's board meeting of the year was to be held in a week's time. The first meeting of the year was always important, as it set the tone for the rest of the year. Apart from the customary financial review, there were two other important items on the agenda.

When the city was rebuilt after World War II, the city fathers had decided on a policy of low-rise buildings, rather than skyscrapers and, with its many green-coppered spires, the city had a particularly elegant look. Hamburg was the most tolerant and open-minded of Germany's cities.

The boardroom was on the fourth floor of the sprawling complex with its lovely views of the lake. The board room contained a horse-shoe table, with nine neatly arranged seats. Pads and pencils were placed in front of each seat. The walls were paneled in African mahogany, and at one end, doors slid away to expose a well-stocked bar. When the sliding doors were closed, the bar was invisible. There were many privileges available to those who had reached boardroom level.

January 19, 1979

The board meeting began promptly at 10:00 a.m. It was a policy of Otto Schtiller to begin strictly on time and run the meeting in a firm and disciplined manner. He never allowed discussions to get out of hand and drag on endlessly.

There were three main items on the agenda that day:

1. Review of the past year's financial performance.
2. Progress report on a new drug being developed by the company's laboratory.
3. Ratification of the purchase of the Cape Town guest house.

Under item one, he was pleased to report sustained growth for the fifth consecutive year. As he, himself, had been in control for the past five years, he paused to allow his fellow directors time to draw the obvious conclusions.

The figures were important, and he was at pains to go into them in minute detail. But as important as the figures were, he was really looking forward to items two and three on the agenda.

"Regarding item two," he said, "I have some exciting news for you. You probably have read in the newspapers that the unseasonable cold weather has precipitated one of the worst outbreaks of influenza and bronchitis in decades, sending thousands of people around the world to bed with bouts of coughing, fever, and chills. In Europe alone, flu cases are running at six times normal levels.

"Presently, there are many flu treatments on the market, but until now all these remedies were designed to treat the symptoms only. I am pleased to report that our research laboratory is on the verge of developing a new high-tech drug, which will combat the flu virus itself instead of just treating its symptoms. This represents a major medical break-through and will cut the duration of the illness by up to 50 percent. The timing could not be better.

"Our trials are now at an advanced stage and will mean a financial bonanza for our company second to none, should we be successful, and could catapult us into the number one position among chemical manufacturers in Europe. This is potentially very exciting news for our company. The down side is that I have heard of a rival company working on the same drug. Therefore, I have instructed our lab to redouble their efforts, and I am confident of making a breakthrough announcement in the near future."

A buzz of excitement reverberated around the room, and the directors secretly weighed up the potential benefits to themselves. In the euphoria of the moment, one of the oldest-serving members of the board rose to propose a vote of full confidence in the chairman and said he spoke for all present in saying how much they valued his inspiring leadership.

In the warm glow of his peer's adulation, Otto confidently broached the final item on the agenda, namely the ratification of the purchase of the Cape Town guest house. However, a sixth sense told him this would be no rubber stamp.

He introduced the subject cautiously. "Gentlemen, we live in an age of incentives. We simply have to reward our best clients for their on-going loyalty to us. Other companies are doing just that, and if we don't keep pace, we will lose vital market share. I have just returned from a visit to Cape Town, South Africa, where I reviewed our branch's activities there.

"I am pleased to report that our African operations are growing steadily. Cape Town is a startlingly beautiful city. During my visit, a marvellous opportunity arose to buy a very special guest house. If I had not acted so forthrightly, I would have lost the deal. Anyhow, I used my initiative and bought it. There was no time to phone everyone.

"I have brought some photographs to show you," he said, passing a batch of pictures down the line. There were a few minutes pause, while the members examined the photographs.

"May we know the cost?" inquired Zigfried Meier.

"It was knocked down for 11.5 million rand in South African currency. It is a magnificent property and will greatly escalate in value over the years."

"Do we need such a large property?" Ziegfried Meier responded. "What is wrong with a nice little property on the French Riviera?" he asked.

"I agree, why do we have to buy something so far away?" enquired Werner Mueller.

Even Heinz Kransdorf, who had always blindly supported him, had doubts. Otto Schtiller remained silent while his fellow directors debated the issue. He observed that the comments varied from lukewarm to negative. He allowed a few further moments to elapse and then brought the meeting to order.

"Gentlemen," he said, "it seems my actions in purchasing the Cape Town guest house have not met with universal approval. I do not want any of you to be unhappy. Consequently, I will purchase the property in my own name and release the company from the sale. That concludes the meeting. Thank you for attending."

As soon as he had reached his office, he put a call through to the auctioneers in Cape Town and instructed them that the purchaser of the property would be Otto Schtiller Nominees, C.C. That evening in the privacy of his apartment, he syndicated the property five ways.

CHAPTER 15

PREPARATIONS

August 30, 1979

As the seller was vacating the property at the end of September, Otto had phoned Gunther to remind him to renegotiate the employment contract with the resident caretaker, Joe Bailey, and his wife, Susan, who was in charge of housekeeping.

Gunther replied that he had already done so and that the Baileys were more than happy to retain their posts. Otto had also informed Gunther that he and four of his colleagues from Hamburg had purchased the Villa in their own names, as the directors felt that the guest house was too far from home for the company's use. None of his partners—Helmut Meyer, Jurgen Kannermeyer, Hans-Joerg Volker, and Willy Weitenkamff—had ever been to Africa before, and he was bringing them out to Cape Town in December to see the property and enjoy a short holiday in the sun. His partners would be arriving on the morning of Wednesday, December 19, but he would be arriving a few days earlier to inspect the property and oversee arrangements for the housewarming party he was planning for the evening of their arrival. He said he would be in touch with him again closer to that time.

September 13, 1979

Otto Schtiller picked up the intercom extension in his office and asked his secretary to contact a Mr. Sid Kaplan in Cape Town. He gave her the phone number. A few minutes later, his secretary phoned and said, "Herr Schtiller, I have Mr. Kaplan on the line from Cape Town."

"Mr. Kaplan," said Otto, "I am pleased to make your acquaintance. Congratulations on your marvelous development in Hout Bay. I am the buyer of your home. The amount of work you have put into it is truly amazing."

"Thank you so much," replied Mr. Kaplan, in his slightly American-accented voice.

"You know, I am in the development business and have excellent contacts in the building world who make things easier for me."

"You are very modest," replied Otto." I have heard that you are a great visionary. Actually, it is about your contacts that I am phoning you. Some German colleagues of mine have never been to Africa, and I am bringing them out to Villa Castello in December to spend a few days with me. I have thought of hosting a housewarming party with a typically African theme. Do you know of anyone who could arrange such an evening for me?"

"It's no problem at all," drawled Kaplan. "We have these kinds of evenings all the time at our game lodges in the northern part of the country. Please give me a few seconds to look up a contact for you." After a few seconds he said, "Phone Luigi Lamberti, Johannesburg, 27-11-3051646, and tell him you got his name from me."

"Are you leaving South Africa?" inquired Otto.

"Well, I feel I have gone as far as I can go in South Africa. This country has been very good to me, but I am now going to try my luck in the U.S. and Caribbean markets."

"Well, good luck with your new venture," replied Otto. "It would be nice to meet you some time."

"You, too," replied Kaplan. "By the way, what did you think of the underground bar with the portholes to the pool? We had many an entertaining evening in that bar, especially at night when the pool lights were on, and the bar lights were dimmed."

"Well, what do you know? No one told me about that bar," exclaimed Otto. "Where is it?"

"In the southern corner of my trophy room is a trap door in the floor below the small Persian carpet. Simply lift the carpet, pull up the trap door, and go down the steps. Come to think of it, I may have left some bottles of excellent wine behind. If so, please help yourself, with my compliments."

"Thanks for the information. I hope to bump into you some time," said Otto again.

"You, too. Goodbye," responded Kaplan.

November 23, 1979

Otto dialed his secretary and asked her to get Luigi Lamberti on the line. "And after I have spoken to him, I need to speak to Gunther Schultz at our Cape Town office."

After a few minutes, his secretary phoned to say that Mr. Lamberti would phone him back shortly. While waiting for the call, he pondered the various uses for Villa Castello. On the one hand, he and his partners could take turns to use the villa and simply lock it up when not in use, as other foreigners do. They certainly had the means. Alternately, with its five large reception rooms and seven *en suite* bedrooms, it would make a wonderful boutique hotel or up-market bed and breakfast. He had noticed on his recent visit to Cape Town that there was a shortage of hotel accommodations in the three- to five=star categories. Wealthy tourists would pay upward of 500U.S. dollars per person per night.

His thoughts were interrupted by the phone. It was his secretary. "Herr Schtiller, Mr. Lamberti returning your call from South Africa."

"Mr. Lamberti, my name is Otto Schtiller. I am the purchaser of Mr. Kaplan's estate in Hout Bay. Mr. Kaplan kindly gave me your number. The reason I am phoning you is that I am bringing four of my colleagues from Germany to South Africa at the end of the year. None of them has been to Africa before, and I intend having a housewarming party on the evening of December 19 for . . . say . . . ten people. I think it would be appropriate to have a party with an African theme, perhaps with some ethnic entertainment thrown in."

"No problem," responded Lamberti. "I do that all the time for Sid. I'll arrange a *boma* evening for you."

"I'm not familiar with that term," said Otto.

"The word boma," explained Lamberti, "originates from East Africa and refers to an open reed structure used by indigenous people as a meeting place and for meals. It is made from reeds, sticks, and grass, which are all tied together and designed in the form of a semi-circle. The entire area is lit with lanterns, seating is arranged around a log fire, and food and entertainment is provided in the true African style. I can get back with you shortly with the menu and costs," said Lamberti.

"Well, that all sounds fabulous. There is something else," added Otto ruefully. "I'm not sure if you are the right person to speak to, but we are five unattached males and a party would be awfully dull without female company. Can you assist us?"

"I understand what you are saying," replied Lamberti, "but this is not exactly my field of expertise. However, I can give you a contact number of a person in Cape Town who may be able to help you. Hold on while I look up his number."

After a few seconds had elapsed, he came back to the phone and said, "Here it is. Phone Cape Town 27-11-3441260 and ask for a guy called Phil Plaatjies. He owns a place called Phil's Night Club and Massage Parlour. By the way, it is none of my business, but you should be aware that under South Africa's strict Immorality Act, sexual acts between different races, if that is what you are contemplating, is against the law."

"Thanks for the advice," said Otto. "I will certainly keep that in mind." Secretly, however, he thought, *What a load of hogwash.* In any case, the property was well hidden from the road and, besides, they were German citizens. No one would dare start with them.

Without going through his secretary, he phoned Cape Town on his private line and asked for Phil Plaatjies. After a short wait, he was put through to him.

"Mr. Plaatjies," he began, "my name is Otto Schtiller, and I am speaking to you from Hamburg, Germany. I have bought a property in Cape Town and intend on having a housewarming party on the night of December 19. There are five of us coming out, all males, and we would like five of your best girls to act as hostesses for the evening . . . if you know what I mean. I don't mind paying you well, but the girls must be top class. Germans like their women to look buxom, you know, full-breasted and not too thin."

Plaatjies quoted him a figure, which was accepted. The night club owner added that he would personally bring the girls out to his house and asked if 8:30 p.m. would be suitable.

Otto, recalling Lamberti's warning, said that would be perfect. By the time the girls reached Hout Bay on the other side of the peninsula, it would already be getting dark. There was no point in tempting fate.

"You will have my best girls," replied Plaatjies, "but remember, my terms are strictly cash in advance."

"That is no problem," replied Schtiller, "I will pay you on delivery of the girls."

As soon as he had finished, he dialed his secretary and asked her to get Gunther Schultz on the line, and after a few moments, she announced that he was on the line.

"Gunther! Otto here. I need a favour from you. My guests, Helmut Meyer, Jurgen Kannermeyer, Hans-Jeorg Volker, and Willy Weitenkamff, will be arriving at Cape Town Airport on Wednesday, December 19 at 7:30 a.m. Do you think you could fetch them and bring them to Villa Castello? They are arriving on Lufthanza flight LH 706."

"I would do it with pleasure," responded Gunther, "but I will be out of town on that date. However, I have a friend, Philip Watermeyer, coming to stay with me, and I am sure he will be able to help you. I'll get him to phone you in the morning."

The next morning Philip phoned Otto Schtiller, introduced himself and said, "Gunther has filled me in on all the details, and I will be happy to fetch your guests at the airport."

Otto replied that he would reimburse him for his time and expenses. Philip declined any form of payment, saying that he was free on that date, and, in any case, he would be using the company's Kombi.

"Well, in that case, I owe you a favour," said Otto. "Goodbye."

CHAPTER 16

BLOEMFONTEIN

December 14, 1979

Jannie was just settling down to dinner with his parents and two sisters, when the phone rang. The maid answered and announced that the call was for Jannie.

"That must be Christine," said Jannie, expecting a call from his girlfriend. It was Johan Kruger, captain of the Stellenbosch 1st XV rugby team.

"Jannie," he said, "you know our first XV is touring Scotland and Wales from mid-December? Well, our regular fly-half, Bryan Van Wyk, has aggravated his knee again and has been ruled out of the tour. I'm pleased to inform you that you've been selected to take his place. We'll be assembling and practicing our drills over the next few days. I might add that it wasn't easy getting seats for a touring party of twenty-five, as the planes are full of people going to Europe for Christmas. We did, however, manage to get a booking aboard a British Airways flight, which departs on the evening of December 24. Sorry to mess up your Christmas, but that was the best we could do. How soon do you think you could get down here?"

Rugby, in sports-mad South Africa, was something of a religion. There was no turning down an invitation like this, even though Jannie was planning to see quite a lot of Christine during the holidays, and his father had planned to take him on a hunting trip.

"I could be there on Monday," replied Jannie excitedly. Nothing beats an opportunity to travel overseas with the 1st XV rugby team.

"Don't forget your passport," interjected Kruger. "I hope it hasn't expired."

"No, it's still valid," answered Jannie.

"Oh, one more thing," said Kruger. "There's a message here for you to call a Warrant Officer Adriaan Pretorius of the Hout Bay Police Station. I hope you're not in any kind of trouble."

"No," replied Jannie, with a chuckle. "I'm a member of the Reserve Police," he said proudly, "and from time to time I'm called out to help whenever they're short staffed."

"Fine. Then we'll see you in a couple of days," concluded Kruger.

December 17, 1979

On his arrival in Stellenbosch, Jannie immediately made two phone calls: one to Johan Kruger to inform him of his arrival and the other to Warrant Officer Adriaan Pretorius of the Hout Bay Police Station. The latter informed him that they were short-staffed and asked if he could report for duty on the 6:00 p.m. shift beginning the week of December 17. Jannie replied that he would be available only until the twenty-third, as he was going overseas on the twenty-fourth.

Jannie looked forward to his duties, as he always felt good in his blue uniform with the Sam Browne and the P38 pistol in his holster. Besides he was doing something for his country and, with a little bit of luck, he might even be able to catch a communist or two.

CHAPTER 17

THE HOUSE- WARMING PARTY

December 19, 1979

Philip Watermeyer had risen early and proceeded to Cape Town International Airport to greet the arrival of the *Hamburg Four*. As the four did not know him, he made a board on which he had boldly written their names; however, he noticed them before they had seen the board.

It wasn't difficult to spot four exuberant German tourists, especially those wearing heavy winter clothing. One in particular had a loud convulsive laugh, which could be heard clearly over the din of the arriving passengers. They obviously were going to make the most of their short holiday in the sun.

After collecting their luggage from the carousel, they spotted Philip with his board and introduced themselves to him before proceeding to the *bureau-de-change* to exchange their deutschemarks into rands. Then they proceeded out of the terminal building, shedding excess clothing along the way, before piling into the kombi for the fifty-minute drive to Hout Bay.

"What time is breakfast?" inquired Willy Weitenkamff.

"Don't they serve breakfast on Lufthansa flights anymore?" asked Philip jokingly.

"Yes, but that was an hour and a half ago," responded Weitenkamff, followed by that convulsive laugh of his. *It obviously did not take much to set this jovial fellow off,* Philip concluded.

They were so engaged in conversation, that they didn't realize they had turned off the main coastal road to Villa Castello. It was obvious to Philip that the four were in a party mood and nothing was going to stop them from having a good time. They entered the main gates of the complex and received a salute from the guards, who were expecting them, and jocularly returned the salute. Philip circled the fountain and brought the Kombi to a halt in the courtyard where they found Otto, and the staff of four waiting to greet them in the old aristocratic manner.

Otto greeted his guests warmly and introduced them to caretaker Joe Bailey, his wife, Susan, the house maid and the cook. He then introduced himself to Philip, thanked him for fetching his guests, and asked him to stay for breakfast. Philip declined with thanks, and after unloading the luggage, wished them all a happy holiday and departed.

Addressing his guests, Otto said, "The maid and Mrs. Bailey will escort you to your rooms, where obviously you'll want to freshen up and get into more appropriate clothing. We'll be serving breakfast in about half an hour in that building over there," he said, pointing to the glazed, pool-house pavilion.

When the guests were assembled in the pool house, Otto announced the programme for the day. He said that after breakfast, he would take them on a conducted tour of the complex and gardens.

"I think we've bought ourselves a very beautiful place here," concluded Hans-Jeorg Volker. Everyone agreed.

"Later on," said Otto, "I'll take you for a drive to show you the quaint little village of Hout Bay, which is a few kilometres from here. I'm only now getting used to driving on the wrong side of the road."

"Well, I hope you don't practice on us," bellowed Willy Weitenkamff and promptly broke into his infectious laughter, which prompted everyone to join in.

"We'll have a late lunch in the village," said Otto, "and I suggest we all get some rest this afternoon to wear off the jetlag. I've planned a special evening for tonight and even organized some beautiful girls for us."

"Well, now you are talking!" responded Willie Weitenkamff, followed by his convulsive laughter. Willie obviously found everything amusing.

"The theme of tonight's party is 'Out of Africa.' I hope you remembered to bring your khaki trousers with you, which I reminded you about a few weeks ago. If not, you can buy yourselves a pair in the village. I've bought each of you a khaki-coloured tee-shirt with an animal imprint on the front, so you'll all look the part tonight. For you, Willy, I've bought an oversized shirt with a lion motif on it."

"I certainly don't have a problem with that," growled Willy.

The evening was to be organized with Germanic precision. Organization was, after all, Otto's strong point. He had alerted the guards at the gate house that a small workforce would be arriving at 3:00 p.m. to set up the *boma*, which, he had instructed, was to be erected adjacent to the pool house. He also alerted the gate to expect three more vehicles: one at about 4:30 p.m. bringing the troupe of Zulu performers and another marked L. L. Caterers, which would be arriving at about 7:30 p.m. with the food and drink. Finally, they were to expect a large white Chevy sedan at about 8:30 p.m. with five ladies and a driver on board. No one else was to be allowed in without first checking with him.

At precisely 3:00 p.m., the workers arrived and began setting up the boma, under the supervision of caretaker Bailey. Otto had instructed Bailey exactly where he wanted the boma to be erected. He said that he would be back from the village shortly after 3:00 p.m.

On their return from the village, his guests retired for a nap, while Otto kept a watchful eye on affairs. He gazed with interest on the unfolding design of the semi-circular reed and grass boma. The operation was slick, as befits workmen who have gone through the exercise many times before.

While some were attending to the erection of the enclosure, others were fetching tables and chairs from the truck and putting them around a central spot, which was destined for the log fire. And hanging lanterns would provide just the right ambiance. Satisfied with the preparations, Otto retired temporarily to his room to freshen up just as the Zulu performers were arriving to set up their act.

At 7:35 p.m., L.L. Caterers' van arrived with the food and wine and began to lay out the buffet dinner, kept hot with warmers. Otto was handed a typed menu which consisted of:

- Fresh home-baked breads
- Garden salads of wild mushrooms, spinach, and sun dried tomatoes.
- Butternut and mango soup
- Marinated chicken kebabs
- Grilled lamb chops
- Crocodile cutlets
- Kudu filet steak
- Barbecue and mushroom sauce
- Corn on the cob
- Cape brandy pudding

- Pecan nut pie
- Fresh fruit salad
- Assorted cheeses with savoury biscuits
- Coffee and tea

A meal fit for a king, Otto thought. The food was laid out on trestle tables buffet style and looked positively mouth-watering. Otto had never tasted wild game before and wondered how the crocodile cutlets and kudu steak would go down. His guests would be thrilled. He had ordered the best Cape wines, which were laid out on a separate table.

As the caterers were providing a waiter service, Otto informed his staff that they could retire to their quarters for the evening. Their quarters were just the right distance from the main villa—convenient but not obtrusive.

As blasé as he was, this was going to be a very special evening, one that he and his guests would never forget. He had, after all, spent a considerable amount of time and money ensuring the success of the function.

CHAPTER 18

THE PIMP

The combined effect of two of the earliest Apartheid laws made it illegal for Whites to marry Blacks and to declare sex across the colour line strictly illegal. To enforce the act, police raided homes and broke into bedrooms to photograph couples breaking the law.

Phil's Night Club and Massage Parlour, located at 130A Buitengracht Street in downtown Cape Town, had been under surveillance by the SA Police for some time. It was known that the innocuous looking nightclub on the ground floor was simply a front for the massage parlour on the first floor where all the action took place. They suspected the owner, Phil Plaatjies, a small balding man in his late fifties, of flouting the government's strict policy regarding inter-racial sex.

Detective Sergeant Roelof Van der Merwe and his colleague, Constable Joe Ntuli, were sitting in their unmarked Ford Cortina parked across the street, keeping a watchful eye on the premises. They were in plain clothes. Sergeant Van der Merwe had noticed that Phil Plaatjies had, from time to time, left the premises in his white Chevy sedan, obviously transporting girls to clients all over the city. His departures were usually timed for approximately 8:00 p.m., when the summer light was beginning to fade.

Sergeant Van der Merwe had joked at the incongruity of such a small man driving such a large American car. He surmised that the large car gave Plaatjies a feeling of power. Once they had even seen him bring a cushion, which he placed below his buttocks, to give him a better view of the road.

Having obtained the evidence he needed, Sergeant Van der Merwe was in a position to file an official report to his superior officer. For the law to succeed, the parties had to be "caught in the act."

At exactly 7:45 p.m. on the night of December 19, 1979, he observed Phil Plaatjies leaving the club with five girls aboard. He decided to follow them in his unmarked squad car at a respectful distance. He watched them as they headed up Kloof Road, into Camps Bay, then along the coastal road. At the crest of the hill, they turned off the main road to a place called Villa Castello.

Sergeant Van der Merwe promptly activated his car radio and made a report to Warrant Officer Adriaan Pretorius of the Hout Bay Police Station, under whose jurisdiction the area fell. He said he believed an offence under the Immorality Act was about to be committed. Warrant Officer Pretorius knew from experience that to catch the miscreants in the act, it was essential to let the proceedings gain momentum. To react too early would be to court failure.

Pretorius decided that between 11:00 p.m. and 11:30 p.m. would be a good time to mount the raid. Having calculated that approximately five couples might be involved, he made arrangements for a convoy of four vehicles.

At 8:15 p.m., Otto and his guests proceeded to the boma to await the arrival of the girls. They all looked comically resplendent in their khaki trousers and animal-print shirts, and none more so than the corpulent Willy Weitenkamff in his oversized shirt with the lion motif.

"Ya," said Willy with a growl, "even lions get hungry." Everyone laughed, even reserved Hans-Jeorg Volker, who was normally a slow starter.

Just then, they heard a short blast of a hooter in the courtyard, as Phil drove up with the girls in his white Chevy. Otto and the men went to the courtyard to meet them. The girls alighted. Phil introduced them as Desiree, Faye, Gerda, Amy, and Sadie. They were unmistakably the top of the crop—young and buxom. Phil had kept his word.

Otto and Phil walked aside, obviously conducting business.

"Are you happy with the girls?" enquired Phil. "They are my top girls."

"Ya," replied Otto, "they are most attractive," and he handed over the cash.

"Thank you," said Phil, "and have a good evening. I'll be back at 10:00 a.m. to fetch the girls. By the way, you have a wonderful place here." He got into his car and, with a surge of V8 power, drove off.

It was a cool, clear evening following a balmy Cape summer's day. The full moon cast its shimmering light over the calm bay below. Otto reflected on the wonders of Africa. Perhaps one day when his career was finally over, he would retire here. The villa was perfect—so beautiful yet so remote. And there was still the nude beach nearby to investigate.

The men escorted the girls to the newly completed boma, which, with its glowing log fire and hanging lanterns swaying gently in the cool evening breeze, looked quite magical. The trestle table with the scrumptious selection of food beckoned invitingly. It was a veritable banquet and Otto made a mental note to phone Luigi Lamberti in the morning to congratulate him on his catering.

Otto had decided to partner with Amy, the most buxom of them all. It was obvious that these girls were professionals and knew exactly how to please their men.

They all sat down, opened some wine, and fell into casual conversation. Soon they were drinking toasts to Germany and South Africa, then Hamburg and Cape Town. The food was consumed with great gusto. Germans enjoy good food. Even the crocodile cutlets and kudu fillet steaks, after initial reticence, went down well—they were determined to try everything.

They had just finished their sweet course, when a narrator came forward to introduce the evening's entertainment. He said, "Dancing and ritual are important facets of African life. The first act will feature a Zulu War Dance."

The narrator once again spoke. "Now I have pleasure in introducing the Muchongolo Tumbling Dance Act."

He clapped his hands, and six dancers and three drummers burst into the arena in a frenzy of energy. With arms outstretched they performed somersaults before forming a line in front of the drums. They were bare, except for kilts of civet skin around their waists and cattle tails which hung from their neck, arms and knees. The dancers of the Muchongolo were hand-picked acrobats, whose tumbling could only be performed by the very fit. The dancers shouted excitedly during their routine and ended up with legs waving in the air before departing.

Otto and his guests clapped enthusiastically; they had never seen anything like this before.

The narrator re-appeared to introduce the second act. "Another facet of African cultural life is ritual. The goal of ritual is to connect the African with the spiritual world. Bizarre masks are worn to create an aura of mystery. Animals and bush spirits feature prominently because of their ancestors' experiences in the bush. The next act is called 'The Dance of the Hunters,' where members of a tribe dance a re-enactment of a hunt in honour of a deceased tribal member."

He clapped his hands and four ghastly apparitions appeared from the shadows, wearing strange masks representing an antelope, warthog, boar, and hyena. Their long shaggy hair tumbled from their necks over their dark woven costumes. The masks were hideously contorted by the light of the flickering log fire. The "animals" were closely followed by a troupe of hunters. The animals cowered before the hunters, who symbolically pointed their rifles at them. To the beat of calabash drums, each animal-like figure took a turn to enact the characteristics of his represented animal. Then they departed.

Otto turned to his guests and said, "Ladies and gentlemen, I believe we've seen something special here this evening. However, the caterers would like to clean up now, so let's take our drinks to the pool house next door and continue our party there. The night is still young."

Within forty minutes, the boma was pulled down, the place cleared, and the caterers and dancers departed. The party continued unabated in the pool house.

In a pre-arranged move, Otto invited Amy to see his underground bar, which he had discovered only recently. They headed for the trophy room, with its collection of stuffed animal heads peering down from the walls—obviously, trophies from successful hunts.

He removed the loose Persian carpet, lifted the trap door, and, before descending the stairs, turned on the dimmer switch, which automatically brought on the air conditioning.

No sooner had they reached bar level, when the large nude figure of Willy Weitenkamff and his partner appeared in the illuminated pool porthole in a riot of bubbles and froth. He and his paramour obviously had decided on a skinny dip. *Now I know what Sid Kaplan meant when he said they'd had plenty of fun in this bar*, Otto thought.

Meanwhile, Hans-Jeorg Volker, Helmut Meyer, and Jurgen Kannermeyer had escorted their partners to the comfort of their respective bedrooms. Except for Willy Weitenkamff in the pool house, a hush descended over the villa.

At precisely 11:00 p.m., Warrant Officer Adriaan Pretorius and his convoy of four vehicles left Hout Bay police station. The men had been properly briefed. The first squad car would carry the two detectives, the two yellow Ford patrol vans carrying two constables each would be in the centre, and he and the reservist Jannie De Beer, would bring up the rear in his 1979 Datsun. Jannie was excited, as he had never been on a raid before—he had the rank of constable.

They ascended the gentle slope outside the village and, at the crest of the hill, turned left off the main road. At this point, as previously arranged, they switched off their lights before stealthily approaching the gates of Villa Castello.

Having caught the guards by surprise, they ordered them to open the gates before handcuffing them to the gate posts. Then, by the light of the moon, they quietly drove over the cobble-stoned driveway and parked their vehicles about seventy metres from the villa.

On entering the courtyard, Warrant Officer Pretorius heard noises coming from the pool house and promptly dispatched Constable De Beer to investigate. Meanwhile, he and the others headed for the front door of the villa, rang the bell, and receiving no answer, entered the premises. Realizing that the bedrooms were upstairs, they quietly ascended the grand, carpeted staircase and burst into three separate bedrooms in which they encountered a startled Helmut Meyer, Jurgen Kannermeyer, and

Hans-Jeorg Volker in bed with their partners. Gathering them all together, he brought them into the hallway.

In a loud authoritarian voice, as he touched each one, Warrant Officer Pretorius announced, "You are committing an offence under the Immorality Act. I am arresting you all and you must accompany me to the Hout Bay police station to be charged." A unique requirement of the law was that he had to touch each person lightly to confirm the arrest.

In a state of shock, the men and women hastily dressed and found a dishevelled and also hastily clad Willy Weitenkamff in the courtyard, noisily protesting his innocence. The men and women were briskly bundled into different police vans to be taken to the Hout Bay Police Station. On the way out, the officers released the guards, who had been handcuffed to the gates. As far as the police were concerned, this was a highly organized and well-rehearsed mission.

As soon as they arrived at the police station, the men and women were separated. The men angrily demanded an explanation, explaining that they were German nationals, who had only arrived in the country that very morning. They demanded to see the German consul.

"It will do you no good," replied Warrant Officer Pretorius, who read them their rights. "You have broken the law. We will need to take your fingerprints, make out a charge sheet, and open a docket. This will explain why you have been arrested. You will spend the night in the cells and tomorrow you will appear in the magistrate's court to be sentenced. There is the possibility of your being deported, but being first time offenders, you may be let off with a fine if you sign an admission of guilt."

That evening the men were issued blankets and served fish and chips obtained from a nearby café. Warrant Officer Pretorius knew that the real purpose of the exercise was to catch the pimp, who was the brains behind the racket, but they would deal with him later.

***

As soon as the guards had been released from the gates, they bounded down the driveway toward the villa to report what had happened. They found the villa deserted, and having spied a dim light on in the caretaker's flat, rang his doorbell. Minutes later, an obviously half asleep Mr. Bailey answered the door. Both guards excitedly spoke at the same time—obviously in a state of shock. It took Mr. Bailey a few minutes to calm them down and obtain a coherent statement.

Eventually one spoke and said, "Sir, the police have come and taken the guests away, but we did not see Mr. Schtiller with them."

"Did the police turn left or right on leaving the gates?" queried Mr. Bailey.

"They went right," said the guard doing the talking.

"Well, then they have gone to the Hout Bay Police Station," said Bailey. "Let's search for the boss," he said with genuine alarm.

They searched the entire complex, picking up loose items of clothing discarded on the pool house floor, but there was no sign of him. Mr. Bailey quizzed the guards again who were adamant that Mr. Schtiller had not left the complex.

"There is one place we have not searched—the underground bar," said an exhausted Mr. Bailey. I'll try the intercom," he said and dialled the number, but there was no answer. He tried again and an irritated voice answered.

"What do you want!" snapped Otto.

"Mr. Schtiller," Mr. Bailey said, "we have a crisis on our hands! The police have come and taken your guests away! I believe they are at the Hout Bay Police Station."

"*Gott in himmel!*" exclaimed Otto, who always broke into his native German when excited. "I'm coming up." Turning to Amy he said, "The cops have been here. I fear the worst. You wait here and don't move until I say so. I'll be back."

He looked at his watch and saw that it was well past midnight. He hastily dressed and went upstairs. On meeting the obviously distraught Mr. Bailey and the two guards, he said, "Mr. Bailey, thank you very much for your help. I'm sorry your evening has been disturbed. Please go back to sleep. I will deal with this matter myself."

After Mr. Bailey and the guards departed, Otto immediately phoned the Hout Bay Police Station and asked for the officer in charge. Warrant Officer Pretorius answered.

In a loud voice, Otto asked, "Are you the person in charge?"

Warrant Officer Pretorius answered, "Yes, I am."

"My name is Otto Schtiller from Villa Castello. My house guests have been taken away by the police. Are they with you?" He gave their names.

"Yes, we have them here," Warrant Officer Pretorius told him. "They are being charged under the Immorality Act of 1950."

Otto Schtiller launched into a verbal tirade. "We are German citizens! Is this the way your country welcomes overseas tourists by invading their private homes?" He threatened a diplomatic row.

Warrant Officer Pretorius listened attentively and replied in a calm voice. "Sir, I am afraid they have broken the law. As a police officer, it is my duty to uphold that law. Your friends will be detained overnight and formally charged in the magistrate's court in the morning. I believe they will be released with a fine, provided they sign an admission of guilt. You can fetch your friends about 10:30 a.m." He then gave Otto the address of the court building.

Otto could not sleep that night, or what was left of it. His thoughts were with his friends, holed up in some cold, inhospitable cell. What a way to spend your first night in a new country. He felt a tinge of guilt at not telling his friends about the Immorality Act. After all, he had been warned by Luigi Lamberti. He just never remotely considered the possibility of his home being invaded by the police. In no country in the world is there a law like this.

At ten o'clock that morning he got into his car. He had made arrangements with Mr. Bailey to drive Amy home. As Otto drove past the gate house, an image of the poor unfortunate guards chained to the gates came to mind. The day guards gave him the customary salute as he passed through.

Shortly after ten o'clock, Phil Plaatjies arrived in his white Chevy to fetch the girls. As he approached the gates, three policemen appeared from behind a bush and arrested him. He was, after all, the main target in the first place.

The magistrate had indeed let the men off with a fine and a warning. Otto's embarrassment knew no end. He was not looking forward to being confronted by his friends. He imagined they would be shattered. To his surprise, however, he discovered that Helmut Meyer had seen the whole episode as a joke and something to tell his friends about back home.

"They even served us breakfast," he said.

Even Willy Weitenkamff, after his initial shock, reported that the station commander had been quite friendly and asked him all about life in Hamburg. Only Hans-Jeorg Volker had taken it badly and threatened to take the matter further, which was bad news, as Hans-Jeorg was a big client of his in Hamburg.

As far as Otto was concerned, an evening that held such promise had ended in complete chaos. He was in no mood for forgiveness. This government with its stupid laws was to blame, and he would not forget this in a hurry.

The following morning, a small article appeared on page two of the morning newspaper, under the headline, FOUR GERMAN TOURISTS APPREHENDED IN IMMORALITY RAID. *It seems*, Otto thought, *that the usually anti-government press is more concerned about selling newspapers than in protecting the privacy of unfortunate citizens, who are victims of this senseless law.*

CHAPTER 19

OFFICE OF THE PRIME MINISTER

In 1978, Peet Bothma came to power in the wake of the "Information Scandal," an event that forced the resignation of his predecessor. His accession to the premiership coincided with serious internal and regional threats to the white regime. The newly independent status of Mozambique and Angola, and the disintegration of rebel Rhodesia, had brought new impetus to South Africa's liberation struggle.

On assuming power, however, Peet Bothma set about changing the political landscape of South Africa. He surprised both his supporters and opponents alike by his reforming rhetoric. Black South Africans were to be brought fully into the economy, he declared, and the wage gap eliminated. In addition, a host of discriminatory legislation was to be dismantled. This was an astonishing about-turn and a major break-through at the time. The new 1984 constitution, which amalgamated the powers of president and prime minister, was to put enormous power in his hands.

Sadly though, events had overtaken him and within twelve months he was faced with foreign disinvestment, acts of violence, and, worse still, a political backlash from his right wing, which had broken away to form its own political party.

A famous poet once wrote, "The most dangerous time for an unpopular regime is not when natural desire for freedom is benumbed by total control, but when people are offered breathing room and a ray of hope."

December 12, 1979. Office of the Prime Minister.

Peet Bothma was in his large, comfortable, oak-lined office. The South African flag stood proudly behind him to one side. One wall was lined completely with books, and the other held portraits of former prime ministers, all benignly looking down upon him. *One day*, he thought, *my own portrait will be added to the wall.* There was space for quite a few more.

He was working on his Christmas Day speech, which was to be televised live to the nation on Christmas Day. He felt good about this speech. The phone rang, interrupting his thoughts; it was his secretary.

"Sir," she said, "General van der Riet is here for his 10 a.m. appointment."

"Please usher him in," responded the prime minister.

A tall, albeit stooped figure entered. General van der Riet was the head of the Bureau of State Security. He was the prime minister's most trusted lieutenant, one on whom he could always rely. In other quarters, though, he was feared, mostly on account of the shadowy activities of the Secret Police, which he headed.

General van der Riet had come to deliver his monthly report on the security situation.

"How are you, Gerhard?" asked the prime minister, smiling.

"I am well," came his reply, "and I trust you are the same?"

The prime minister nodded. "Will you have tea?" he enquired.

"Thank you," replied the general, nodding.

Lifting the phone to his secretary the prime minister said, "Annemarie, one black with two spoons of sugar for the general and the usual for me."

Impressed with the prime minister's memory for detail, the general suppressed a smile.

"Well, general," said the prime minister, "what do you have for me today?"

The general read from a prepared report. "As you know," he said, "there were three incidents of bombings in the past few weeks. I have to report that major damage was done to some government installations but, luckily, loss of life was comparatively limited. Obviously, it was the work of the UAC, which is resorting to hit-and-run tactics. In one of the attacks, the bomber blew himself up."

"Serves him right," said the prime minister.

"The situation is, however, under control," added the general, "and the townships are comparatively quiet." The general continued on for a while, and then handed the prime minister his typed report.

"Thank you," said the prime minister. "It is my firm conviction that world opinion is slowly coming around to our point of view. Here at the tip of Africa we are of immense strategic importance to the West. As you know, we closely monitor all shipping around the southern coast of Africa, including, of course, all Soviet shipping."

Wagging his finger, as was his habit, the prime minister said, "You would be amazed at the collaboration that goes on behind the scenes. Britain, for example, has a special relationship with us because of our long-standing economic ties and does not believe in harming our economy, unlike some other countries."

"That's most interesting," observed the general.

"And what is the situation on Robben Island?" enquired the prime minister, gazing out of his window across Table Bay.

"Everything is under control on the island," said General Van der Riet. "The prisoners, led of course by Khumalo, are always grumbling. One can never satisfy them. They want improved food, better treatment, and larger rations of tobacco. From time to time, we get visits from the International Red Cross and Human Rights delegations."

"Obviously, we are notified in advance of these visits, and when this happens, we issue the prisoners with fresh uniforms and put meat in their diet for the day. It is important to show the world that we treat our prisoners humanely. Some of the prisoners have been there for sixteen years, you know."

"Incidentally, Khumalo has had to be taken to hospital in Cape Town."

"What happened to him?" asked the prime minister, his voice rising an octave.

"Well," explained the general, "he hurt his right heel while exercising in the courtyard. It's an old injury, and the x-rays revealed bone fragmentation. However, he is back on the island again. That is all I have to tell you."

The prime minister thanked him for his comprehensive report and personally escorted him to the door.

On seeing him at the door his secretary interrupted, "Sir, I have the head of police in the Western Cape, Colonel Albert Du Toit, on the line. He says it is urgent."

"Okay, put him through," said the prime minister. Waving a brief goodbye to General Van der Riet, the prime minister returned to his office.

"I am sorry to disturb you sir," said Colonel Du Toit, "but my undercover agents have informed me of a rumour that Truman

Khumalo is planning an escape. My informants are usually reliable, and I thought you should know."

"Well," replied the prime minister, "I have just had a meeting with General van der Riet. The general normally has his ear close to the ground, and he mentioned nothing of this. It's probably just another rumour. Thank you anyway for calling."

He sat back gazing at the ceiling and reflected on his first fourteen months in office. He had introduced meaningful reforms, which had been welcomed by both the Indian and Coloured communities. Even the usually critical opposition press had praised him for his reforms. Yes, he had lost support to the Right, but had gained from the Centre.

As the previous Minister of Defence, he had transformed South Africa's armed forces into a formidable fighting unit. He would deal with international sanctions. He had reason to feel satisfied and continued writing his speech.

Suddenly he stopped writing. *What if the rumours are true*, he mused. Having Khumalo and all his cohorts behind bars was a major coup for his government. If Khumalo did somehow manage to escape, he would leave the country and probably join the UAC. in exile. Then the situation would really escalate. *Yes*, he thought, *it wouldn't hurt to tighten security*. He would give the order in the morning.

He resumed writing his speech.

CHAPTER 20

ROBBEN ISLAND

Early July 1964

Each morning loads of stones about the size of volley balls were dumped at the entrance to the courtyard. Using wheelbarrows, the prisoners had to move the stones to the centre of the yard, where they had to crush them with hammers. They wore makeshift wire masks to protect their eyes. The work was tedious and difficult. The repetitive routine of prison life was designed to break their spirits and destroy their resolve. At 4:00 p.m., they were allowed half an hour to clean up. There was no hot water. At 8:00 p.m., they were ordered to go to sleep. A single mesh-covered bulb in the cells burned day and night.

One morning in early January, they were lined up and marched to a covered truck. It was the first time they had left the compound. A few minutes later, they emerged at a lime quarry, an enormous white crater cut into the hillside. The idea was to use picks to extract the lime. It was strenuous work. They would work on the quarry for thirteen years. They worked until 4:00 p.m., at which time they had to carry the lime to waiting trucks.

The glare of the white lime hurt their eyes. Their requests for sunglasses were turned down initially, but thanks to the Red Cross, conditions gradually improved.

Communication with the outside world was accomplished in two ways: via those prisoners whose sentences were complete and who were leaving the island and through contact with visitors. Prisoners who were leaving would smuggle out letters in their clothing or baggage. Passing letters to visiting lawyers was another method of getting information out, as lawyers were never searched.

The struggle would prove neither short nor easy. After the Rivonia Raid, much of the underground machinery had been destroyed. Virtually every one of the UAC's senior leaders was either in jail or in exile.

For as long as Robben Island had been used as a prison, people have tried to escape. Khumalo and his men considered various escape plans—even one involving a helicopter painted with South African military colours—but all of these plans had been rejected by the UAC high command as being either impractical or too dangerous.

CHAPTER 21

EVE OF DEPARTURE

December 14, 1979

Philip was relaxing on the porch of his friend Gunther Schultz's house when the phone rang. It was Arthur.

"Philip," he asked, "are you alone? May I speak freely?" Philip assured him that he could. "I don't know if you realize it, but the temperature in Moscow at this time of the year is negative eight degrees Celsius. You'll need ultra-warm clothing. Please go to Ahmed's Outfitters in Plein Street in Cape Town and get yourself suitably outfitted. You'll need vests, long underpants, polo-neck sweaters, jerseys, and one or two padded coats. Also, you must get a few track suits for the training sessions.

"Oh, and don't forget some stout boots and long, thick socks. Don't pay for them. That has been taken care of already. I'll have all your documents ready for you by next week. Meet me at the usual place at six o'clock on the evening of December 20. I've arranged for transportation to bring you to Riz's house and take you back.

"Meanwhile, I suggest you learn some Russian phrases and read up about the country. Get yourself a book on Russia at the travel section of the Executive Book Shop. Oh, and once again I must ask you to be discreet and not discuss your plans with anyone. If you do, you'll be jeopardizing not only your safety but also the safety of others. See you next week."

It had been a quiet week for Philip. Time had dragged somewhat. He had been to Ahmed's shop and obtained the requisite clothing. It was not every day that one was able to obtain a free wardrobe of clothes. Ahmed had been very helpful. No questions had been asked."

Philip had jogged every morning and been to the beach a few times. He felt fit and in good condition. As far as his host was concerned, he would be leaving for a holiday soon.

At 5:00 p.m., on the December 20, his driver arrived to take him to Riz Kahn's house for his meeting with Arthur and the others. On arrival at the house, he was ushered into the back office to be greeted by Vincent, Sipho, Faizil, and Arthur. As usual, Arthur was the first to speak. He never wasted time or words.

"Philip, I am pleased to inform you that your appointment has been ratified by UAC's high command in Dar es Salaam. So, how have you been passing the time?"

"Well, I've been to Ahmed's shop and obtained the necessary clothing, as you requested," replied Philip. "Also, I've been keeping fit and reading up about Russia, a country that seems to have had quite a fascinating history."

"Yes, she has," said Arthur knowingly. "She's been through some interesting times. I've been there many times and know the country well. It's vast. You're going to find it fascinating, especially as you've never been abroad before." Reaching for his briefcase, Arthur produced a wallet.

"Here are your traveling documents, including traveler's cheques and some loose English change. You can start using the English currency on the plane, as you'll be travelling on British Airways. Use this credit card in case of emergencies only. You'll be traveling under the assumed name of Philip Jordan and, ostensibly, will be going on a student-study tour.

"Here is your itinerary," he said, handing Philip a typed document. "Let me just go over it with you quickly. On December 24, you'll leave Cape Town Airport for London at 7:25 p.m. on flight BA 058 and arrive at Heathrow Airport on the 25th at 6:25 a.m.

"You'll go through passport control, fetch your luggage, and proceed through customs. When you're in the general concourse, go directly to the ABC Book Shop. One of our operatives, who has received a photograph of you, will approach you with the words, 'Excuse me sir, what operation are you from?' You will answer, 'Operation Khulula', and he will then hand you your new passport and other documents for Russia and Tanzania. The purpose of this exercise is to obliterate all references to these countries which would attract suspicion with your South African passport.

"You'll then leave Heathrow Airport for Moscow on BA 872 at 9:20 a.m., so you won't have much time there. You'll arrive that evening at Sheremetyeva Airport in Moscow at 4:15 p.m. where you'll be met by Captain Valeriya Checkov, who will escort you to your quarters and brief you. The captain speaks good English and will act as your mentor and interpreter during your stay. You'll spend a month in Moscow at the Moscow Institute of Strategic Studies, where you will undergo the necessary training.

"On January 26, you'll depart Moscow for London on BA 873 at 5:30 p.m. and arrive at 10:30 p.m. at Heathrow and spend the night at one of the airport hotels.

"On the 28th, you'll leave Gatwick Airport at 10:25 p.m. for Dar es Salaam, Tanzania, on BA 2069. You'll arrive at Dar es Salaam the next morning, the 29th, at 11:55. You'll be met at the airport and taken to your hotel. While there, you will meet members of the external organization of the UAC and the High Command, to whom you will debrief on your activities in Russia. You will discuss the plan in detail.

"On January 30, you'll depart Dar es Salaam on BA 2068 at 7:30 p.m. and arrive the next day at Gatwick Airport at 5:15 a.m. where you'll be met by the same operative you met before. Spend a few days in London and relax before coming home. Destroy your old documents and resume using your original traveling documents.

"On February 3, you'll depart Heathrow Airport for Cape Town at 7:50 p.m. on BA 58 and arrive the next day at Cape Town Airport at 8:25 a.m. You'll be met at the airport by one of our drivers. Do not attempt to contact us here in South Africa while you are away. In an emergency, contact our London operative."

Turning to the committee, Arthur asked, "Does anyone have any questions regarding Philip's mission?"

"I do," said Sipho, turning to Philip. "How are you going to explain your absence to your parents and the university authorities, when university reopens?"

"Well," answered Philip, "I think we should let the immediate future take care of itself. However, I, too, have a question that I have been meaning to ask for some time. Can anyone here explain to me why my training has to take place in the Soviet Union and not in any of the Western countries, with which South Africa has traditional ties?"

"I think, Arthur, that you are in the best position to answer that one," Sipho responded.

"Well," said Arthur, "it goes to the very core of our international connections. I'll try to explain it as well as Barney Pityana did. Pityana was one of the founders of the South African Student's Organization. Black consciousness has always had a particular aversion to capitalism, which, in South Africa, has led to racism. The South African Communist Party was founded in 1921, nine years after the UAC. Although its appeal was limited, it did afford a bridge between White and Black that was not available elsewhere. As the ally of the UAC from its early days, Moscow developed into its principle backer when the movement was in exile. When the UAC changed its policy from one of passive resistance to one of armed struggle, the only source of arms was from the USSR and some Eastern European countries. The USSR not only supplied us with arms, but training and counseling as well. That's why you're going to the USSR. Does that make sense?"

Philip nodded. As usual, Arthur had summed up the situation perfectly.

Addressing Philip, Arthur said, "We'll arrange transportation to the airport for you on December 24, but we'll say goodbye to you here, so as not to arouse suspicion at the airport. Oh, by the way, the money you requested for your father's medical bills has already been taken care of."

"That's wonderful," replied Philip. "That's something off my mind."

"You need to leave here with a clear mind," said Arthur.

"Why don't we drink a toast to Operation Khulula?" Vincent suggested.

A bottle of whisky and five glasses were produced. "On behalf of all of us and a grateful population, we wish you the best of luck and God speed," Arthur said, raising his glass.

"To Operation Khulula," they all chorused.

Philip shook hands with everyone and left the room. He was met at the front door by Riz and Zakkiya, who had come to say goodbye. Each hugged him in turn and wished him well. On seeing him climbing into the car, Zakkiya remarked with a glint in her eye, "So young to be going on such a dangerous mission. He carries the hopes of millions on his shoulders."

On the way home, Philip's mood suddenly changed to one of introspection, and he began to question the events which led to his present situation, and yet, equally, all self-doubts were suddenly erased. He had always been a fatalist, believing that everything in life happens for a purpose. One thing was certain: life as he knew it would never be the same again.

He still had some tricky tasks to overcome. His commitment to the mission made his immediate future uncertain. He would write to the university authorities telling them that he had been invited to join a church group on a study tour overseas and was not sure of the return date. Then he would phone his dad to inquire about his health and give him the welcome news that funding for his medical bills had been arranged.

A new chapter in his life was beginning, and he was not at all sure of its ending. Strange that his first trip abroad should be to the USSR.

December 24, 1979

The great day dawned. It occurred to Philip that this was the first Christmas he would spend away from home. Was it an omen that he would be travelling on Christmas day, of all days?

Packing wasn't easy. London and Moscow would be very cold, but Dar es Salaam being near the equator, would be excruciatingly hot. However, he would be there only for a few days.

His lift to the airport arrived at 4:25 p.m., three hours before departure. The ride to Cape Town International Airport would take approximately thirty minutes. His emotions were a mixture of excitement and anxiety. He had never set foot outside the borders of his country before and here he was off to some exotic, far off land and a rendezvous with people he had never met.

Checking in at the British Airways counter was uneventful; however, a strange feeling of guilt came over him, and he privately hoped he would not see anyone he knew. He decided to go straight through passport control to the international departure hall and await his call to board BA 058 to London. Before he could board the plane, however, there was a shock in store for him.

CHAPTER 22

THE MISSION BEGINS

December 24, 1979. Cape Town International Airport

Philip was about to take a seat when he heard a familiar voice calling his name. He turned in consternation and saw that it was his friend Jannie De Beer. Jannie was with a group of varsity colleagues, all wearing maroon university blazers and scarves. Having got over his initial surprise, he stammered, "Jannie, what are you doing here? I thought you were in Bloemfontein with your parents."

"Well," answered Jannie proudly, "I received a last minute call-up to join our First Rugby XV. We're touring Scotland and Wales in our off-season. And where are you going to?"

"Remember I mentioned to you the possibility of getting a short, all-expenses-paid holiday with my church group? Well it came off," said Philip convincingly. "That's my group over there," he said, pointing vaguely to a small group across the room. "What a coincidence that we should both be on the same plane, but I suppose life is full of these little coincidences. We're going to Holland," he added with a straight face. If Jannie knew the real purpose of his trip, he would explode. They had chosen positions and would henceforth be on opposite sides of the political fence. He wasn't at all sure what the outcome would be.

"I'll speak to you later," Jannie said and went off to join his team-mates. Philip grabbed a chair and passed the time reading an abandoned newspaper.

At exactly 6:45 p.m., an announcement came over the public address system. "Will all passengers traveling on British Airways Flight BA 058 to London, please board now at gate twenty-five." The enormity of what he was undertaking hit him. He rose slowly from his seat and walked briskly to gate twenty-five. Jannie and his group were not far behind.

At the boarding gate, Philip inquired if he had been allocated a window seat and was met with the reply, "Yes, Mr. Jordan, you have window seat. Twenty-five A. Have a good flight."

It took some moments for him to get used to his assumed name, but it was absolutely essential that he did. He boarded the aircraft, stowed away his overnight bag in the overhead storage compartment, and settled into his seat. Jannie passed down the aisle giving him a friendly wink.

The plane took off at precisely 7:25 p.m., and within minutes they were airborne. As it was his first flight abroad, he marveled at the apparent ease with which such a large aircraft could take off. Drinks were served, and dinner followed.

After dinner, he met up with Jannie again, who asked him rather smugly if this was his first trip overseas. He said it was. He remembered Jannie telling him that whenever his father traveled overseas, he always took the whole family with him, but then his family could easily afford such an indulgence.

It was at this point that Jannie dropped his bombshell. "Tell me, Philip," he said, "I might have heard wrong, but I thought the airline attendant addressed you as Mr. Jordan when you went through the boarding gate."

Philip's cheeks turned a pale red, but with a presence of mind that impressed even himself, he answered, "She must have been addressing the person behind me," an explanation that was readily accepted. The rest of the evening was uneventful and, after he had seen the in-flight movie, he slipped on his eye patch and dozed off to sleep. Even the *whoopee* made by the rugby fellows at the rear of the plane failed to disturb him. He had always been a good sleeper.

Philip awoke early and went to the toilet to freshen up. Soon the plane started its descent to Heathrow Airport. He remembered to set his watch back two hours. Before touching down, the captain made an announcement to thank everyone for travelling with British Airways and to wish everyone a Merry Christmas, which was followed by a chorus of "Merry Christmases" from the passengers. They touched down at 6:25 a.m.

December 25, 1979

At the airport, Philip followed the other passengers, collected his luggage, and went through customs before heading for the ABC Book Shop in the general concourse. Within minutes, he was approached by a person who enquired, "Excuse me, sir, what operation are you from?"

"Operation Khulula," Philip answered.

He was handed an envelope, after which his contact disappeared into the concourse as quickly as he had come. As he had three hours to kill before his Moscow flight, he attended to his luggage and passport formalities. However, there was something of vital importance he had to do before anything else. Using the spare English change given to him by Arthur, he sought out a phone booth and dialled home. As the uncertainties facing him were daunting, he needed to be re-assured that all was well at home.

He had just settled into a chair in the departure lounge, when a BBC newsreader on an overhead TV monitor, interrupted the programme to announce that the USSR had just invaded Afghanistan. This was startling news. Could they not have waited until after he had left? He fished out the book on Russia, which he had bought in Cape Town, and began to read. It might be beneficial to know more about this vast, mysterious country to which he was headed. Because of the *Iron Curtain*, so little was known of this land. This curtain must be lifting as the XX11 Olympiad was due to be held in Moscow in July, and the focus of the world would be on that city.

Philip lifted his head momentarily and pondered on Russia's complex history. All countries have had their tumultuous pasts: America had her War of Independence, Britain various conquests and wars, France her Napoleonic adventures, and Germany has started two world wars. Apart from minor diversions, all of these countries have since settled down.

It occurred to him that as far as South Africa and the USSR are concerned, their stories are still being written. Just then, there was an announcement that Flight 872 to Moscow was now boarding through Gate 75.

CHAPTER 23

MOSCOW ODYSSEY

The flight to Moscow was uneventful. The aircraft made a wide circle over the outskirts of Moscow and touched down at approximately 4:15 p.m. Russian time—he had remembered to set his watch three hours ahead. Sheremetyevo Airport was about twenty-nine kilometres to the north of Moscow and well-sited with regard to the river port, seas, and motorways. Philip's immediate task was to make contact with Captain Valeriy Checkov.

On entering the terminal building, he noticed that Sheremetyevo Airport was a little different from Western airports he had seen illustrated. The men at passport control looked incredibly young, Philip thought. They checked his passport and visa and compared his photo to his face.

"What is the purpose of your visit?" he was asked rather brusquely.

"A study tour," answered Philip, not wanting to go into too much detail. After what seemed like an eternity, but which was in reality only a few minutes, they stamped his passport and waved him through.

When he arrived at the carousel, luggage was already tumbling out of the hatch and after retrieving his suitcase he re-joined the queue at customs. He was met by a customs official, a large burly man in his fifties, wearing a uniform clearly too small for him. He noticed that the customs officials were searching cases at random.

He was politely asked to open his case. The official expertly padded his hands through it, disturbing nothing, before waiving him on. A glimpse through a window revealed blizzard conditions outside. He stopped, opened his suitcase, and fished out his thick, polo-neck jersey and overcoat. The next step was to make contact with Captain Valeriya Checkov. He wondered what he would look like.

On entering the Arrivals Hall, he saw his name on a sign board held aloft by a strikingly beautiful female army officer. She was statuesque, about twenty-four years old, with long, flowing auburn hair. He went up to her, introduced himself, and said he was expecting a Captain Checkov.

"I am Captain Checkov," she said, explaining that the forename Valeriya was unisexual in Russia. "You simply add the suffix 'a' for a female. I have been assigned to you to ensure that your stay in Moscow is as comfortable and as enjoyable as possible. If there is anything you need, you are to ask me."

Besides her obvious good looks, she appeared to be most agreeable. Catching a glimpse of the *Bureau de Change*, he asked if she could look after his luggage while he exchanged his pounds for roubles. At the bureau, he noticed he had received a good rate for his pounds.

On leaving the airport, he was met by an icy, arctic blast. He had never experienced such cold before. Observing his discomfort, his host said, "The first thing you must do is purchase an *ushanka*, a fur hat with ear flaps, to protect your ears." She said they were experiencing a somewhat warmer spell as the temperature had risen to negative three degrees Celsius. It could go down to negative fifteen degrees Celsius again.

Everything was new to Philip. He inquired the make of car she was driving, and she replied that it was a 1976 Moskvitch, made right here in Moscow at the AZLK plant.

"Cars were scarce until 1960, but now the plant produces 200,000 of these compact cars per year," she added proudly. "Spare parts are still scarce, and some drivers automatically remove their windscreen wipers when they park their cars to prevent pilfering." Philip observed that many of the features of her car were outdated by Western standards.

They left the airport and travelled down Leningradsky Prospekt, a six-lane, concrete highway linking the airport to Moscow. Hundreds of women, wearing thick yellow waistcoats, were cleaning debris off the large centre island.

"Every adult, male and female, has a job," she observed. "That is the beauty of our communist system."

As they drove on, great, ten-to-twenty storey, monolithic, apartment blocks began to appear on both sides of the highway. To speed up construction, every component had been pre-fabricated, giving a dreary conformity to the environment.

The trees had long since shed their leaves and the grey winter light did nothing to relieve the monotony of the landscape. Sensing Philip's interest, Captain Checkov said, "The government has never been able to meet the demand for housing, a problem worsened by the destruction of six million housing units during World War II."

Maybe the Russians have developed a fetish for gigantism, Philip thought, but he felt that the buildings had lost all scale. Further on they passed the Memorial to the Heroes erected in memory of the Red Army, who defended the city against the German invaders during World War II.

"The German advance halted at this point, only a short distance from the city centre," Captain Checkov proclaimed.

"Our forces responded magnificently." Subconsciously she slowed the car down out of respect. "I know you are here for special training," she said, "but may I ask the purpose of this training?"

"All I can tell you," answered Philip, "is that the people of South Africa live under an oppressive regime. We hope to accelerate a process of change enabling us to install a truly democratic government. It might have to be done by force, and your country is going to assist us with the necessary training and plan of action. The USSR always has been most sympathetic to our cause."

"We can certainly identify with your people's struggle for freedom," she said. "Everything here has changed for the better since the revolution. The government is here to serve the people, unlike some Western countries."

Closer to Moscow, as they moved away from the urban sprawl, the architecture had become more interesting but the traffic heavier. Reading Philip's thoughts, Captain Checkov told him that Russia builds upward to save space as well as the forests, and that there is little demand for private homes.

"Let me tell you about Russian life," Captain Checkov said. "Russian families are very hospitable. Our gatherings are often spontaneous and unplanned and not restricted to one particular class. Vodka is our national drink, and no party is complete without it. You had better get used to the taste and also to smoke-filled rooms. Smoking and drinking are national pastimes. Often parties start in one place and move quite naturally to the next."

"In the old days, the whole family—parents and grown-up children—lived in one big room, with sections curtained off for privacy. Because of the shortage of space, they had to sleep in shifts. Nowadays things have changed, and everyone has a flat that includes a stove and refrigerator. Telephones, however, are hard to get, and people still have to queue for basic necessities like meat and butter. Other than that, life is very good for us."

"Tell me, Mr. Philip," she inquired, her mood becoming less formal, "are you married? Do you have a girlfriend?"

"No, I'm not married. Actually, I'm still at university and don't have a steady girlfriend at the moment. And, please, call me Philip." Sensing her interest in his background, he continued. "I was brought up on a farm near the small town of Vryburg. I'm an only child and am studying to become a mechanical engineer."

"How is it that a mechanical engineering student is getting involved in such dangerous politics?" she asked pointedly.

"Well, there's always been something of a rebel in me," he answered.

"I am interested in astrology," she said. "What sign of the zodiac were you born under?"

"I'm an Aires. My birthday is the second of April. What about you?" he asked. "Where did you learn to speak such good English?"

"I learned English at school, and after I graduated, I spent a year in London working as an *au pair* for a London couple who had two little girls. Then I returned to Moscow to join the army. It is a steady job, and I don't have to worry about clothes so much, as I am in uniform most of the time."

Philip thought she could be a real beauty if she took a little more interest in her appearance. Her heavy overcoat seemed to be concealing a really stunning figure.

Suddenly her mood changed. She had momentarily let her guard down and realized it. "Let's discuss your programme," she said with an authoritative voice. "You will be stationed at the Moscow Institute of Strategic Studies for the duration of your stay. Owing to the freezing weather, your training will be mostly indoors. However, they have excellent facilities and the building is centrally heated. As you will be under the direct control of Colonel Aleksandr Leonov, the director of the institute, your mission must be important. Please contact me if you need anything. Here are my particulars," she said, handing him a card.

"Let me explain your programme to you. Today is Tuesday, December 25. As your course only starts on Wednesday, January 2, this will give you a few free days to see our great city. I have been instructed by the colonel to show you around, as he is keen for you to see something of our way of life during your stay here."

"Tonight my parents are having a little get together at their flat, and they would like you to join them. It will give you an opportunity to see how we Russians live."

"I would be delighted to come," replied Philip.

"In that case," she said, "I suggest that we go directly to the institute, where you can sign the register and put your things in your room. Then we can drive straight to my parents' home and get there before the others arrive."

They drove to the Institute of Strategic Studies on Moskovoretskaya Nab, a wide tree-lined street overlooking the Moscow River. *So this is to be my home for the next few weeks*, Philip mused.

The complex of buildings had been designed in the eighteenth century and was considered to be a masterpiece of baroque architecture. The wings of the building formed a perfect parade ground, which was reputed to be a favourite spot of the tsars.

The courtyard was accessed from the street through an impressive triple-storey archway, surmounted by a base-relief sculpture composed of a charioteer urging on a team of horses. On entering the archway, they were stopped by two guards wearing great coats and *ushankas*. Philip noticed that everyone was wearing *ushankas*. Valeriya produced her security card and was waved on. They parked in the courtyard and entered the west wing via a large double-volume lobby. She introduced Philip to the registrar, who helped him fill out some forms and handed him the keys to his room.

He entered his room and was pleased that it had a view of the impressive courtyard. After dropping off his suitcase, they headed for her parents' flat, about a forty-minute drive through the western side of town. Most of the buildings were designed in the neo-classical style. Unlike a relatively young country like South Africa, there were very few modern buildings to be seen, and yet many of the old buildings were quite charming. The roads, though, seemed in urgent need of repair.

Women, with buckets and trolleys and wearing those same yellow waistcoats, were cleaning the streets. Philip had read that Russian men seldom helped at home and that Russian women were the backbone of the economy.

Philip noticed a brown car following them. They turned a corner, and it was still there. Were they being shadowed? He found himself silently tracking it in his rear-view mirror. They turned another corner, and it disappeared. He was overcome with a sense of relief.

As they approached the flat in Pavelski Street, Valeriya told him that her mother's name was Olga, her father's name Yuri, and her brother was Surgei. The names of the couple coming over were Tanya and Konstantin Kournikhova, friends of the family. Although they did not speak English, she assured him that he would be made to feel very much at home. At 125 Pavelski Street, they parked the car and walked up three flights of stairs. Valeriya introduced Philip to her parents, and her father promptly gave him a bone-breaking bear hug, her mother a large toothy, gold-filled smile. He immediately felt at home.

The other couple and her brother had not arrived yet, which gave Valeriya a chance to show him around the flat.

Yuri and Olga Checkov lived in a three-room flat, which they shared with Olga's mother until her recent demise. Olga was a woman of ample proportions, with thinning grey hair which she wore in a bun, while Yuri was a rotund, jovial man who worked as a supervisor at an engineering works. He had grown podgy through lack of exercise and too much vodka. But he enjoyed life, especially his food.

For the party, the centre of focus was undoubtedly the kitchen table, which was crammed with food to be served in no particular order. There were mounds of boiled potatoes, sliced roast, vegetables, caviar, sausage, and bread. Caviar was served on special occasions only, which this was.

To buy food for the dinner table, Olga has to queue up to select the items, then join another queue to pay the cashier, and a third to obtain a receipt. At each store she visits, she is shoved and jostled by the customers. It is around this large kitchen table that all entertainment takes place. Such is the intensity of Russian friendship that they linger for hours and indulge in talk ranging from the shortage of certain foodstuffs to the Russian space programme. They were pleased to be living in Moscow, as they felt that all good things in Russian life tended to flow there first.

Philip was shown around the flat. A large print depicting a wheat harvest hung behind the main bed. In the bathroom, the Checkovs had installed a washing machine, which cleaned the laundry, but was not capable of spinning or drying it.

A large bookcase dominated the living room. Valeriya explained that Soviet people spent an eighth of their spare time pouring over books and magazines; hence, no living room was complete without a bookcase. The living room windows were covered with lace curtains, and a gold-plated chandelier hung from the ceiling. The flat was modestly furnished but cosy.

A ring at the door announced the arrival of Valeriya's brother, Surgei, and Tanya and Konstantin Khournikova. They were introduced to Philip, after which everyone sat down around the kitchen table. Valeriya's father, Yuri, poured neat vodka into seven small tumblers. It was served chilled and taken with a bite of marinated fish or pickled cucumber. In broken English, he proposed a toast to their special guest from South Africa. Everyone raised their glass, the contents of which were gulped, not sipped. Philip, although reticent at first, was encouraged to do likewise.

He gasped and everyone laughed. Thereafter, he was much more cautious. It was the first of many toasts, all tossed back neatly. It is considered bad luck to leave half-empty bottles of Vodka on the table.

Everyone helped themselves to the food with great gusto. The caviar was the first to go. There was much laughter and camaraderie. A second bottle of vodka was opened. Valeriya excused herself from the table and headed for the spare bedroom, where the phone was kept after the death of Olga's mother.

She dialed and Colonel Leonov answered. "Comrade Colonel, I am reporting to you as requested. We are now at my parents' home. He seems to be who he says he is. His birthday correlates with our records, and the photograph fits."

"Does he know the real reason you were in London?"

"No. I told him I worked there as an *au pair*. He suspects nothing."

"Well, it is one thing to be a freedom fighter from South Africa, whose cause we support, but it is quite another to be an Amerikansky spy, posing as a freedom fighter. It would be a disaster if we allowed a spy to inspect the inner workings of the institute. Show him around the well-known tourist spots and keep a sharp lookout for anything irregular. You know the drill—make him fall for you."

"As you say, Comrade Colonel," she said and re-joined the party.

With the meal over, Yuri produced a guitar, and everyone joined in singing Russian folk songs. The atmosphere was most convivial, and at one stage, Yuri did an impromptu jig.

Valeriya turned to Philip and said, "My father says he does not like the name Philip. He will call you Tavaresh. He has a pet name for me too—he calls me his little Babushka." It was obvious that Yuri was the soul of the party. Philip was asked to sing a South African song, and he obliged with the national anthem, which was followed by much clapping. A third bottle of vodka was produced, and the room began to fill with smoke. Yuri loosened his belt, took his boots off, and encouraged others to do the same.

The evening wore on, and Philip asked Valeriya to drive him back to the institute. He has had a long day.

"My father says I must bring you back again. He likes you," she said.

On the way home, she informed him that she would call for him at 9:00 a.m. As Colonel Leonov felt that it would be most useful for him to imbibe a bit of Russian culture, she would be taking him to see the Kremlin and Red Square. She parked the car in the courtyard of the institute and, to Philip's surprise, kissed him gently on the cheek.

December 26, 1979

They met in the courtyard at 9:00 am. "Good morning, Tavaresh," Captain Checkov said. "How are you this morning?"

"A little bit of a hangover, Babushka, otherwise okay."

"Well, today we are going to visit the spiritual heart of our city, namely the Kremlin and Red Square." They drove along the river-fronted Muskovoretskaya Nab, took a right, and parked the car opposite the huge Hotel Rosslya, which was near the Gum Department Store and a stone's throw from Red Square.

"The first thing we must do, Tavaresh, is to get you a *ushanka*. Otherwise your ears will freeze off," she said. They stopped at a small street stall to purchase one, which he immediately slipped on.

"That feels a lot better," he remarked.

"Now you are beginning to look like a real Russki," she added with a chuckle.

Right next to the *ushanka* stall was a newspaper kiosk. Philip glanced at the English language *Moscow News* and was surprised to find no mention of the Russian invasion of Afghanistan. In the West, this was big news. *Maybe*, he thought, *the Russian government has an instinctive resolve to cover up certain news or perhaps protect the people from bad news.* Whatever it was, it appeared to him to be some form of censorship.

Glancing at a map of Moscow, Philip noticed that the city was laid out in a series of rings with the Kremlin and Red Square in the centre. Each ring marked an historical boundary of the city. All roads led to the gates of the Kremlin, the very hub of Imperial and Soviet might. For Philip, Red Square was immediately associated with TV images of stern-faced Soviet leaders, standing in the bitter cold, as a presentation of military might rumbled past the review stand atop Lenin's mausoleum. The magnificent square, over 70,000 square metres in extent, is framed by the walls of the Kremlin, the exuberantly coloured St. Basil's Cathedral, the stark serenity of Lenin's Tomb, and the expansive facade of the Dan Department Store. A strict route ensured that everyone pass St. Basil's Cathedral. Philip marveled at the unusual Russian-styled onion domes atop the cathedral.

As they entered the square, Philip was approached by a *fartsovchiki*, a black market dealer, who offered his services for currency exchange. Valeriya advised Philip to have nothing to do with him.

Lenin died in 1924, but his preserved body still draws the faithful. Philip and Valeriya joined the long queue. Once inside, visitors were not allowed to pause and hold up the line.

Eventually they emerged. "Now we will be heading for the Kremlin," Valeriya advised, "which is right next to Red Square and an outstanding monument of Russian history. The Kremlin dates back to 1147 and the very beginning of Moscow," she added. "It is the seat of our Soviet Government." Her patter seemed word perfect, and it was obvious to Philip that she had been through this routine many times before. They joined a tour group and emerged a few hours later.

They walked to the car along one of the streets, and he could not help noticing a three-storey high poster, illustrating a heroic military figure, with the slogan "Glory to the Communist Party." The city seemed a charming blend of anarchy and nostalgia. Large anachronistic Gothic skyscrapers dominated the skyline, but it also had plenty of character, with whole streets lined with neo-classical mansions of the old aristocracy. Wandering into a back alley off the main roads was like entering a time warp—little had changed from the time of Tolstoy and Dostoevsky. In one area, street musicians were playing lively music and in another, long lines of people were queuing up for scarce goods.

Heavily built women were conscientiously cleaning the streets, while older women were begging for a few roubles. The street scene was lively and vibrant. Philip made a mental note to come back again on his own. From the car park, it was but a short drive to the river.

Although the weak winter light was beginning to fade, Valeriya observed that there were lovely city views to be had from the embankment at this time of day. They parked the car and, as they walked, her hand momentarily sought out his, but remembering she was in uniform, she swiftly withdrew it again.

A warm and unexpected feeling enveloped Philip. Was he developing feelings for this lovely but different Russian girl? They seemed quite happy in each other's company. Conversation wasn't necessary.

After a brisk walk, they headed back to the car. Philip was feeling the delayed effects of his long flight and asked to be taken back to his lodgings. In the courtyard of the institute, under the cover of darkness, she fondly kissed him good night. Without thinking, he retaliated by planting a passionate kiss squarely on her lips. Funny, that this kiss should have such an effect on him.

She said she would phone him in the morning.

An office of the KGB, Lybyanka Square

"Did you gain access to the captain's flat?" asked the major.

"No problem, comrade major," answered the subordinate. "I have placed bugs in the living room, bedroom, and bathroom."

"Why the bathroom?"

"Well," he answered wryly, "there is no harm in mixing business with pleasure."

Thursday, December 27, 1979. 9:00 a.m.

The phone rang, and Philip slowly raised his sleepy head. "Hello," he growled after picking up the receiver.

"Tavaresh? It is me, Babushka."

"Sorry, Babushka. I was in a deep sleep. What time is it?"

"It is nine a.m. How soon can you be ready?"

"I can be ready in thirty minutes."

"Fine. See you downstairs in thirty minutes," she said.

Philip got ready and met Valeriya in the courtyard. "Today," she said, "I would like to take you to Gorky Park. I suggest we leave the car here and go by Metro."

On the way to the station, Philip observed that there were signs that said rather impersonally *Aptyeka* (pharmacy), *Bulochnaya* (bakery), and *Myasa* (meat) but nothing that could convey an element of ownership like Vladimir's Pharmacy, Igor's Bakery, or Gorky Street Butchery. They entered the underground under a red neon sign marked M. As part of the Stalin plan for the reconstruction of Moscow, an underground railway was built that would convey a spirit of entrepreneurship. It was planned by Stalin as a showpiece of Soviet engineering capable of transporting the workers rapidly in socialist luxury.

Inside was a hive of activity. People were selling bread, vodka, lottery tickets, and ball-point pens. An ex-army guy in a blue army overcoat was playing a double bass.

Valeriya informed Philip that this activity goes on until late at night. "During the war," she said, "many of the stations had doubled as air-raid shelters." Philip noticed that some of the escalators went on forever, leading seemingly deeper and deeper into the bowels of the earth. They boarded a train and emerged at Park Kultury Station in the Frunze District. From there it was but a short walk over the Moskva River to Gorky Park.

Philip had never seen such a large park before. It contained boat rentals, open-air theatres, and ice rinks. Cross-country skiers careened down slopes, and people were towing their children around on toboggans. Some men were breaking the ice in ponds and swimming in the freezing black water. Others were stripping to the waist and rubbing their bare chest with snow in an impressive display of virility. No one was without their *ushankas*. It was obvious that Muscovites had a passion for outdoors and enjoyed their park in any weather. Philip and Valeriya spent the day in the park.

On the way back to the institute, Valeriya informed Philip that Colonel Leonov wanted him to spend a few days in the library. He had prescribed some reading matter, which needed to be reviewed prior to the commencement of the course.

She said that Sunday would be their last free day for a while and asked him if he would like to see something of the countryside followed by a home-cooked meal at her flat. He said that sounded great and her face lit up.

"I will call for you at 10:30 Sunday morning," she said and embraced him in a passionate kiss. She had now thrown all caution to the wind.

Sunday, December 30, 1979

Philip and Valeriya rendezvoused in the courtyard at 10:30 a.m. The temperature had dropped.

"The weather has been unseasonably high," she remarked. "It was bound to drop." They drove south and out of town. Light snow was beginning to fall. Their drive took them past lovely villages, scattered amid dark forests. Although the highways were in good shape, Philip observed that the country roads were in poor condition. She explained that it was a question of houses before roads.

Farther on they passed a few *dachas*, which are used as second or vacation homes. "For Muscovites, the perfect destination over weekends is a *dacha*," she said. A few were quite grand, but most tended to be simple wooden cottages. For the vast majority who have no dachas, there are state-controlled resorts on the warm southern beaches of the Black Sea.

They drove alongside a river. "Do you feel like braving the weather and going for a walk in the snow?" she asked. "It might be cold, but it is very fresh."

Philip agreed and adjusted his *ushanka*. They strolled hand in hand alongside the river, stopping only for the occasional hug and kiss. He realized he was falling for her.

The snow was beginning to fall a little harder, and the temperature was dropping fast. Valeriya felt they should be getting home, which, for her, was a one-bedroom flat she was lucky to get, as it was not far from her parents' flat.

On arriving at the flat, she invited him to watch TV while she prepared dinner. The news came on. Philip noticed that there still was no mention of the Russian occupation of Afghanistan. As far as the Russian people were concerned, it was not an issue.

Soon dinner was ready—a romantic candle-lit affair. She had made duck with gravy and potatoes. It was piping hot and delicious. She opened a small bottle of vodka and admitted that she was not really keen on the drink. She poured the contents into two small tumblers, and it was swallowed in the prescribed manner. Philip choked, as he was not used to it. She laughed, and he joined in.

"The dessert course," she explained, "is a cream-filled gateau, bought at the nearby deli." She proposed a toast to the successful conclusion of his course and felt sure that, under Colonel Leonov's tutelage, he would acquit himself well.

The radio was switched on, and they danced closely to the music. She then made coffee. Suddenly it was 11:00 p.m. The weather outside had deteriorated further, making driving hazardous. He would have to stay the night, and she would drive him back in the morning. The flat was heated and cosy.

The walk along the river had numbed Valeriya's fingers and feet, which were still very cold. She felt she needed a hot bath before retiring, but, unfortunately, there was water enough in the system for only one hot bath. She suggested that he bathe first, and she would use his water. He said politely that she must go first, but she stuck to her proposal. It was a stalemate.

Emboldened by the vodka, he proposed a solution—they bathe together. She remained silent and he took her silence to mean acquiescence. The very thought of it was beginning to create a tingle in his groins. He had undressed her so many times with his eyes.

In a separate room, she modestly slipped into her dressing gown, fetched the still-flickering candle from the dining room, and took it to the bathroom. She ran the water and climbed in. Philip undressed and knocked tentatively on the partially-opened bathroom door. The voice inside bade him enter. She observed that he was adequate in all departments. Her senses were on red alert.

He climbed in behind her, so that they were both facing the same way. The water level rose, but it was warm and soothing. It was snowing steadily outside.

He asked her if she would like to experience his famous South African back-rub. She nodded her approval. He soaped his hand and glided it over her back and neck. She purred.

He slipped his hands below her arms and soaped her breasts. They were just the right size, and he felt her nipples begin to tighten. She nestled her back into his chest in a gesture of submission. His manhood was beginning to press into her back, and she adjusted it with her left hand. Her touch was electric.

He soaped her stomach in ever-declining circles until her whole body was in a state of heightened excitement. She moved subtly in sync with his hands. The water level ebbed and flowed.

Suddenly for the first time she spoke, "Philip, take me now."

They climbed out of the bath, dripping soap suds and water. There was no time to dry off and reach the bed. Hastily she spread a large towel on the floor.

She looked up at him expectantly as he lowered himself to dock inside her. The soap suds had made the process easier. *Soyuz* and *Explorer* met in a perfect manoeuvre, the action slow and rhythmical.

Within minutes, Valeriya let out a scream. "Tavaresh!" The voice trailed off.

Across the road, a tramp hovering over a brazier in an alleyway momentarily looked up startled, and then resumed his original position again.

The next day, when there was a break in the weather, Valeriya drove Philip back to the institute. On parting, she said, "Good luck on the course, Tavaresh, and please keep in touch."

He promised he would.

His course was about to begin, and he still had to finish reading the books in the library that Colonel Leonov had prescribed. Also, he needed to get a few nights of good sleep before his meeting with the indomitable colonel on Wednesday.

On the eve of his special training, the irony of the situation struck him again. Here he was on a pioneering mission that could possibly lead to a new order. A fleeting comparison with Louis De La Caille came to mind. The latter was a young, self-taught mathematician and astrologer, who, in a daring pioneering spirit, came to Cape Town in 1750 to set up an observatory. Within a year, he had managed to catalogue nearly 10,000 stars. *Was Louis*

De La Caille's pioneering mission any less dangerous than his own, he wondered.

On returning to her flat, Captain Checkov dialed the colonel. Recognizing her voice, the colonel responded, "Yes, comrade captain, what is your final report?"

"He is genuine."

"Thank you. You have done well."

CHAPTER 24

THE PLAN UNFOLDS

On arriving at his room, Phil found a note under his door which read:

Dear Comrade Philip,

Please meet me in my office, no. 312, on the third floor at 0830 on Wednesday for the start of your course.

Signed,
Colonel A. Leonov

Wednesday, January 2, 1980 at 0830.

Philip rose early, had a shower, and proceeded to office number 312. Not knowing what to wear, he put on his track suit. He was slightly apprehensive as he knocked on the door. The voice inside bade him enter.

Colonel Leonov had been born into a military family. His father, a tank commander, had regaled him with countless tales of how he and his tank corps had heroically pushed the Germans back all the way from Leningrad to Berlin. His father had taught him the benefit of discipline and of taking pride in serving the Motherland.

The young Leonov could not wait to join the army. At age sixteen, he had travelled to Moscow from the small town of Smolensk, to attend the elite Suvorov School. At this school, a significant number of boys were the sons of officers. The purpose of the Suvorov School was to prepare its pupils for military college. He graduated from the school first in his class and was welcomed at the prestigious Viroshilov College Academy, where he spent five years specializing in operational and strategic matters. This was his first love. After graduating with honours, he chose a posting to the Institute of Strategic Studies, where he rapidly worked himself up the ranks to become chief director.

On entering the room, Philip was met by Colonel Leonov, who had left his chair to greet him. The colonel had the classical look of a northern Russian—pale skin, blonde hair, and piercing blue eyes. He looked impressive in his uniform and appeared to be in his early forties.

"We meet at last, comrade. Welcome to Russia. I take it Captain Checkov has taken good care of you during the past week?"

"Very much so," answered Philip.

"And what is your impression of our country so far?"

"Very different from my own and most interesting."

"Well," said the colonel, opening a file, "let's get down to business. I see that you are going to be with us for approximately three weeks. I do not think we can make a soldier out of you in that time, but then this seems to be a one-off mission. Am I correct?"

"That is correct," answered Philip. He had known the colonel only for a few minutes, but it was obvious that this was a man possessed of a large measure of self-confidence and charm.

"We have had good reports about you, particularly from our Cape Town operative, Arthur Norman."

So I was right about him all the time, thought Philip. *So these are his masters.*

"I am sorry that Comrade Norman has injured his foot and was unable to come. Please give him my best regards, when you return."

"I certainly will," replied Philip.

"Have you had any formal military training?"

"Only at school."

"Sometimes that is not a bad thing. It is better to come here without any preconceived ideas. Now, please tell me in your own words about your mission and what you hope to achieve."

The colonel slumped back in his chair, closed his eyes with his forefinger and thumb, and settled back into a listening mode. He had a reputation for being thoroughly professional in these matters. Although he had already been properly briefed, he was prepared to listen again just in case he had missed something.

"South Africa," Philip began, "is a multi-racial country, with the Black population out-numbering the White population by about five to one, yet only the Whites are enfranchised. To entrench themselves in power, the present, exclusively White government has adopted a policy called Apartheid, which regulates every facet of a Black person's life. It is oppressive in the extreme. The people yearn for a democracy where everyone is treated equally."

"Why don't they organize a revolution and throw off the yoke of the oppressor? After all, they have the manpower to do so," interjected the colonel.

"There are good reasons why they can't. First, the White regime is highly organized and well-armed. Second, the Whites have the support of some of the most powerful countries in the

West. Remember, South Africa's mineral reserves are the envy of the world. Any revolution would have a detrimental effect on the West's strategic and business interests. Another issue is that the United Kingdom has hundreds of thousands of their own kin living in South Africa, and any violent uprising would give them a refugee problem of unimaginable proportions. So they maintain the status quo, while doing good business with South Africa. From time to time they make little anti-apartheid noises to placate the rest of the world."

"And to complicate the picture even further, the West sees South Africa as a bastion against communism in that strategic part of the world. The party representing the Blacks—the United African Congress, or the UAC—is in total disarray, as most of its leaders are behind bars. It's worth mentioning that not all the members of the UAC are Black, as the South African Communist Party has formed an alliance with them. Apart from a small government-in-exile in Dar es Salaam, the UAC is virtually leaderless at present. The situation is desperate."

Philip paused.

"Please continue," said the colonel.

"The only ray of hope lies in the release of their leader, Truman Khumalo. He is charismatic and has great leadership qualities. He could be a rallying call for change, especially as he has an open invitation to address the United Nations on the treatment of Blacks in South Africa. But he, too, is behind bars in a place called Robben Island, together with most of the UAC's top brass. His escape would make a big difference to the cause. That's why I am here."

The colonel opened his eyes and resumed his normal posture. "Tell me about this Robben Island," he said.

"Robben Island is a fortress-like island in Table Bay, about eleven kilometres from Cape Town, our second largest city. The island is 575 hectares in extent and has a harbour, maximum security prison, warder's houses, and a church.

"There are no beaches, but it is green and low-lying. Approximately half the island on the eastern side is covered with small trees and bushes, while the other half on the western side is bare. The bare portion contains an aircraft runway, which is in the shape of a cross. I have been shown a plan of the island, which I have committed to memory. Let me show you."

He asked for paper and sketched the island and its major features.

"It is a maximum-security prison, and no ships are allowed within 1.6 kilometres off its coast."

"What is the daily routine of these inmates?" asked the colonel.

"They used to do manual labour at a lime quarry, but that was stopped about three years ago. At present, conditions are less harsh, and they are now expected to do something useful, like learning a trade. At eight-thirty every week day, about twenty top political prisoners, who are housed in a special area of the prison called Section B, are marched from the prison to a workshop a kilometre down the road. This group contains Khumalo. We have information that that they're accompanied by five guards, one of whom is a dog handler.

"Are these guards armed?"

"No, they are not armed purposely, as the authorities believe that arming them would only pose a security risk, especially as they consider the island to be escape-proof."

"How far is this road from the coast?" enquired the colonel.

"About five to six-hundred metres," replied Philip. "At 1500 hours every day, they return to the prison, so they can wash before the evening meal. Their day ends at 2100 hours."

"Is there any way of communicating with the political prisoners?"

"Yes, there are ways without the authorities knowing."

"Let's discuss Cape Town," suggested the colonel, unfolding what appeared to be an up-to-date map of the city. "We keep strategic information and maps of most of the world's major cities. As you may have realized, intelligence-gathering is our business. Let's see, Cape Town International airport is over there, and the main roads out of the city all lead north," he said, pin-pointing their location on the map. "And Western Province Command Headquarters is over here."

My God, thought Philip, *he knows more about Cape Town than I do.*

"Tell me, comrade, has anyone ever successfully escaped from Robben Island?"

"Only one," answered Philip, "but that was a long time ago, before the introduction of the sophisticated security measures."

"And what is the weather like in January and February?" asked the colonel.

"It's usually hot, with not much chance of rain. The bay, though, is blanketed in fog from time to time."

"Please continue, comrade Philip."

"Cape Town is on a peninsula at the very tip of Africa. Sheltering the city to the south is Table Mountain, and this range of mountains stretches all the way to Cape Point, about as far south as you can go in Africa. This is the point where the two great oceans meet: the warm Indian Ocean and the cold Atlantic Ocean. Cape Point is a rocky promontory in the shape of a finger, which defines False Bay on the eastern side where the main naval base at Simon's Town is situated.

"It's worth noting that the area around Cape Point has not been called the "Cape of Storms" for nothing. There are lighthouses there, but many ships have foundered in the thick fog and stormy seas where the two oceans meet. The remains of no fewer than twenty-three shipwrecks lie strewn along the coastline."

"Is there a prominent landmark on the Atlantic side, away from the naval base?" inquired the colonel.

"Yes, the Slangkop Lighthouse near the fishing village of Kommetjie is the tallest lighthouse on the South African Coast. It's thirty-three metres high and because of its precarious position, took five years to construct."

"Please pin-point the exact position of the lighthouse on this map, Philip," the colonel said, producing a hydrographical map, comparing it to the map of the peninsula.

"I believe the exact position is at latitude 34 degrees, 8 minutes, 55 seconds south and longitude 18 degrees, 19 minutes, 12 seconds east," he said.

"Are there any beaches close by?"

"Yes, there is a small beach, but it is virtually inaccessible on foot because of the steep terrain."

"You said that all major roads lead north, but are there any roads leading south?"

"There are, but they all lead to a dead end. This is the end of the continent," replied Philip.

"Reverting to Robben Island, what did you mean by the word 'fortress'?"

"Well, it's classed as a high-security prison. There are seven observation towers: four around the prison and three positioned around the island. These towers, called Alphas one through seven, are manned on a twenty-four-hour basis and equipped with radar scanners and two-way radios. Alpha Three is close to the workshop I referred to. No ships are allowed within 1.8 kilometres of its coast, and this area is protected with underwater scanners.

"The moment the sonar and radar are activated, an alarm is automatically set off in the central control room. They also have two high-speed patrol boats capable of doing forty-eight knots. That's ultra-fast. These boats are armed with L.M.S. machine guns and have two-way communication with the island."

"When do these boats patrol the island?"

"Regularly at night, between 2100 and 2400 hours and during the day on special orders. In addition to the above, there are about 240 guards and trained dogs."

"You realize, comrade Philip, that in the eyes of the regime, Truman Khumalo is public enemy number one and within an hour of his escape, all harbours, airports, and roads will be sealed. The authorities will have the whole country out looking for him."

"It sounds hopeless, doesn't it?" said Philip resignedly.

"Not at all," replied the colonel nonchalantly. "In fact, I already have it figured out." Leaving his seat, the colonel said, "Let's leave it at that for today. I have arranged for Lieutenant Ivanov to show you around the complex tomorrow. Please finish reading those books on combat that I prescribed and carry on with your gym work. I will see you at the same time on Friday."

Wednesday, January 2, 1980 at 11:00 a.m.

General Chernenko was enjoying a well-earned rest in his country *dacha* near the village of Peredelkino, a thirty-minute drive from Moscow. Organizing the Afghan invasion had left him mentally and physically exhausted. The four-room *dacha*, nestling amongst the tall elm and spruce trees near a babbling stream, was the perfect retreat to unwind and relax.

Peredelkino, a writer's colony, was also popular with the military. Boris Pasternak, the great Russian poet and novelist, once lived there.

The phone rang at the *dacha*, and Madame Chernenko answered.

"Madame Chernenko, Colonel Leonov here from the Moscow Institute of Strategic Studies. May I have an urgent word with the general?"

"Just a second," she said, and a few minutes later, the general answered.

"This had better be good, Colonel. I have given instructions for no one to disturb me."

"Comrade general, a thousand pardons for disturbing your well-deserved rest, but something important has come up, and frankly I would be failing in my duty if I did not personally report it you. The matter is of national importance, and I believe requires an immediate meeting at the highest level."

"It sounds urgent."

"It is, Comrade General, most urgent."

"Well, knowing your record and reputation, Comrade Colonel, it must be important. I'd better get the others to join us."

"That will be a good idea, Comrade General. Can we meet in my boardroom, office number 320 at 9:30 a.m. tomorrow?"

"We'll be there."

In the Soviet Union, the Institute of Strategic Studies reported directly to Main Military Council, which, together with the Minister of Defence, controlled the armed forces.

Thursday, January 3, 1980

At 9:15 a.m., a sleek, black, chauffeur-driven Zil limousine swept through the monumental archway of the Institute of Strategic Studies. Heavy steel gates clanked closed behind it. Judging from the colour of the uniform and the elaborate braid on the collar and cap, the rear passenger was a person of the highest rank. The Zil was followed closely by a second, a third, and a fourth black limousine, all chauffeur-driven and carrying similar-ranking passengers in the rear seat. The startled guards saluted smartly as each car entered and parked in the courtyard.

In every instance, as the cars came to a stop, a bodyguard hastily emerged to open the door for his V.I.P. passenger. On entering the lobby, the registrar snapped to attention and saluted. The military men knew exactly where they were going.

Colonel Leonov was waiting at the boardroom table, being careful not to occupy the seat at its head. General Chernenko went directly to that seat and the others took up seats adjacent to the chief of staff. Colonel Leonov remained standing.

"Comrade Colonel," said the chief of staff, "I take it you know comrade Admiral Dimitri Rutskoi and Generals Vassili Varenikof and Valentine Ostrovsky?"

"Yes, I do. Good morning, gentlemen. Once again, my apologies for this hastily convened meeting, but there has been an important development which holds great strategic benefits for our country. As usual, timing is of the essence."

"Please proceed," said the chief of staff with a swift wave of his right hand.

Unfurling a large map of Southern Africa on the wall, the colonel proceeded to explain his hypothesis.

Comrades, as you know, we support liberation struggles in various parts of the globe. Our reward comes in the form of regional influence when backing the right side. The world today is a battle for influence, and we must constantly be on the lookout for opportunities.

The southern part of Africa holds great economic and strategic value for whomever controls the region. There has been a stalemate in the past, but recently, events have tilted the pendulum in our favour, and we must not let the opportunity slip. In Angola, for example, we support the governing party, the M.P.L.A., in its fight against the Western-supported Unita Rebels led by Jonas Savimby. Angola is rich in diamonds and oil.

South Africa is staunchly Western. With the encouragement of the American imperialists, they sent a battalion deep into Angola in support of the rebels. Their battalion was heavily armed, and they thought they could drive right through to the capital, Luanda. However, with the help of our Cuban comrades and superior air power, we drove them off with heavier than expected casualties. I believe we can control Angola into the foreseeable future.

In neighbouring Rhodesia, now named Zimbabwe, the previous illegitimate White regime, under Ian Smith, declared a Unilateral Declaration of Independence. However, in terms of the Lancaster Agreement now being brokered by the British Government, the Patriotic Front, led by Robert Mugabe and Joshua Nkomo, are destined to form the new government. Smith and his discredited minority are earmarked to play a minor role. Both Mugabe and Nkomo are avowed Marxists, and I believe we can count on them.

Similarly, in Mozambique on the east coast, the long-running civil war has ended, resulting in a victory for Samora Machel's socialist forces. On the West Coast, South West Africa is administered by South Africa under a U.N. charter. South Africa is under enormous pressure to give up its mandate. In fact, U.N. Resolution 435 demands that supervised elections be held in South West Africa. It is now only a matter of time before South Africa hands over control. As you can see, gentlemen the noose is tightening.

The final piece in the jig-saw is the biggest prize of all: South Africa. Besides being the industrial giant of Africa, it also contains a treasure trove of some of the world's most important minerals. It's the world's largest producer of gold, platinum, chromium, and vanadium. In addition, it possesses one-fifth of the world's known uranium deposits. Uranium, as you know, is an essential component in the manufacture of nuclear weapons. It is this supply line that gives the Americans the edge on us in the nuclear field. The only strategic mineral not available in reasonable quantities is crude oil, which Angola has in abundance.

From the above, you can readily deduce what control of South Africa would mean to us.

"That's very impressive," interrupted Admiral Rutskoi, "but as we all know, South Africa has a mighty efficient army, is well-organized, and more important, has the support of the West."

"Yes," said General Varenikov, "I agree. You can't compare South Africa to the smaller and less developed countries to the north. South Africa is not going to hand over her country without a bloody fight."

The chief of staff listened patiently and then spoke (it was his custom to have the last word). "Comrade Colonel, I agree with the others, that's where your hypothesis falls down. We all know you are a master strategist, but tell us how we can get our hands on South Africa without directly confronting the West?"

"Those are all good questions, comrade generals," replied the colonel. "In fact, our intelligence tells us that South Africa has already advanced to the stage where she may be developing nuclear weapons. As long ago as 1977, aerial reconnaissance photographs revealed what looked suspiciously like an atomic test site in the Kalahari Desert . . . right here," said the colonel, pointing to a spot on the map. "And on September 22 of the same year, a low-yield nuclear explosion occurred in an area of the ocean between South Africa and the Antarctic. Only South Africa had the capability to set it off and keep quiet about it. The nuclear club is not confined to the big-league players anymore. Some smaller countries, like South Africa and possibly India and Pakistan, may have joined already."

"Yes, yes," said the chief of staff, a little irritably, "but tell us how we can complete the jig-saw. Otherwise there is no point to this discussion."

The colonel continued unruffled.

With all the countries to the north now falling into Black majority hands, South Africa, as the last White-ruling government in Africa, is steadily and swiftly being drawn into a position of isolation. The White regime, with its racist policies, cannot continue to subjugate the volatile masses for much longer.

The South African Communist Party has formed an alliance with the UAC, which has discarded its previous policy of passive resistance in favour of armed resistance. This is a major shift in policy. As a result, our country and some Eastern European countries have been asked to supply weapons and financial aid. We also provide their cadres with basic training right here at the institute.

Strategic government installations have now been bombed, and there are reports of civilian casualties.

Through the good offices of the president of Tanzania, the UAC has been allowed to establish a government in-exile, and we are in direct contact with them.

Comrade generals, you have been most patient, but now we come to the crux of the matter. Truman Khumalo, their leader, and most of the UAC top brass are behind bars on a place called Robben Island, just off Cape Town. The island is right here [pointing to a spot on the map].

As Khumalo is a very charismatic and natural leader, the UAC is currently planning his escape. I have received a personal letter from Alexander Thembo, the acting president of the UAC, apprising me of the situation and formally requesting our assistance in planning the escape. In fact, the leader of the task force, comrade Philip Jordan, is already here, and I have personally taken him under my wing. I have information, comrade generals, that Truman Khumalo's escape will be a turning point and act as a catalyst for a major popular uprising.

That is the final piece in the puzzle. We have been asked for help and must not be found wanting. A national sense of grievance is a most potent revolutionary force, and we can harness it if we play our cards right.

I believe that, for the oppressed people of South Africa, the day of reckoning is near.

For a second or two there was silence. The colonel had, as usual, been most convincing.

The first to react was the chief of staff. "With all the changes taking place in that part of the world, there is bound to be a power vacuum," he said. "Should we succeed in our endeavours, I believe it will be our greatest diplomatic victory ever. We will control the whole of southern Africa and its mineral resources."

"Comrade generals," said Admiral Rutskoi, "we have just launched a new class of attack submarine. It is undergoing sea trials and is presently on its way to the Kamchatskiy Peninsula near Vladivostok to join the Pacific Fleet. It might be a useful exercise for us to conduct sea trials in warmer as well as colder waters. I could make the new sub, the *Admiral Federov*, available for the rescue mission, but on one condition."

"And what is that, Comrade Admiral?" asked the chief of staff.

"That the rendezvous be swift. After all, we are in unfriendly waters. We can only afford a limited time there before having to move out. It would be too risky to stay longer."

"Then its settled," said the chief of staff. "Are we all agreed?"

There was general agreement.

"Congratulations, Comrade Colonel, on your well-thought-out appraisal. I'll leave it to you and comrade admiral to work out the finer details. When you have done so, please let me have your report, so that I can brief Secretary General Podgorny."

The general arose, closely followed by the others, and they all left as swiftly as they had come. The colonel had good reason to feel satisfied with himself. He had lost none of his old skill.

Friday, January 4, 1980 at 08:30. Colonel Leonov's office.

"Good morning, comrade Philip. How are you today?"

"Fine, thank you, Colonel."

"Did you get through those books on combat training I prescribed?"

"Yes."

"Good. Since the last time we met, I have formulated a plan of action. Today I'm going to go into the practical implementation of the plan with you. Oh, by the way, I would prefer it if during the week you would have early nights, as your course is going to be very strenuous. Captain Checkov can show you around the city over weekends.

"On any mission such as this, you must understand the dangers involved. Much as one puts effort into planning, something can always go wrong. There are no guarantees in this business. Are you quite clear on that point?" asked the colonel, hammering the point home.

"Yes."

"One can, of course, lessen the risk by observing a few basic rules. They are the following:

- The element of surprise. Surprise is your strongest weapon, as the enemy won't be expecting you.
- Speed and silence. Get in and out as speedily and as quietly as possible. Don't spend more time on the island than is absolutely necessary.
- Planning. Attention to detail is important. Keep the plan simple and try at all times to keep the other side guessing.
- Personnel. Involve as few people as possible.

"You must be well prepared, after all your life and the lives of others are at stake. During the next few weeks, we shall instruct you in sabotage, hand-to-hand combat, and how to handle guns. You also will need crash courses in learning to fly a microlight aircraft and ride a motorbike.

"I have worked out the escape route for comrade Khumalo and am now going to go through the plan with you. Stop me anytime if you wish to add anything."

Seeing Philip groping for his pen, he added, "No need to write anything down. I will have these notes typed out for you in the morning. Study the notes and commit everything to memory.

"Here is the plan:

We know that comrade Khumalo leaves the prison compound every weekday morning about 8:30 and goes to the workshop with a group of political prisoners. We also know that they are supervised by five guards, accompanied by a dog handler and his German shepherd dog.

You have told me that thick fog blankets the bay on certain days. We need to launch a boat from Cape Town under the cover of this fog. I believe the English call it a pea-souper. Fog cover is vital. The raid has to be conducted during the day, as the prisoners are securely locked up at night. The thicker the fog, the better, of course. So wait for a dense fog and be prepared to launch at a moment's notice. Let's call it D-Day.

You will need a quiet take off, so use paddles to get away from the shore before starting the motor. The boat must be big enough to accommodate six persons on the return journey: five from the task force, plus, of course, comrade Khumalo.

Remember that speed is of the essence. After you have made contact with your target, you may have fifty to sixty minutes at the most before all outlets are sealed. If the fog lifts too soon, you will be in trouble, but that is the risk one takes. Most important, you will need a compass to guide you in the fog. Keep a look out for other boats in the fog, as well, because a collision would be disastrous, which is why you must use a rubber dinghy.

Comrade Khumalo must not be taken by surprise, so it is essential to get a communication through to him that Operation Khulula, as you call it, has begun and to expect your team on the first foggy day after a certain date.

The rescuer must use the code words "Operation Khulula is on," or your target may become suspicious of you. You will wear black wetsuits, as the operation takes place over water and anything can happen. Don't forget to take an extra wet suit and pair of running shoes with you for comrade Khumalo, as he will need to discard his prison uniform and shoes.

Each of you must be armed. Arthur Norman has an arsenal, and I recommend the use of the AK-47 fully automatic rifle or the 9-mm silencer-fitted Makarov, which is deadly up to thirty metres. You must also have dart guns, for reasons I shall explain later. In this game of espionage, it's often kill or be killed, he said with a glint in his eye. Learn to master your weapon.

Your best plan is to intercept the posse taking the prisoners to the workshop. To do so, you must beach your boat just north of Murray's Bay Harbour in the penguin-nesting area. I believe there is a small beach there.

Thoroughly familiarize yourself with the layout of the island, in particular the position of the road leading from the prison to the workshop. It would be a disaster if, after having made contact with your target, you became disorientated and went off in the wrong direction. If any of the task force fails to return to the boat within a given period, the boat must leave without him. The mission can't be jeopardized. So memorize your position on the island by using visual check points.

I shall give you some whistles, which, when blown, sound like a frog's mating call. In the event that you lose contact with the boat, all parties can keep in touch by using the whistles. No one will suspect a frog's call.

Your map shows plenty of bush cover in this part of the island. Get into position early and as near the workshop as possible. Wait for the posse to come down the road and at a convenient time, use your dart guns to tranquillize the guards and the dog. Thereafter, get the prisoners to move the darted bodies behind the workshop.

When you have done the job, get out as soon as possible. By the time the guards wake up and perform a count, you should be back in Cape Town. Your take-off point in Cape Town must be carefully chosen. The task force must vigilantly reconnoitre the coast line to find an abandoned boat house or store, which will be necessary to house the boat and other equipment.

"I've already explored the coast line," Philip interjected. "There's a group of unused boat houses that were damaged by last month's floods. They're at a suburb called Mouille Point where the coastline takes a fork. These boat houses are below beach-road level and completely out of sight. Also, there's an old boat ramp alongside, leading up to road level. And what's more, about three-hundred metres down the road is the Mouille Point Lighthouse, which activates the fog horn as a warning to ships whenever the fog envelopes the bay."

"That's perfect," said the colonel. "When you get back, make sure the boat house is still available. On arriving back at Mouille

Point, hide the boat in the boat house. All of you, including comrade Khumalo, must abandon your wet suits and get into motorcycle gear—the full ensemble: T-shirt, leather trousers and jacket, gloves, full-face helmet, bandana, goggles, and boots. The jackets must have a club logo on the back.

"The moment you emerge at the top of the ramp, you will join a prearranged mock Harley Davidson club ride. The gloves, goggles, and helmet are essential to cover the skin, as the authorities will be looking for a person of colour. A motorcycle rally won't attract much attention or suspicion.

"Obviously, the rallyists will be UAC sympathizers, who must be carefully screened beforehand. In regards to the task force, you will ride a spare bike, with comrade Khumalo as your pillion passenger. The rest of your team will ride pillion on the other bikes.

"It is essential for the rally to move in a southerly direction, as the authorities will be concentrating on the airport, harbour, and northern exit roads. I am aware that the south is a dead end. Consequently, I have arranged for a submarine, the *Admiral Federov*, to pick both of you up. I say both of you, because you do realize, comrade Philip, that by this time you will be hot property, and you can't stay behind."

Philip shifted uncomfortably. He hadn't thought that far ahead.

"Maybe we will give you a rank in the Soviet Army," said the colonel jokingly.

"It is essential to use the fog as cover and, as no one can foresee the onset of fog, the D-Day of the mission will only be known at the last moment. Consequently, you must get a coded message to your colleagues, so that all other facets fall into place. Your colleagues must then get a coded message through to us that D-Day has begun so that we can liaise with the submarine.

"Remember, the *Admiral Federov* can't wait in unfriendly waters for any length of time. Otherwise she runs the risk of being spotted by maritime patrol or surveillance aircraft. It would be tragic, if after a successful rescue attempt, you arrived at the rendezvous point only to find that the submarine has had to leave without you. It is better for you to be waiting for the sub, than the other way round.

"Consequently, we will need a transition station in the form of a safe house. The use of a safe house for a few days will allow the situation to cool off and perhaps, with a bit of luck, the authorities may even start believing that you are already out of the country. More important, this will give you the opportunity of planning your rendezvous more accurately. Do you know of such a safe house, comrade Philip, in the south of the city?"

"Yes I do," replied Philip. "I know the perfect property. One of my close friends, Gunther Schultz, works for a German firm called B.A.S.E. Pharmaceuticals, and the house is owned by his chief executive, Otto Schtiller. I can vouch for both Gunther and Otto. Otto Schtiller has a long-standing grudge against the government. The house, which is called the Villa Castello, would be perfect, as it is well-hidden from the road. I must confirm whether the house will be available at that time of the year."

"Well, that sounds great," said the colonel. "Where actually is the house?"

"It's about twenty minutes from Cape Town, along the southern coastal road, just outside the village of Hout Bay. Let me show you on the map," said Philip.

"The rally must head for this Villa Castello," said the colonel, "and drop you and comrade Khumalo off with your bike. The rest of the riders will move on and disperse as soon as possible. At the house, you must have mountaineering clothes ready."

154

"Why?" Philip asked incredulously.

"Can you imagine the furor when comrade Khumalo escapes? There will be road blocks on all the major roads. On the day of your rendezvous with the submarine, the two of you will leave in the morning on the motor bike and head for the nearest southerly mountain route. There you will abandon the bike and take to the mountain to avoid the roads.

"As soon as you get back to Cape Town, discuss the best mountain route with comrade Arthur Norman, who is a member of the Cape Town Mountain Club. It must not be too strenuous a route, as we do not know what physical condition comrade Khumalo is in."

"And then what?" asked Philip, still as mystified as before. "How do we make contact with a submarine from the top of a mountain?"

"Well, that's the beauty of the concept, comrade. No one will know where you are or, less still, look for you on top of a mountain.

"I still don't understand," said Philip.

"From the top of the mountain, you will take off in a light-weight microlight aircraft. I have made enquiries and discovered that there is a microlight club in Cape Town called the Zeekoevlei Club," said the colonel, struggling over the name. "These microlight aircraft are the latest fad and are powered by a small two-stroke engine. It looks like a motorized kite, requires hardly any runway, and can take off from a mountain top. It is important that comrade Arthur Norman makes arrangements for five microlites to be available."

"Why five?" asked Philip, overwhelmed by the colonel's mastery of detail.

"Well, should the authorities catch up with you, it will save valuable time by creating a diversion. The microlites will fly off in different directions to confuse the enemy, but only one craft will have the navigational link.

"The submarine will be keeping a look-out for you and, on sighting you, will surface for a short time. You must head straight for it and ditch your craft. Remember, you must rendezvous with the *Admiral Federov* on D-Day plus three. In other words, you have three days after D-Day to make contact at a time to be decided.

"Regarding piercing the island's security, I would like to discuss this matter further with my colleagues here the institute. I will be in touch with comrade Arthur Norman directly regarding this. You have enough on your shoulders for the time being. Do you have any comments?" asked the colonel.

"Yes, I do. It's quite brilliant. Congratulations."

"Thank you, but bear in mind that theory is one thing and reality is another. On Monday, your practical training will start. Please report to Lieutenant Ivanov at 8:30 at the combat centre on the second floor. Your track suit will be fine. You will be under his control for a while. Contact me if you require anything. Enjoy the course."

The two men shook hands and parted.

CHAPTER 25

TRAINING

Monday, January 7, 1980 at 8:30 a.m.

It was bitterly cold outside as Philip made his way toward the combat centre on the second floor as directed. Although the institute was centrally heated, there were distinct draughts in every corner of the old eighteenth century building.

He pushed open the wooden, double doors revealing a huge, double-volume hall, which was a revelation. In one section, clusters of men were practicing mountain-climbing exercises up simulated mountainous terrain. In another section, others were firing at cardboard silhouettes of moving human figures. In the far corner, commandos in black tunics were practising emergency procedures at would-be hijackers aboard a mock commercial jet.

This is going to be very interesting, mused Philip, not knowing what lay in store for him.

Although he was early, Lieutenant Nikolai Petrovich Ivanov was already waiting for him. The lieutenant had a strong, square-faced jaw, with blonde crew-cut hair. He looked to be in his late twenties and was built like a pocket battleship. His uniform strained to conceal his bulging form. *I wouldn't like to tangle with this guy*, Philip thought. Obviously, he was a career soldier who took his fitness very seriously.

Nikolai Petrovich Ivanov had decided early on to make a career of the army. He was not alone in his choice. A career in the army had always had its attractions for Soviet men, as there were many to whom the rugged adventure of army life appealed.

In any case, he was not cut out for the mental rigours of academic life. He had realized that the best way to start his career was to attend one of the Suvorov schools, a military boarding school which gave preference to boys brought up in a children's home. There was a great deal of competition for these places, but the school seemed more interested in the boy's motivation than in academic brilliance, and Nikolai Petrovich Ivanov had this in abundance.

From Suvorov school, he went to military college, where he spent four years specializing in weapons and tactics. After graduation, he was given a choice of postings and chose a permanent position as a combat instructor at the Institute of Strategic Studies.

"Good morning comrade," barked lieutenant Ivanov, offering his hand. "I will be your combat instructor for the next few weeks. Today we are going to learn the ins and outs of this little beauty," he said, holding up a 9-mm semi-automatic Makarov in his right hand. "It is the very latest design and also a good weapon to use for training purposes. Its strength lies in its superb balance, making it easy to use. It holds nine bullets.

"What is important is to keep the gun clean at all times, so as to ensure a clean shot every time. Before cleaning it, always make sure the gun is unloaded to avoid accidents. Once dismembered, the gun will be in four main parts: the frame, the slide, the barrel, and the magazine. Then it has to be assembled again. We shall repeat this exercise until we get it right and can do it in double quick time." He handed Philip the gun.

To Philip this was all new. He had never handled a gun before. While Lieutenant Ivanov had none of the classic sophistication of his chief, it was evident that he was ultra-efficient at what he was trained to do. The officer knew exactly how to get the best out of his pupils—by repetition, repetition, and more repetition.

"I'll show you, and then you can do it yourself."

In a matter of seconds, the lieutenant had dismantled the gun and reassembled it again. It was a dazzling exhibition of gunmanship. Then it was Philip's turn.

"No, no, no!" shouted the instructor impatiently. "Not like that! You are not doing it right. In mortal combat you would be dead by now! It is either your life or theirs. Do it again."

The exercise was performed perhaps a hundred times until, somewhat miraculously, Philip had managed to strip, clean, and reassemble the gun in seconds. By afternoon, the instructor had allowed himself the luxury of a half-smile.

"Tomorrow we will learn how to fire this little thing. That's all for today."

Philip realized why the director had advised early nights. He was in a bath of perspiration.

Tuesday, January 8, 1980 at 8:30 a.m.

"Yesterday we learned how to handle a 9-mm Makarov. Is there any part of yesterday's drill that you do not fully understand?"

"No, I am fine with it," replied Philip, reluctant to go through it again.

"Good, then today we are going to fire real bullets at a target. I want you to remember what I taught you yesterday, particularly about safety and reassembly. I will show you the correct posture, and once you have fired your shots, you must strip your weapon, reassemble it, and reload."

A heavy wooden door led them off the main combat hall into a chamber that was sectioned off into long corridors, each with firing stations at one end and targets at the other. There were ten of these stations, all well-lit.

Philip noticed instructional posters on the wall indicating various correct-firing positions and how to take aim. Interestingly, there also were posters of U.S. tanks, missiles, and infantry weapons. Observing Philip's interest, the lieutenant advised him that infantrymen must be able to recognize foreign weapons, equipment, and uniforms, especially those of the American imperialists.

Philip was shown to his position. His gun had been laid ready on a metal stand, with, for the first time, live bullets alongside. *The organization*, he thought, *is first class*. He swallowed hard, acknowledging to himself that the bullets he was about to insert into the spring-loaded magazine were real. His hands felt lifeless.

He picked up the live bullets, one by one, and inserted eight of them into the magazine and one in the chamber. On instruction, he lifted the gun with both hands and held them stretched out in front of him. Closing his left eye, he married up the silhouette at the end of the range with the small raised sight at the top of his gun.

He then lined it up with the target—a black silhouetted figure of a storm-trouper. Repositioning his finger on the trigger and closing one eye, he leveled the gun and pulled the trigger slowly. *Bang!* Even with the headphones on, the noise was incredible. The automatic mechanism flew back and a millisecond later the bullet blasted a neat hole into the silhouette's left shoulder. He was thrown slightly back by the force of the recoil.

"A couple of inches lower and you have his heart," remarked the lieutenant.

Philip didn't mention he was aiming for the head. He felt like sitting down. Funny, the guy next door was doing it so effortlessly. Obviously this calmness came with practice.

Bang! Bang! Bang!

Each time he hit the target, the fear lessened until it became almost manageable. Once he had got over his initial shock, he became quite intoxicated and couldn't wait to fire again.

"Now let's see you dismantle your weapon and reassemble it, as I taught you yesterday. And remember to keep your finger out of the way."

This sequence was repeated and repeated, until Philip felt that there was no one else in the room, just him and his storm-trouper, and he wanted to blast its head off.

"Not at all bad for a beginner. In fact, I am rather pleased with your progress," said the lieutenant in a rare moment of levity. "Let's leave it at that for the day. We shall meet again tomorrow. Same time and place."

On the way back to his room, Philip couldn't help wondering what it must feel like to be facing a real flesh and blood target instead of a paper cut-out stuck onto a wooden board. Now that he had experienced the myriad emotions of firing a gun, he was surprised at how much he had enjoyed it.

Wednesday, January 9, 1980 at 8:30 a.m. Combat Centre.

"Good morning, comrade," said the lieutenant. "Today we are going to learn to fire one of the finest guns ever produced, the 7.62-mm AK 47. It is a little beaut," he said bringing the barrel fondly to his lips. "The AK-47 is a gas-operated rifle designed by that master gunsmith, Mikhail Kalashnikov. It is fully automatic and very hard-wearing but, unlike other semi-automatics, does not require regular cleaning. Believe it or not, it is even more popular than the American M-16. It is readily recognized by its curved magazine. As long you hold the trigger, it will fire. It is dynamite.

"For best results, you must cock the weapon and hold it firmly to your shoulder. Although it is fully automatic, it is best used in short bursts of say three to five rounds."

"Why is that?" enquired Philip.

"Because of its recoil action," answered the lieutenant. "The gun lifts a little on recoil, and you must learn to handle this recoil and bring the aim back to target. I will demonstrate to you once again, and you will follow me."

The same cut-out targets were produced, and after the lieutenant demonstrated, it was Philip's turn. The recoil took time to master, but by early afternoon, he felt he was getting the hang of it.

"We will come back tomorrow," said the lieutenant. "It is important that you are fully comfortable with it."

By the following day, Philip could confidently say he had made satisfactory progress.

Thursday, January 10, 1980 at 8:30 a.m. Combat Centre.

The lieutenant led Philip to a far corner of the combat hall, where there was a large mat on the floor.

"Self-defence is important in man-to-man combat where both you and your adversary are unarmed and within short range of each other," he said. "You could get killed by someone hell-bent on doing you bodily harm. In such a situation, you must use the armoury of your natural weapons, such as your fist, feet, knees, and teeth on your opponent's vulnerable areas. Where your life is concerned, there is no such thing as dishonourable moves. There is also the effective use of ad-hoc weapons, such as chairs and table legs. I am going to produce a dummy, and we will spend the rest of the day practicing some moves."

By the end, Philip was exhausted. His instructor had hardly raised a sweat.

"Well, comrade," the lieutenant said finally, "that completes my section of the combat training course. I am told that next week you will receive training in the final part of your course, namely, how to ride a motorbike and fly a microlight aircraft. I certainly hope that in the short time available, you have learned something."

"It has been a revelation," said Philip.

On parting, the lieutenant gave him a crunching handshake and said, "I hope to see you before you leave."

Monday, January 14, 1980 at 9:00 a.m. Office of the Chief Director, Institute of Strategic Studies.

"Good morning, Philip. I called you in to get an update on how your course is going. Is the lieutenant treating you well?" Colonel Leonov asked.

"Well, he's a hard taskmaster," replied Philip.

"Good, then he is doing his job. You should find learning to ride a motorbike and flying a microlight, the final part of your course, much easier. I have arranged for Corporal Sushkevich to meet you in the courtyard every morning for the next eight days. He has a 1977 XLCR Harley- Davidson and will transport you on his bike to Tushenko Airfield, a forty-minute drive from here. There is an improvised track at the airfield, where he will teach you the rudiments of motorbike riding.

"I rode a motorbike in my youth, and it is my contention that if you can ride a bicycle, you can master a motorbike. It is all a question of balance. Such issues as starting, stopping, balancing, and pulling off should, with a little practice, become second nature to you. The corporal will give you a helmet, a pair of gloves, and a thick army jacket, as it is going to be very cold riding pillion *en route* to the airfield. You will use the same field for the microlight lessons. And regarding the microlight course, don't take it lightly. I don't want you to be under any illusions. It might be—how do you say in English—no picnic.

"Microlites in Russia are presently only manufactured in one-seaters. Consequently, as there will be two of you, we have had to specially modify the craft at our MIG factory here in Moscow to incorporate two seats. Oh, one more thing, crash landing on water is not that simple."

"Why is that?" Philip asked.

"Because the swell, which I believe can be as high as three metres at Cape Point, makes it impossible to gauge the water level. To solve this problem, your microlight will be fitted with a weighted pendulum on its undercarriage, to which a light will be attached. The pendulum will be about five metres long, and you will know when you are close to water surface by watching the light. Don't forget to wear your life jackets.

"As soon as the light hits the water, the engines must be switched off, and with your known vertical speed, you will have three seconds to jump off. Position yourself for a two- to three-metre jump. You will have to explain the evacuation procedure to Comrade Khumalo, and let's hope he can cope. After all, he is not a young man.

"The regime is going to hound you. They won't take the loss of Khumalo lightly. Should the government forces be in hot pursuit, head out to sea as fast as you can and crash land in the ocean as close to the submarine as possible. On seeing you, the sub will surface and send a small boat out to rescue the two of you. At this stage, the sub will be most vulnerable. I would say that the most the sub can afford to stay on the surface is fifteen minutes. Timing is crucial. Use your radio beacon to guide you to the sub.

"As this is a tricky exercise and requires practice, I have instructed your microlight instructor to rehearse this procedure over the Moskva River, because, if not done correctly, you could hurt yourself. Your aircraft here will also be fitted with this pendulum/light attachment and, of course, a life jacket.

"Once aboard the sub, get the hell out of there. And now, enjoy the rest of your course and I will see you at eleven next Friday, the day before your departure."

Thursday, January 24, 1980 at 7:30 p.m. Bolshoi Theatre.

"I was lucky to get these tickets," Valeriya said, as she and Philip jostled in the foyer with the to-capacity crowd. People were excitedly greeting one another. For Russians it was an evening out, an evening of enchantment, one in which they could forget the deprivations of everyday life.

Everyone was eager to see *The Nutcracker*, produced by the master Tchaikovsky, who was famous for his brooding and romantic melodies. She remarked that Tchaikovsky was undoubtedly the greatest composer of Russia's Golden Age, an age that later spawned such giants of the stage as Anna Pavlova, Vaslav Nijinsky, Rudolph Nureyev, and Mikhail Baryshnikov.

"Russians have a passion for ballet, which is why there are no fewer than forty dance companies in the nation. Tavaresh, do you know that Tchaikovsky trained as a lawyer before turning to music in his twenties. He was also responsible for the music of such magnificent ballets as *Swan Lake* and *The Sleeping Beauty*."

For a soldier, Philip thought, *her knowledge of ballet is quite outstanding.*

The stage was brightly lit. The faces of the audience reflected a sense of expectancy. The curtain rose and the show began. Philip noticed that the audience was totally involved. The performance was exhilarating, but overhanging everything was the silently shared thought that Philip's day of departure was drawing closer. His sojourn in Moscow had developed into a pattern: combat training during the week and weekends spent with the lovely Captain Checkov. Many of their evenings were spent in quiet, relaxed conversation. On one such occasion, some friends of Valeriya's had dropped by to take them to a jazz club in downtown Moscow. He also had visited her parents again.

"Tavaresh," Valeriya said, "you are leaving on Saturday. Will I ever see you again? I am afraid of losing you."

"No more than I am of you," he replied. "I'm embarking on a very dangerous journey, and the outcome is unknown. It seems as if my whole life so far has been a prelude to the coming events, and I simply cannot see beyond that point. Should everything turn out successfully, I'll come back for you. That's a promise.

"Colonel Leonov has scheduled a final meeting for eleven tomorrow. Can you call for me at two on Saturday and take me to the airport?"

"Of course," she replied dolefully.

Friday, January 25, 1980 at 11:00 a.m. Office of the Chief Director of the I.S.S.

Philip knocked on the door and was told to enter. Waiting inside were Colonel Leonov and Lieutenant Ivanov.

"So, comrade, how was the balance of your course?" asked the colonel.

"Apart from the fact that I almost drowned in the Moskwa River, it was enjoyable."

They all laughed. "Well, Comrade Philip, this is goodbye. We have enjoyed having you with us," said the colonel. "You have been an apt pupil."

"I hope I haven't been too tough on you?" chirped in the lieutenant. "You were rather raw when you came to us. However, I believe we have turned you into something of a soldier, both technically and mentally."

"I've come a long way in the past few weeks," said Philip, "and feel equipped for the rigours that lie ahead. If I fail, it certainly won't be due to any omissions on your part. I wish to thank you both for your efforts and the special interest you have shown in me. I will be taking the warmest feelings of your hospitality back with me to my country."

Both the colonel and the lieutenant nodded their appreciation.

"By the way, we have established that the Villa Castello will be available for the month of February, as the owner has made a special gesture to your cause," commented the colonel.

Good old Otto, thought Philip, *has come through for us.*

"The staff, except for the cook and two guards, has been given leave. We have established that the cook and guards are card-carrying members of the UAC and can be vouched for. They will be expecting you," said the colonel.

"As you are heading for Dar es Salaam, don't forget to pop into the downstairs clinic before leaving to get yourself immunized against yellow fever and malaria."

Does this man ever forget anything, Philip wondered.

The colonel stood up, and they walked to the door. "You will give comrade Arthur Norman my best regards, won't you?"

"I certainly will."

"I take it that Captain Checkov will be taking you to the airport tomorrow?"

"Yes."

"Please let us know how things turn out. Best of luck."

Philip shook hands with his mentors and departed. Another chapter in his life was over. What would the next hold?

"Well, Comrade Colonel," asked the lieutenant, "what do you think of his chances?"

"No more than fifty-fifty," answered the colonel.

The mood *en route* to the airport was in sharp contrast to the inward ride. The last thing Philip had banked on was falling in love with his host. He knew that parting would be difficult, but his immediate crystal ball was hazy.

They parked the car and entered the concourse. He hugged her and kissed her passionately, but could not find the right words. She understood. He headed for the check-in area and, with a final wave, disappeared. After a brief pause to collect her emotions, she too left. No sooner had she left the concourse, than two thick-set men appeared from nowhere and bundled her into a brown car.

"You are under arrest, comrade captain," snapped one. "You will come with us."

"What is the meaning of this?" she protested. "What about my car?"

"Someone will fetch your car," said the one doing the talking. "Our orders are to bring you into headquarters for questioning."

They drove to Lubyanka Square, the headquarters of the KGB, parked in the basement lot, and took the lift to the twentieth floor. A senior officer addressed her.

"Captain Checkov, you have been observed excessively fraternizing with a foreigner. You should know that this is strictly forbidden."

"Who says I was fraternizing?" she answered unconvincingly.

The senior officer pressed a button on a video recording machine and instantly a scene of the captain cavorting in the bath with her foreign lover came onto the screen.

"How did you get this?" she stammered.

"It does not matter how we got this," he said. "What do you have to say?"

"I have been instructed by Colonel Leonov of the Institute of Strategic Studies to fraternize with this person, comrade Philip Jordan. He is a guest in our country and the colonel wanted to make sure he was on the level, before admitting him to the institute. This is how things are done here," she explained.

"Well, let's phone Colonel Leonov at the institute and find out," he said.

He phoned the colonel and listened intently to what he had to say.

Addressing Captain Checkov, he said, "It seems you are telling the truth. Be more careful next time."

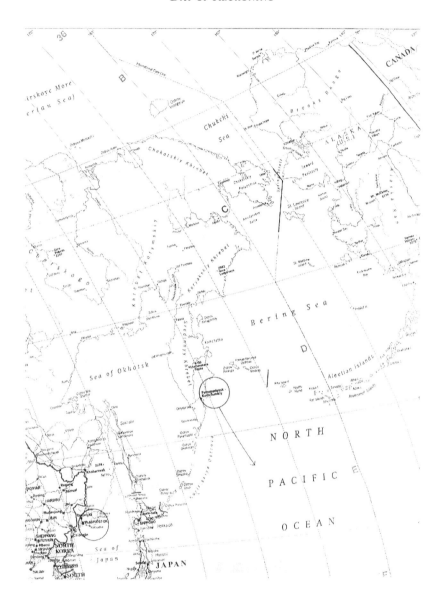

CHAPTER 26

THE ADMIRAL FEDEROV

Wednesday, January 9, 1980 at 9:00 a.m.
Colonel Leonov's Office at the I.S.S.

The intercom buzzed. "Comrade Colonel," said his secretary, "Comrade General Chernenko on line one for you."

"Good morning, Comrade General. How may I help you?"

"I am phoning to tell you that the meeting with Secretary General Podgorny went well. He has approved the plan, with one or two conditions. As you know, because of the assistance we give to the UAC in South Africa, relations between our countries are cool, to say the least. However, sending our latest hunter-killer submarine into South African territorial waters to aid the escape of their top prisoner will be considered a provocation equal to an act of war. Are you aware of that?"

"Yes, Comrade General."

"Not only that, but we would be placing the *Admiral Federov* in an extremely vulnerable situation, especially so far from home. Therefore, although the secretary general approves the plan, he insists that the submarine not enter South African territorial waters.

"Considering the clandestine nature of the mission, it is quite feasible that, even outside their territorial limits, the submarine might be detected and attacked. I have spoken to comrade Admiral Rutskoi, and we both agree that it would be advisable to prepare for such an eventuality.

"Consequently, it is imperative that the commander of the submarine, Captain of the first rank Yakutin, be informed of the rules of engagement in the event of his being attacked."

"And what are those, comrade general?"

"The rules are that he is to try and remain undetected just beyond the fifteen-mile nautical limit. However, in the event of his being attacked, he is to defend himself."

"Begging your pardon, Comrade General, but as you know, our hunter-killer class submarines are not equipped to attack aircraft."

"I am all too aware of that, Comrade Colonel," said the general tersely. "That is why the *Admiral Federov* will be supplied with machine guns and specially fitted with surface-launch anti - aircraft missiles, or SLAMS. The *Admiral Federov* will be departing on January 12. Do you have any questions?"

"No, Comrade General. Thank you for including me in the picture."

The general omitted to mention that at his meeting with the secretary general, he had taken most of the credit for the operation.

Vladivostok, on Russia's eastern seaboard, is one of the Soviet Union's more attractive cities. Lying at the base of the Sikhole-Alin Mountains and bordered by China to the west and the Sea of Japan to the east, it is sometimes called the San Francisco of Russia, which is in reference to its Pacific location and steep streets, but that is as far as the comparison goes. This naval city, founded in 1860, has a colourful history. Originally taken from the Chinese, it was closed to Soviet shipping between 1958 and 1961.

Being the headquarters of the Pacific Fleet and the country's main port in the Far East, the new Vladivostok is rapidly reinventing itself. The twists and turns of its steep streets offer visitors many beautiful views of the city and bay.

Thursday, January 10, 1980. Vladivostok.

Captain Anatoly Yakutin was sitting in the lounge of his apartment, looking wistfully out across Golden Horn Bay. His only daughter, Tanya, aged ten, was at school. The commander was enjoying his last few days of shore leave.

"Darling," he said to his wife, "this is one time I can't wait for my shore leave to end."

"Why is that?" his wife enquired, looking up from her magazine and lowering her reading glasses. "You submariners usually enjoy your shore leave so much."

"Well, our latest beauty is about to be launched, and I shall be taking her out for her first run. In fact, she is being brought all the way from Mermansk for our next mission."

Normally this appointment would have been a cause for celebration, except that the commander had had the privilege of commanding many new, top-secret subs over the past few years. During that period, his superb seamanship and guile had earned him the appellation of The Silver Fox, so creating a reputation for mystique and glamour that had even spread to the West. A posting to one of his ships was considered a rare honour.

He was, in fact, a different breed of Soviet commander—calm and professional but with an additional string to his bow: an expert in the analysis of Soviet naval technology. Many recent technological innovations had sprung from his fertile mind. For this he had received the coveted Order of the Red Star. Yet, he longed for a new challenge, something that would tax his brain.

He was growing weary of the continual seek-and-run tactics of the never-ending Cold War with never a shot being fired.

"And where are you going this time?" she asked. It was a rhetorical question to which she already knew the answer.

"Darling, you know I can't answer that one," he answered blithely. "In fact, I won't know myself until I am aboard ship. I expect it will be another of those jaunts around the North Atlantic. What I can tell you is that the new sub, the *Admiral Federov*, named after one of our naval heroes, is the fastest and most advanced submarine ever built. This time our naval architects have really excelled, and I am looking forward to testing some of my own innovations."

Captain Anatoly Yakutin was born in May 1940 in the district of Mermansk. He was the only child of Vladimir and Maria Yakutin. He had graduated secondary school in 1959, Higher Naval College in 1963, and the Naval Academy with honours in 1967. He commanded his first ship at age thirty.

The Soviet Navy consists of four fleets: The Black Sea Fleet, the Pacific Fleet, the Northern Fleet, and the Baltic Fleet. Since World War II, the Soviet Union has invested colossal resources into developing its submarine fleet. Major breakthroughs in hull design and methods of propulsion have revolutionized naval warfare.

Despite the extraordinary restrictions of submarine life, a normal routine has to be maintained. Compulsory physical training is required for, all as well as political and naval education for the officers. The *Zampolit*, the deputy responsible for political affairs, accompanies all vessels. It is his duty to oversee the moulding of young minds. Lectures are usually held in designated rooms where party books and other ideological material is kept.

In 1973, the Russians rushed the *November Class* into service and, besides being noisy, there were many instances of radiation-related illnesses among its crew. The November Class was quickly phased out and followed by the ultra-advanced Victor Class, which was fitted with the latest silent-drive system, making it the fastest and quietest modern submarine ever built.

First off the line was the *Admiral Federov*, which was completing its sea trials. This new type of vessel, the attack or hunter class, was the pride of the admiralty. It was smaller than the conventional boomer type of subs, could operate from a depth of four-hundred metres, and was capable of launching both torpedoes and cruise missiles. Its torpedoes could hit a ship twenty-five kilometres away and its missiles, launched from below the sea, could hit a target 1,500 kilometres away with deadly accuracy. It had a crew of ninety men and could transit at eighteen knots, with a maximum speed of thirty knots. It was, in fact, the ultimate weapon.

Petropavlovsk- Kamchatskiy—main submarine base for the Pacific Fleet.

About a three-hour flight from Vladivostok lies Petropavlovsk-Kamchatskiy, home of the Pacific Fleet's main submarine base on the Kamchatskiy Peninsula. The latter is a strange-looking proboscis on Russia's eastern face. The supreme command had ordered that the latest Victor Class sub, the *Admiral Federov*, be delivered from Reindeers Lip Shipyard on the Puloma River near Mermansk, to Petropavlovsk-Kamchatskiy in the far east. Her trials passage would take her through the ice-ridden Barents Sea, into the Kara Sea, through the Bering Strait near Alaska, and finally into the Bering Sea. In near arctic conditions, no ship ever had a more stringent test.

There were strict procedures for taking a newly built submarine into service. All vessels would be taken on sea trials by a test crew. As diving safety was at stake, the water-tightness of the submarine had to be proven. Individual equipment concerned with safety, such as bilge pumps, compressors, main propulsion, masts, etc. had to be thoroughly checked, as did operational equipment, such as sonar detection devices, radar, and torpedo attack systems.

The Submarine Operational Authority (SOA) usually appoints a senior ex-submarine commander and staff to oversee the workup and compile a report. Prior to sailing, a systems check is carried out. Only when *all systems are go*, will the submarine be allowed to sail.

Friday, January 11, 1980. Petropavlovsk.

As was his habit, Captain Yakutin had flown to Petropavlovsk-Kamchatskiy a day earlier to supervise arrangements and take on the crew. He was pleased to see his old cook come aboard. This man knew how to cook his favourite dish, *taranka*, a dry fish delicacy.

The captain was standing at the quayside with ex-sub Commander Mironenko, who, a few days earlier, had completed his workup report. The two were admiring the lines of the new sub.

"She is fully operational now," said the ex-sub commander. "There was some trouble with the air-conditioning system, but that's been sorted out. Apparently she handles like a dream."

"That's wonderful," said Yakutin. "I can't wait for tomorrow to try her out. I see she has a sonar pod on her tail fin. That's a new feature."

"Yes, that's the latest listening device," replied the ex-commander.

"I must say, I am surprised to see S.L.A.M. anti-aircraft missiles mounted on one of the hoisting masts. Can you explain that?"

"Beats me," said the ex-commander. "My job is to test submarines, not to ask questions."

Saturday, January 12, 1980 at 3:00 p.m.

The captain, first officer, and the *zampolit* were on the control tower, supervising the loading of the torpedoes and missiles. A cold easterly wind was blowing, creating choppy conditions. The captain instinctively raised his fleece-lined collar to shield his neck from the biting wind. He wondered how many voyages were in store for him. He was approaching his fortieth birthday.

Turning to the *zampolit*, he said, "You know, a maiden voyage on a brand new sub never fails to stir the emotions in me. There is something special about it. Standing here breathing in the clean air, I feels as if I'm alone in the world on a tiny island. Anyway, I suppose we had better go below and check our orders."

With one last scan of the darkening horizon, they descended.

The mooring lines having been slipped, the submarine backed away from the quay and sailed slowly out of the harbour to begin her maiden voyage. Water began to lap over her bow, as the force of her twin, phosphor bronze screws took effect. No sooner had they left the base, than a dummy submarine, an exact replica of the *Admiral Federov*, was towed into the berth previously occupied by the departing submarine. This was a successful ploy to fool American satellites.

Safely away from the harbour approaches, the captain handed the con to the second in-command, Andrei Smirnov, as they headed for deeper waters.

Once in the diving area, he gave the order to dive. "Smirnov, dive to twenty metres. Check the trim," he ordered.

"Dive! Dive! Dive!" ordered the second in-command

Ballast tanks were vented, speed increased, and the hatch to the bridge clanged close. The diving panel in the control room indicated that all hull openings were closed. The submarine slowly settled in the grey sea and eventually disappeared below the surface. Up came the periscope to keep a lookout for contacts.

Speed was reduced to assist in getting the submarine trimmed to neutral buoyancy. Smirnov began the process. He found that his shore calculations for the trim were out. The submarine was too heavy. He surmised that possibly it was due to all the extra victuals that had been taken aboard.

"Pump two tons," he ordered the auxiliary compartment, as the too-heavy submarine struggled to remain at periscope depth. Two tons were pumped. Still too heavy.

"Pump another ton," he ordered.

The submarine approached neutral buoyancy, but was heavy forward. Must be the full torpedo load, he mused. "Pass five hundred litres aft," he ordered.

The submarine achieved zero trim. It had taken fifteen minutes.

"Submarine trimmed," he reported.

"Two hundred metres," ordered the captain. The submarine tilted forward ten degrees and glided into the depths. In each compartment, the crew kept a watchful eye on the water-tightness of the vessel. Flooding, like fire, was a sub-mariner's worst nightmare.

"Depth two-hundred metres. Submarine watertight," reported the control room.

"Assume cruising stations," ordered the captain. "Remain at 200 metres, steer course 170 degrees."

And so began the long and secret mission of the *Admiral Federov*.

Captain Yakutin and his *zampolit* went directly to the ward room, where the ship's orders were kept in a safe. Regulations required that the safe be opened with both men present. The captain retrieved the envelope containing the ship's orders and broke the seal. He read the contents carefully and, as he read, his mouth opened in amazement.

"Fascinating," he said, "quite fascinating. In all my years at sea, I have never seen such fascinating orders."

The political officer moved forward in his chair expectantly. He had sailed with Captain Yakutin on many missions, but had never seen him so animated. Was this the challenge the captain had yearned for, one last hurrah before perhaps calling it a day?

"Listen to this comrade," said Yakutin.

"First, we are to sail due south through the North Pacific Ocean, past the Marshall Islands, and head for Australia and New Zealand. Then, when in the Tasman Sea, we are to swing due west through the Bass Strait between Australia and Tasmania and head west to a place called Cape Point in South Africa.

"The transit will be dived deep to minimize leaving a heat trail, and we are to be extra careful to avoid under-water collisions. The usual check reports indicating that all is well are to be dispensed with. When we reach South Africa, we are to be careful to avoid transiting their submarine exercise areas, a map of which is enclosed. Check reports are only to be resumed when we leave their waters.

"That is most interesting, don't you think? Obviously a security precaution."

The captain paused to take it all in and then continued.

"Near Cape Point, at the tip of the continent, we are to rendezvous at a position approximately fifteen nautical miles due west of the Slangkop Lighthouse, which is on the Atlantic

Coast near a small fishing village by the name of Kommetjie. This position is just outside South African territorial waters, which we are not to enter under any circumstances. The exact time, date, and position of the rendezvous will be signalled to us later. In the interests of security, this instruction will be encrypted and sent to us in a burst transmission. To avoid interception, we are not to acknowledge. To receive this instruction, we are to be in a pre-determined loitering position, three hundred sixty kilometres west of Cape Point."

"Well, that *is* interesting," replied the *zampolit*, joining in the unaccustomed banter. "But who are we to rendezvous with?"

"At the rendezvous point, we are to keep a lookout for and await the arrival of a two-seater microlight aircraft carrying two freedom fighters: comrades Truman Khumalo and Philip Jordan! They are going to crash-land their aircraft near our vessel, and we are to pick them up with minimum delay!"

The captain's voice rose an octave as he spoke those words.

"What happens if these freedom fighters crash-land inside the territorial limit?" asked the *zampolit*.

"Too bad for them, I would say. We can't disobey orders. If we are successful with the rescue, we are to transport them up the east coast of Africa to a place called Dar es Salaam in Tanzania. At this point, the crew will be allowed three days shore leave, before beginning our homeward journey. It goes on to say that the importance of this mission cannot be overestimated.

"The final paragraph is entitled 'Rules of Engagement'. As one of the persons being rescued is South Africa's most important political prisoner, it is quite possible that, if detected, we might be attacked. If attacked, we are to defend ourselves with the SLAMS fitted to our mast. Well, that explains why we have SLAMS, as well as torpedoes and missiles."

The captain looked up. There was fire in his eyes. This was the challenge he had been waiting for, a challenge worthy of the Silver Fox.

It was customary for the commanding officer to outline the ship's operational orders and simultaneously give the crew a pep talk. For security reasons, he did this once they had left the harbour. On this occasion, however, he was deliberately vague as he addressed his men over the main broadcast.

The captain looked forward to these pep talks. He saw it as a two-way street where he could communicate with the crew, many of whom were young and raw, while they in turn could get to know more about the fabled Captain Jakutin. He was all too aware that his reputation had preceded him and took a delight in watching the wonderment in their faces as he moved about the vessel.

He began by saying that they were on a mission of the greatest importance to the Motherland and their success would depend on everyone playing his part. He announced that they were heading for the southern tip of Africa and East Africa, but stopped short of giving the identity of the VIPs to be uplifted.

He told them that it was necessary, in the nuclear age, to have a basic knowledge of some of the technical innovations in this new class of ship. He mentioned some of these and subtly slipped in a few of his own for good measure. He urged them to be aware of everything. As long trips could be boring, movies, quizzes, and talks had been laid on for those off-watch. He urged them to use these facilities and to occupy their time profitably.

The chef had been especially recruited by him, and they could be assured of excellent food; in particular, wine would be available, as he had found that a little wine relaxed the nerves.

By his estimate, transiting at an average speed of eighteen knots, the voyage to Africa would take approximately thirty days with a further eight days to Dar es Salaam in East Africa. Should the mission be successful, they would be rewarded with three days shore leave in Dar es Salaam, where the climate is warm and the people friendly. He wished them all a fruitful and enjoyable voyage.

CHAPTER 27

RETURNING HOME

Back in London, Philip booked into Hilton Gatwick hotel and left the next day for Dar es Salaam. He was met at the airport and taken to an office in town. He noticed that Dar es Salaam possessed a certain distinctive charm, due, no doubt, to the cultural diversity of its people. There were German, British, and Asian influences, and, because of the heat, the inhabitants were in no particular hurry to go anywhere. It was hot, very hot.

At the headquarters of the UAC in exile, Philip gave a thorough account of his activities to the president of the organization, Alexander Thembo and members of the high command, and the plan was discussed in great detail. Although everyone agreed that there were grave risks involved in the execution of the plan, the benefits, nevertheless, of having Truman Khumalo free again and taking up his rightful position in the organization outweighed all other considerations. Besides there still was the unfulfilled invitation for their leader to address the United Nations, a rare opportunity that could only come about if he were freed. It was now or never!

The plan was approved without amendment.

On January 30, Philip boarded flight BA 2068 at 7:30 p.m. for London and arrived at Gatwick Airport at 5:15 a.m.

January 31, 1980

Philip was met at the airport by the same operative he had met before. On instructions, he spent three days in London relaxing from his exertions. His original passport was handed back to him, and on February 3, he departed London on BA 58 at 7:50 p.m. for South Africa.

Next day

From Cape Town Airport, Philip was driven to Riz Khan's house in Rylands Estate where Arthur, Vincent, Sipho, and Faizil were waiting expectantly for him. This time, however, it would be he who would be supplying the answers.

CHAPTER 28

DEBRIEFING

February 4, 1980

"It's good to have you back," said Arthur, who seemed to have recovered from his ankle injury.

"Tell us about Russia. Did you learn a lot?" Sipho enquired excitedly

"Well, so much has happened. Where do I start?"

"The beginning would be a good place," said Arthur, adept at bringing proceedings to order.

Philip's thoughts were focused already. He had rehearsed his report mentally in the plane a number of times.

"I went there as an enthusiastic rookie," he began, "and I believe I've returned as a trained operative. As you know, in Moscow I was under the direct control of the chief director of the Institute of Strategic Studies, Colonel Aleksandr Leonov— who, by the way, sends his warmest regards to you, Arthur."

"Thank you," responded Arthur. "Our relationship goes back a long way. Actually, he has been in touch with us already regarding certain specific aspects of the mission. Please continue, comrade Philip."

"The facilities at the institute are world-class, and there are pupils from all over the world. Yet, somehow, I had the funny feeling that I was getting special treatment. I can't put my finger on why. I was trained in the use of hand guns and automatic rifles as well as how to handle myself in hand-to-hand combat. In addition, I learned to ride a motorbike and fly a microlight aircraft."

"A microlight aircraft?" queried Vincent.

"Yes, the microlight is the key to the final stage of the operation."

"And your contact, Captain Checkov, was he useful to you?" asked Arthur.

"Well, *he* turned out to be a *she* and, yes, she was exceptionally useful to me," replied Philip. "The plan is ingenious and based on the twin elements of surprise and keeping the enemy guessing," he said, paraphrasing the colonel's exact words. "We have to match the regime's ruthless approach, as they will have no mercy on us if we get caught."

Philip described the plan in great detail, omitting all references to his affair with the lovely Captain Checkov, which he considered to be none of their business.

Arthur noted that this was a more confident and hardened Philip than the one who had left the country only a few weeks earlier. Any doubts he might have harboured about this maverick Stellenbosch University student, were soon dispelled.

"That's an ingenious plan," retorted Arthur. "You and your mentors have done well. Our party's high command in Dar es Salaam has already endorsed the plan, and, in order to save time, Colonel Leonov in Moscow has been in touch with us regarding three vital aspects of the plan."

"What are those?" queried Sipho.

"The availability of Otto Schtiller's house in February, securing an abandoned boat house on the shore line where we can launch our attack, and the weather patterns at this time of the year. I am able to report positively on all three aspects," continued Arthur. "Schtiller is committed to our cause and has made his house available for the entire month of February. The Mouille Point boat-houses are still abandoned after the storms, and I have put a combination lock on one of them to secure it. Regarding the weather patterns at this time of the year, I have been in touch with the South African Weather Service. The vital sea fog cover we require is called advection fog, which is formed by the cooling of moist air in contact with the cold sea. These favourable conditions are very prevalent in Table Bay at this time of the year. What is unpredictable is how long the fog will last on any one day."

"I have a question," said Vincent. "As the success of the entire operation depends on fog cover, how are we to know what type of fog is suitable?"

"When horizontal visibility in the bay gets down to fifty metres, you will hear the intermittent wailing of a foghorn. Those are the right conditions," answered Arthur.

"And if the fog lifts while the operation is still in progress and our cover is blown, what then?" asked Faizil.

"That is unfortunately the chance we have to take," answered Arthur. "Sipho, once on the island, it will be your job to guard the dinghy. The rest of us will try to intercept the prisoners on their way from the prison to the workshop. Faizil, I want you to contact Peter Campbell, one of our party members, and have him arrange for a mock motorbike ride of about twenty riders to meet us in Beach Road when we return to Mouille Point. We will merge with the bikes there and become part of the ride. You, Philip, will ride a spare bike with comrade Truman Khumalo as your pillion passenger. The rest of us will ride pillion on the other bikes. The ride will head south in the direction of Otto Schtiller's house in Hout Bay, where comrades Truman and Philip will peel off to hide for a few days. The rest of us will disperse as soon as possible.

"I will arrange for the dinghy, wet suits, and motorcycle gear to be stored in the boat house, together with the rifles. Any other questions at this stage?"

"Yes," said Philip. "I believe that it would be better if we all knew the number of the combination lock on the boat house door, just in case of accidents."

"Agreed," replied Arthur. "We should all know the combination. When weather conditions are suitable, that is, when D-Day arrives, we must get a signal out that Operation Khulula has begun, so that all other facets will fall into place. And most important of all, we must get a message to Moscow that the mission is on, so that the submarine can get final instructions on the exact timing of the rendezvous. We will need to lease an apartment, so that we are all together and ready to launch at a moment's notice when conditions are favourable. Sooner or later someone will lay claim to the boat house, so I believe the sooner we get started the better."

"There's a large furnished apartment block opposite the boathouse, called Savoy Holiday Apartments," interjected Philip. "I remember seeing a to-let sign outside the building a little while ago. Let me phone them and rent an apartment."

Philip left the room to make the call in the hall. He returned a few minutes later to say he had rented an apartment from the following day.

"As Mouille Point is designated a *white area* according to the Group Areas Act," said Arthur. "Sipho, Faizil, and Vincent are not allowed to take up residence there. To get around this, we will purchase plumber's overalls and you three will slip in under this disguise. We will all move in tomorrow afternoon. I suggest that anything you may need for a few days' stay should be brought here, and I will take it across.

"Once there, unfortunately, you won't be able to leave the apartment until D-Day. I suggest you bring some books and cards to occupy your time. There is also TV. I will stock up on food and drink and either Philip or I can pop out to get anything you may need."

"What about the island's security?" interjected Philip. "Colonel Leonov assured me that he would be in touch with you regarding this vital issue. Without this information, we can't get started."

"Quite so," replied Arthur. "We have gone into this thoroughly. As we see it, the island is protected by sonar, radar, manned observation posts, guards, dogs, and high-speed patrol boats. This is typical of a high-security prison. We have been advised by our informant on the island, that the activities of the large penguin colony regularly interfere with radar signals on the eastern side. These penguins, called jackass penguins because of their donkey-like braying, apparently make quite a racket. The colony is to the right of the harbour, where they occupy a small beach. This is the island's Achilles' heel.

"I have obtained a white noise jammer, which, when turned on, kills the echo and nullifies the display on radar screens. This device was used quite effectively by the Japanese during their attack on Pearl Harbour."

"What's it look like, and how does it function?" queried Philip.

"It is the size of a shoe box and has an antenna. The antenna allows the jammer to radiate in all directions. It is powered by a battery, which has a life of about ten hours. For maximum effect, we must switch the jammer on as we reach the Island's two kilometre radar-sonar zone. The chances are good that the radar operator will blame the penguins for the malfunction, as he has so often done in the past.

"As an added precaution, we have had the external face of the dinghy coated with a special compound which will absorb any stray signals. As far as sonar is concerned, only metal objects can be detected, which is one of the reasons we are using a rubber dinghy, as rubber absorbs sonar signals."

"What about the outboard motor?" queried Philip.

"A special leather jacket has been made to cover it," responded Arthur. "And when we reach the two kilometre limit, we will lift the outboard motor out of the water and paddle in quietly. This should take care of both radar and sonar. Regarding the manned observation posts, only Alpha Three to the right of the penguin colony is of concern to us. Our information is that high-speed boats only patrol at night. Of course, during an emergency they could be called out during the day, but I believe the crew takes fully twenty minutes to assemble. We should be gone by then. We know that at 8:30 on weekdays, a group of prisoners from Section B are marched from the prison to the workshop down a narrow road. Khumalo will be in this group. They are accompanied by about six warders, one of whom will have a dog. These dogs are trained to be vicious, so we must be extra careful. This narrow road is only about 500 metres from our landing point on the coast.

"To summarize, then," said Arthur, "our plan is as follows: We must plot a course for the eastern side of the island and land our boat in the middle of Penguin Beach, just to the right of Murray's Bay Harbour. As I have said, this spot has the added advantage of being closest to the road leading to the workshop. The noisy penguins should provide us with adequate cover. When we reach the island, you guys must immediately head for the road to intercept the group, while I take off for Alpha Three, which is manned, and I need to take the guard out of the equation.

"Because of the danger of hitting prisoners, we will be using dart guns to tranquillize the guards. If, by mistake, we do hit a prisoner, the worst that can happen is he will be asleep for a few hours. Don't forget to dart the dog as well.

"Then we must move out as soon as possible," concluded Arthur.

CHAPTER 29

OPERATION KHULULA BEGINS

February 6, 1980. Robben Island

In early 1980, the political prisoners on Robben Island were granted the right for the first time to buy newspapers. This was a victory, but, as always, each new privilege contained a catch. Although they were allowed to buy one English language and one Afrikaans language newspaper per day, the prison censors cut out articles they deemed unsafe to read. Because of this censorship, attempts to slip coded messages to the prisoners via newspapers failed.

It was necessary for Khumalo to consult with his attorney from time to time. It was at one of these visits, as he was leaving, that his attorney deftly slipped him a piece of paper. This was hastily hidden in his trousers' pocket. On returning to his cell, Khumalo opened the paper which tersely read, "Operation Khulula is on. Wait for first foggy day and contact by operative Philip." He knew instinctively what was up.

February 5–10, 1980. 401 Savoy Holiday Apartments, Mouille Point, Cape Town.

Minutes seemed like hours, as the task team frittered away the time playing cards, reading magazines, and watching TV. The weather, unfortunately, had been perfect. There was nothing to do but wait for conditions to change. Throughout the long wait each was preoccupied with his own thoughts; all acutely aware that for them and their people, the day of reckoning had finally arrived. Arthur, meanwhile, was keeping his binoculars firmly focused on the harbour.

"Our information is correct," he said finally. "Those high-speed boats only patrol at night. That's good news."

CHAPTER 30

ASSAULT ON ROBBEN ISLAND

Monday, February 11, 1980 at 6:00 a.m. D-DAY.

They were woken up by the gnawing and persistent blast of a foghorn.

"Comrades," Arthur said excitedly, "wake up! This is it!" Poking his head out of the window and observing near zero visibility, he picked up the phone and dialed one of his operatives in the city. His message was cryptic. "Operation Khulula is on."

The recipient of the call went to a private room and, within twenty minutes, had notified Moscow. A second call was made to Peter Marshall of the University of Cape Town.

Arthur called his group together for a last minute briefing. "Comrades, remember we were specially chosen for this mission. If we succeed, this day, February 11 will be remembered forever and ever. This has to be a slick in-and-out operation. Don't lose your way. If you do, you will have to stay behind."

Mentally, Author did a quick inventory check: dinghy, paddles, compass, jammer, guns, wetsuits, running shoes, frog whistles, and riding gear. The mountain gear would be delivered directly to Villa Castello. The assault on the island had to be organized with military precision. There was no margin for error.

"I have arranged for one of our guys to come and clean up in the morning, as we can't leave any evidence behind. The monthly rental for the apartment has been paid in advance," Arthur stated.

"I suggest we synchronize our watches," said Philip. "It would attract less attention if we leave the apartment singly at, say, five-minute intervals before regrouping at the boathouse below the promenade. By my calculations, we should launch at 7:30."

"Yes, I agree," responded Arthur. "Vincent, you go first and open the boathouse, followed by Sipho, then Faizil, and then you, Philip. I will close up and meet you all down there."

At the boathouse at sea level, visibility was down to fifty metres. A final last-minute check of the inventory revealed that everything was in order. They donned their wet suits and, with a furtive glance from left to right, launched the dingy at precisely 7:30 a.m.

They paddled out quietly and when a safe distance from shore, started the eighty horse-power motor and set an 11-degree course for the eastern side of Robben Island just north of Murray's Bay Harbour.

Meanwhile, the foghorn kept up its persistent cry, the dense fog intensifying the sound. Far from bringing a jangle to the ears, however, it brought a comforting reassurance that, while in operation, their cover was in place. A light south-westerly was blowing, allowing them to do a steady twelve knots. The bay was fairly calm.

Suddenly, from out of nowhere, a large hulking form of a freighter appeared straight ahead.

"Watch out! We are going to collide!" shouted Vincent. Just in time, Sipho veered off to starboard, narrowly avoiding a fatal collision.

"That was a close call. Let's take it easy," gasped Arthur, who was never quite at home on water.

Within two kilometres of the island, they cut the motor and lifted it out of the water. At the same time, Arthur switched on the radar jammer. Everything now depended on this device doing its job. They paddled quietly to shore. The fog was still holding up—for the fog to lift at this point would be disastrous.

"Sipho," Arthur whispered, "when we land, stay with the boat, and if any of us get lost, listen for the frog whistles."

Except for the penguins, all seemed quiet. They touched down at 8:15 a.m. in the middle of Penguin Beach.

"I am heading for Alpha Three," said Arthur. "The rest of you head for the workshop road. Our target group should be coming down the road in fifteen minutes. When I have completed my task, I'll double back to cover your escape." Arthur set off at a brisk pace in a northerly direction.

"We must be stationed on both sides of the road, as planned," said Philip. "I'll take the western side, and you two stay on the eastern side. Keep an eye on me. When I raise my hand, we must all fire our dart guns at once. We have to be accurate. We can't have anyone escaping and giving the alarm. Let's hope that there are no more than five or six guards and that they're unarmed, as was our information."

As Philip, Vincent, and Faizil scurried to their positions, the penguins objected by letting off a cacophony of sound, simultaneously jerking their heads from side to side. They were not at all happy with their space being invaded.

The fog on the island was slowly starting to drift out to sea as Arthur reached Alpha Three. From behind a minnatokka bush, he had a perfect view of the tower and the road linking the prison to the workshop. If he mistimed his shot, the Alpha Three guard would have time to warn the rest of the guards, which would scuttle the entire mission, one that depended on perfect coordination.

In the distance, he noticed a group coming around a bend in the road. Meanwhile, the Alpha Three Tower guard was concerned with the malfunction of his radar screen.

"Damn penguins," he muttered. "They're at it again. I'll have to get the technicians back. My screen is particularly bad today. If I had my way, I'd shoot the lot of them. They do seem a lot noisier than usual, however."

He stepped outside to have a look. Arthur took careful aim—there was no room for error. If he missed, the guard would have time to radio for help. He pulled the trigger, and the bullet from his silencer-fitted Makarov unerringly found its mark. The guard dropped to the ground. Groaning with pain, he lay on his back, looking around. Stumbling to his feet, he half rose, then stumbled again, and, drawing on the last remnants of his strength, reached for his two-way radio.

A final volley brought him to the ground for good. Arthur dragged the limp body to the tower and propped him up in a seated position in front of the screen, which, by this time, had totally malfunctioned. The two-way radio fixed to the guard's belt started buzzing. Someone was trying to contact Alpha Three. There was no time to lose. Pretty soon the place would be crawling with guards.

Mission accomplished, Author turned back to cover his colleague's retreat. The group was marching down the road, kicking up little puffs of dust. There were six guards: two on each side of the prisoners and two at the rear. One of the rear guards had a vicious-looking dog on a leash.

The island fog definitely seemed to be lifting and drifting out to sea.

As the group drew alongside, Philip raised his left hand. A second later, a volley of drugged darts split the air, all three finding their mark with practiced accuracy. A second volley caught the other three, and a third the startled dog. The victims dropped like hot potatoes. Just then, a shot rang out. It seemed to be coming from a northerly direction, the area where Arthur was reconnoitring. Philip broke cover and ran toward Khumalo.

"Operation Khulula is on," he said. "I am Philip. Quickly follow me. We have a wet suit for you in our boat, where you can discard your prison uniform."

Khumalo understood and gave a command to his colleagues. They knew what they had to do: the prostrate guards had to be moved out of sight.

On the run, Khumalo gave each of his rescuers a high-five salute as they scurried off through the bushes and across Penguin Beach toward the boat.

"Ouch!" cried Vincent, as a nesting penguin took a peck at his ankle.

"Where's the boat?" whispered Philip, in a state of near panic. Just then a frog whistle rang out in the gloom. "It's this way," he said, "follow me." Philip looked at his watch. It was 8:40 a.m. as they reached the boat.

"Where's Arthur?" asked Sipho. In the heat of the moment no one had noticed his absence.

"Keep blowing the whistle," urged Philip.

"We can't hang around here any longer," said Sipho. "We have to go."

Just then, a hunched figure appeared out of the half-light. Instinctively they raised their rifles.

"For God's sake, don't shoot," whispered Vincent. "It's Arthur." Arthur was holding his left shoulder, bleeding from a bullet wound.

Splashing into the cold water, he said, "I came across a stray guard, and he took a shot at me. I returned the fire and managed to bring him down."

They paddled out quietly, and when a safe distance from shore, started the outboard motor, setting a 191-degree course for Mouille Point. Khumalo donned his wet suit for the short passage across the bay. There was no point in taking chances with their precious cargo—anything could happen. The bay was crowded with ships wanting to enter the harbour and, remembering the near collision on the inward journey, they proceeded with due caution.

"Hello, I'm Truman," Khumalo said to Arthur, as he tore off the trouser leg of his prison uniform to form a tourniquet to the wound. "This should stem the flow of blood for a while."

"Thanks," responded Arthur. "I am afraid I'm not terribly good company right now."

They battled slightly into the stiff south-westerly. Three-quarters across the bay, the island's sirens started up.

"That's it," remarked Philip. "Khumalo's absence has been noticed. This is sooner than we thought."

To the cacophony of siren and foghorn was added another sound, the distant whine of a high-speed patrol boat. The sound appeared eerily to advance and retreat amplified by the dense fog. It seemed the entire bay had come alive in a symphony of metallic sounds.

Addressing Khumalo, Philip said, "We'll be landing at Mouille Point soon, where the plan is to merge with a group of motorbike riders heading south. With luck, you could be out of the country in a few days, and I'll be coming with you."

"Approaching shore," Sipho announced.

"Cut the engines," Arthur instructed in considerable pain, but still conscious of his authority. "Let's paddle in."

The fog was lifting fast. Suddenly the foghorn stopped.

"Abandon boat!" shouted Philip. "Our cover is blown."

The boat missed the mark by fifty metres, forcing them to scamper over rocks and seaweed.

"Be careful," warned Faizil, "it's very slippery."

Khumalo helped Arthur over the rocks toward the boat house.

CHAPTER 31

THE RIDE

9:15 a.m.

Back at the boathouse, Vincent fiddled with the combination lock.

Oh God, Philip thought, *don't tell me he has jammed the lock.* A jammed lock was certainly not part of the plan. Suddenly, with a click, it opened. The noise of an approaching chopper could clearly be heard as they hurriedly entered the boathouse.

"Slip these on," Philip said, handing Khumalo his riding gear. "This will cover you from view."

They all hurriedly donned their riding gear—the black leather jacket and trousers, tee-shirt, visors, bandanna, gloves, and shoes. As they exited the boathouse, they looked for all the world-like experienced members of the Harley Owners Group (HOG), and no one looked more resplendent than Comrade Khumalo, with his tall, lean physique.

Philip looked at his watch. They were a little late, but not seriously so.

At the top of the ramp, waiting for them on cue, were twenty *members* of the HOG, all appropriately attired with natty club emblems on the backs of their jackets. They had already formed up in formation awaiting the arrival of the task force. Onlookers could be forgiven for believing that this was a genuine *Harley Experience*.

Philip approached Arthur, who was in obvious distress. "We can't leave you like this," he said.

"You have to move on," replied Arthur. "I'll go to our rented apartment across the road and phone for medical assistance. It's over to you now. Good luck."

Philip shook him by the hand in a silent gesture of comradeship, and then rushed to his Sportster, which was waiting for him. He started his bike, and within seconds, it roared into life. The engine beneath him gave a reassuring feeling of power. Khumalo took up his pillion position behind Philip. Sipho, Faizil, and Vincent did likewise behind other riders.

They were placed in the centre of the group. The polished chrome work on the bikes shone impressively in the early morning sunlight. Comrade Peter Campbell, the leader of the ride, looked back and smilingly gave them the thumbs up.

9:27 a.m.

With a roar of engines and screech of tyres, the riders moved off in a southerly direction. Although Philip was an inexperienced rider, he was impressed with the exquisite balance and comfortable riding position of his Sportster. The group took a right and continued along Beach Road onto Victoria Road, passing the palm-fringed promenade of Camps Bay, which eventually led them out of town.

So far, so good, thought Philip.

Just then they heard the blaring wail of a police siren behind them. The siren got louder as a police vehicle drew level. Philip felt his skin tightening. The police seemed to be looking directly at them. The vehicle accelerated and then passed them, bringing a collective sigh of relief.

An army truck, filled with soldiers passed them in the opposite direction and waived at them. Nervously they returned the wave.

Twenty minutes later, they reached the cobbled road leading to Villa Castello. *First objective attained*, thought Philip.

The group slowed to allow Philip to peel off to the right. His colleagues gave him a farewell wave, as the bikers increased speed on the down slope leading to the village of Hout Bay where they were to disperse.

Philip looked at his watch—it was 9:50 a.m.

10:40 a.m. Office of the Prime Minister.

The prime minister's intercom buzzed. "Yes Annamarie?" he answered.

"Director of State Security General Van der Riet on line one for you, sir."

"Good morning, Gerhard," said the prime minister good-naturedly. "What can I do for you today?"

"I regret to inform you prime minister that Truman Khumalo has escaped from Robben Island."

"What?" exploded the prime minister. "How is that possible? I thought you told me security on the island was impenetrable."

"We think it might have been an inside job. He won't get very far, however. We are confident of his recapture within twenty-four hours. This is only a temporary setback."

"What actions have been taken?"

"The local police, security police, and national security have all been alerted. Helicopters are at this moment scanning the city. The coastguard has been notified, and the media informed.

Regular broadcasts are taking place on TV and radio, and we are offering a one million rand reward for any information leading to his capture, dead or alive.

"In addition, we have sealed off the airport and the harbour and installed roadblocks on all the major exit roads. House-to-house searches are being conducted also."

"This is shocking news indeed," replied the prime minister. "I must inform the Cabinet immediately. Please keep me personally abreast of all developments."

CHAPTER 32

INSIDE THE SAFE HOUSE

At the ornamental gates leading to the villa, they received the customary salute from the guards, who had been expecting them. Once inside the comparative safety of the gates, Philip turned to his passenger.

"With all the tensions of the past few hours, I really haven't had a chance to speak to you properly. How are you feeling?"

"A little breathless, but otherwise okay," replied Khumalo. "Fortunately, I have been keeping fit."

"We'll be spending the next three days at this villa, where you can get your breath back. The property is owned by a Mr. Otto Schtiller, who hails from Hamburg in West Germany. He is sympathetic to our cause and wants to help in any way he can. Being isolated, we should be comparatively safe here.

"On our third day—let's call it D-Day plus three—we'll use our motorbike and head for the mountains on the other side of the village. At a predetermined spot on the mountain, we'll fly a short distance in a microlight aircraft to a rendezvous with a Russian sub—and don't worry, I've taken a course in microlight flying.

"The submarine will take us as far as Dar es Salaam, where, all being well, you'll be united with your colleagues again."

"I take it this particular type of aircraft is equipped to land on the sub?" queried Khumalo, who had not lost any of his sense of humour.

"No, that's the tricky part. Our microlight has to be ditched in the sea as close to the sub as possible. To do so, we have to wear life jackets, and when two or three metres above the water, we'll jump. Take your cue from me."

Khumalo looked a little uncomfortable.

"Before we take off in the microlight, we have to do a little mountaineering. Are you up to it?" asked Philip.

"Well," said Khumalo smiling, "after the hell I have been through on the island, this should be a cake-walk."

"All the same, we'll take it slowly," said Philip.

The threatening sound of sirens emanating from nearby Victoria Road could be heard clearly from the grounds of the villa. As they arrived at the courtyard with its playing fountains, a figure stepped out from under the shadows of the entrance portal. Philip's heart skipped a beat.

"Oh, hello Mr. Schtiller," Philip said, taken a little by surprise. "I wasn't expecting you to be here. Anyhow it's good to see you again. May I introduce Truman Khumalo."

"Pleased to meet you," Schtiller said, shaking his hand warmly. "Better come inside straight away. There are helicopters everywhere. I'll have your bike moved to a store." He led them to the dining room.

"I have laid on breakfast," he said "You guys must be starving."

"Yes," said Khumalo with a chuckle. "I have not had a proper meal in sixteen years. Thanks for placing your lovely home at our disposal. Your brave gesture will not be forgotten."

"I, too, have had an embarrassing brush with Apartheid which I will never forget," said Schtiller. "My Cape Town director, Gunther Schultz, was only able to fill me in with the sketchiest of details. So I have flown out from Hamburg to place my services at your disposal. How can I be of further assistance?"

Noting Khumalo's unease, Philip said, "We can trust him. If we couldn't, we'd have been in custody by now." Addressing Schtiller he said, "The plan calls for us to head for a mountain trail near the village, avoiding all roads. At a predetermined point on the mountain, we'll fly out in a microlight aircraft to a rendezvous with a submarine."

"How do you expect to get to the mountain undetected from here?" asked Schtiller.

"On the motorbike," answered Philip, "which we'll then abandon."

"That's far too risky," answered Schtiller. "What if you are recognized? I suggest that I take the car out and report back to you on what I have seen."

"That sounds like a sensible idea," said Khumalo. "What do you think Philip?"

"Yes, I'll go along with that, but we have to leave here on the third day in order to make the rendezvous. Speaking of that, we still don't know the exact time and location of the rendezvous," he said nervously.

At 3:00 p.m. Schtiller took his car out and headed for the village, where he spent an hour driving around. On his return he said, "There is a police road block at the junction of Chapman's Peak Drive and Princess Street. As you are heading for Chapman's Peak Drive, I suggest that you circumvent the road block by cutting across the beach, linking up with Chapman's Peak Drive beyond the road-block. On the day of your departure, I'll drive you to the beach concealed in the boot of my car.

"Have a look at this," he said, throwing the *Cape Times* on the table, in which banner headlines proclaimed KHUMALO ESCAPES from robben island—massive reward offered for his recapture.

"There is a colossal manhunt out for you guys," he said. "You have done well to get this far."

Just then the doorbell rang.

"*Gott in himmel!*" exclaimed Schtiller. "I have given strict instructions at the gate for no one to enter unannounced. This is not good." He jumped up and said, "Quickly! Follow me," and led them to the trophy room. He removed the loose Persian carpet and opened the trap door, which provided access to the underground bar. At the head of the staircase, he switched on the light, which automatically switched on the air conditioning.

"You will be safe down here," he said. "Please do not come up until I say so."

Replacing the loose carpet neatly, he hurried to the front door. Taking a few deep breaths to compose himself, he opened the door.

"We have a search warrant and are conducting house-to-house searches for an escaped prisoner," announced Warrant Officer Pretorius. He was accompanied by six heavily armed men.

"Are you harbouring any fugitives here?" he asked rather brusquely.

"No, of course not," replied Schtiller, "but please feel free to look around."

Warrant Officer Pretorius dispatched his men to all parts of the complex, while he himself browsed around the main house.

"I have been here before," he said.

"I believe so," responded Schtiller, the memory of his ruined house-warming party still fresh in his mind.

"I see you have today's newspaper here," remarked Pretorius, looking at the headlines.

"Yes, we have it delivered," responded Schtiller tersely.

A few minutes later a senior officer returned to say the house was clean.

"Sorry to have disturbed you," said Pretorius. "We'll be leaving now."

It is a successful ploy of police all over the world to leave a premise they have just searched and return almost immediately to catch their prey unaware. Schtiller, being aware of this, returned to his lounge. He would leave his guests in the underground bar a little longer. Not five minutes later, the front door bell rang. Schtiller smiled as he opened the door.

"Did you forget anything warrant officer?" he asked nonchalantly.

"We would like to have another look," the officer answered.

"Be my guest."

After another careful search, they left. This time for good.

Schtiller went to the trap door and called down. "You guys can come up now. We have had a visit from the local police, who have searched the place and left. You will be safe here for the next few days. I believe we can all do with a strong cup of coffee."

Pouring the coffee he said, "Truman, things must look very different to you after sixteen years in prison."

"It's quite unbelievable," he answered. "I am amazed at the development of the city, especially the many new skyscrapers, the dramatic freeways, and the elegant homes. I even saw a Free-Khumalo sign," he said to spontaneous laughter. "It's like I have been in a deep sleep."

"Incidentally," said Otto, "an unmarked parcel was delivered here a few days ago. It contains two sets of boots, light weight cotton shirts, trousers, and wind breakers."

"Oh, those are our mountaineering clothes," replied Philip.

"As I imagined you guys would be travelling light," said Otto, "I have taken the liberty of buying you some casual clothes to use over the next few days. You will find them packed away in your drawers, as well as a wallet containing some dollars which might come in useful when you reach your ultimate destination." Waving his hands, he said, "Please don't thank me. It is but a small gesture on my part. Perhaps one day we will meet again under less stressful circumstances."

"When we form a new government," Truman said with a grin, "I'm going to make you minister of organization."

CHAPTER 33

THE REGIME REACTS

Monday, February 11, 1980 at 3:30 p.m. D-DAY, Western Cape Divisional Police Headquarters.

"Any progress on the case, brigadier?"

"Yes, commissioner," replied Brigadier Meiring. "One of our helicopters has spotted a motorized dinghy abandoned on the rocks at Mouille Point. A thorough search of the area revealed a boathouse close by with six wet suits inside. We believe this was the launching point for the assault. From this we can deduce that the task force was composed of five people—plus Khumalo, of course. From here, they could have gone anywhere. However, statements taken from people in the area and also petrol pump attendants at a garage in Mouille Point have confirmed that a group from the Harley Davidson Club formed up a few hundred metres down the road and passed the garage at approximately 9:35 a.m."

"Let's see," said the commissioner, "a few hundred metres down the road would be opposite the boathouse you spoke of. And the timing is perfect."

"Quite so, commissioner, and from that we have deduced that the fugitives joined the bike ride pre-arranged, obviously. This is quite ingenious, as the goggles, visors, and gloves would provide the perfect camouflage. We also know that they were heading south, as garages further south in Bantry Bay and Camps Bay also saw them pass. They have probably dispersed by now, but it does narrow the search down to the south. Consequently, we have called off the search in other areas."

"Excellent work. That certainly narrows the search area down. Any other clues, brigadier?"

"Yes, one of our agents who has infiltrated UAC ranks keeps mentioning the name of Philip Jordan. He feels sure that this person was sent to Russia to mastermind the escape."

"Any description of this person?"

"No, commissioner, only the name."

"Well, that's an important clue. Circulate posters immediately of Khumalo and this Philip Jordan. Keep up the house-to-house searches, especially those of known sympathizers, and let's concentrate on the south. It's important that they don't leave the country."

Tuesday, February 12, 1980 at 2:30 p.m. D-DAY+ 1

In late January, the Stellenbosch University rugby club arrived back from their tour of Scotland and Wales, where they had won five games and drawn two.

The first term of the year had already started. Jannie De Beer noticed that his friend Philip Watermeyer had not yet returned from his overseas tour. This was a little strange, as he had never missed the start of a new term before.

Jannie was relaxing in his room. There was a knock on the door.

A voice from the corridor shouted, "Jannie, phone call for you in the lobby!" Jannie hurried to the lobby.

"Constable De Beer, this is Warrant Officer Adriaan Pretorius from the Hout Bay Police Station. You've probably heard that Truman Khumalo has escaped from Robben Island."

"Yes, I have," answered De Beer. "Shocking news isn't it? Probably sprung by his communist buddies. He needs to be taught a lesson he'll not forget. You can't trust these people."

"Yes, and I would not like to be him when we catch up with him. We are presently conducting house-to-house searches in our area and are calling up all reservists. When can you report for duty?"

"I can be there later this afternoon," he said enthusiastically, happy in the knowledge that all those who opposed the government were either communists or traitors and deserved to be behind bars, and he was doing his bit for his country.

"Good, I'll see you later," said the warrant officer.

5:00 p.m.

On arrival at the Hout Bay Police Station, Jannie De Beer's attention was immediately drawn to two posters of *wanted men* on the walls of the charge office: one of Khumalo with a picture and one of a Philip Jordan with no picture. The latter struck a chord in his memory. Philip Jordan, Philip Jordan— the name reverberated through his mind. Where had he heard that name before? For a moment, he stood transfixed. If only he could remember where he had heard that name before, he could provide some valuable information. He mentally traced and re-traced his recent movements.

Suddenly the penny dropped. "I've got it!" he said to himself. "I was at Cape Town Airport and was about to embark on the plane with the rugby team. It was at the boarding gate that I heard the British Airways attendant address the person behind

Philip as 'Yes, Mr. Jordan, you have window seat twenty-nine A. Have a good flight'. Philip Jordan, the traitor, must have been on our plane."

He went directly to Warrant Officer Pretorius's office, knocked, and entered.

"Warrant Officer," he said "I am reporting for duty. Also, I have something important to tell you in connection with the Khumalo escape."

The Warrant Officer lifted his head, his eye brows arching. "What is it?" he asked eagerly.

Jannie relayed the incident at the airport. "In fact, come to think of it, I was convinced at the time that she was actually addressing my friend, Philip Watermeyer, who was also going overseas. I remember mentioning it to him at the time. It was he who persuaded me otherwise. Is it possible that Philip Watermeyer is actually Philip Jordan travelling under an alias?"

"Quite possibly. Can you give me a profile of your friend?"

"Well, he's twenty years old, about 1.8-metres tall, keeps himself super fit, and is a good swimmer. Politically, he's a bit soft on Blacks and has frequently been seen fraternizing with an Indian waiter, Faizil Khan, at the Golden Fig Restaurant where they both work part time. He doesn't seem to mind hanging out with people of colour. One thing that bothers me, though, is where he was going if he wasn't going on a church tour?"

"There's a simple explanation," replied the warrant officer. "These chaps are recruited by the UAC and sent to the USSR for training. The younger they are, the more gullible. They have this misguided notion that the country would be better off under communism. A Stellenbosch University student would be the last one to be suspected."

"My God!" blustered Jannie. "It all adds up! He was perpetually short of funds, and to add to it, his father has been seriously ill.

Maybe he was tempted by the money? The university term has begun, and he's nowhere to be seen. Maybe I'm wrong, but it bears looking into."

"I think I'd better get Brigadier Meiring on the line. He's in charge of the investigation. Please repeat to him what you've told me."

Warrant Officer Pretorius phoned Brigadier Meiring. "How is the Khumalo case going, sir?" he enquired.

"We have some interesting leads, but no arrests yet. We would appreciate any help we can get. Khumalo could do a lot of damage if he were to get away."

"Well sir," said the warrant officer," Constable De Beer, one of our reservists, has some interesting information for you. I will put him on."

Constable De Beer repeated his story.

"Good work, constable. I'll send a squad car to pick up this Faizil Khan. If he's mixed up in this, we'll make him talk. One call to British Airways will establish if there was both a Philip Jordan *and* a Philip Watermeyer on the flight you mentioned. If there was no Philip Watermeyer registered, then he's our man. Please have Warrant Officer Pretorius bring you over to police headquarters first thing in the morning. You might have to miss a lecture or two. And please bring a photograph of Philip Watermeyer with you."

5:30 p.m. Villa Castello

"This envelope was just delivered at the gate," said Schtiller, handing Philip the envelope. "I think it must be for you."

Philip opened the envelope. "I've been waiting for this," he said. "It's the final rendezvous position of the submarine. We're to meet fifteen nautical miles west of the Slangkop Lighthouse.

The *Admiral Federov* will surface between 8:50 and 9:05 on the morning of Thursday, February 14. There's no margin for error. If we're not on time, the submarine will have to leave without us."

February 13, 1980 at 8:00 a.m. Brigadier Meiring's Office, Police Headquarters. D-DAY+ 2.

Addressing Warrant Officer Pretorius and Constable De Beer, the brigadier said, "This new information is a major breakthrough. I've contacted British Airways. There was no one called Philip Watermeyer on the passenger list, which means that Watermeyer was traveling under an alias.

"We've also picked up the waiter Faizil Khan and taken him in for questioning. After giving him the *squeezed testicle* treatment, he sang like a baby."

"May I ask what that is, sir?" asked De Beer.

"We take out his testicles and squeeze them until they become the size of golf balls. Take it from me, this is excruciatingly painful. It's enough to make the strongest man break down. It's only a matter of time before we round up the ringleaders. Watermeyer is obviously our man."

"I am absolutely shocked," said De Beer, "to think that I befriended a traitor all this time, one that was in league with communists and Blacks. How could I have been so blind?"

"You had no way of knowing," replied the brigadier. "Anyhow, you've more than made up for it. The raid on Robben Island was daring and carefully planned. It looks certain they had outside help. Some people think Khumalo may already be out of the country, but I don't think so. However, if he is heading south, how would he get way? The south is a dead end."

"Maybe he has bribed some Coloured fishermen in Hout Bay or Llandudno to take him out to a waiting ship," ventured De Beer.

"A waiting ship would have no chance," replied the brigadier. "Our territorial waters are well guarded. Also, there are road blocks on all the major roads. He wouldn't get very far."

"Couldn't a helicopter airlift him to a waiting submarine?" asked the warrant officer.

"It's a possibility," answered the brigadier, "but the sub would be picked up on sonar, and our continental shelf is notoriously shallow for subs to get close. Regarding the use of a helicopter, even if the pilot were to avoid detection, he'd have no chance of escape. It's a tricky one. Let's all think about it," concluded the brigadier. "Thank you both for your valuable contributions—especially you, Constable."

"Glad to have been of service, sir," said De Beer, conscious of both his duty and the one million rand reward.

"I may need you again soon, Constable. Please leave your contact number with my secretary on the way out." The brigadier slumped back in his chair. He was not easily stumped. After all, he had solved some of South Africa's most complex cases over the past few years. He phoned his secretary and instructed her to hold all but the most pressing calls until further notice. He needed time, free of interruptions, to think.

The case was close to a solution, but a vital element was missing. He sieved through the available information again and again.

If Khumalo was already out of the country, he would have known about it by now. That being the case, he was obviously in hiding and being sheltered by some of his supporters and probably waiting for the right moment to make a break-out. With a one million rand reward on his head, the house would have to be isolated from public gaze. That reward would be awfully tempting, especially as the government would guarantee confidentiality.

It seems certain that his hideaway is somewhere in the south, probably an isolated house in Hout Bay or Llandudno. As these suburbs are designated white areas, his host would have to be a white person—either a white member of the UAC or a sympathizer.

Regarding the motorbike ride, it's safe to assume that Khumalo would be in no condition to drive. It would have to have been Watermeyer, who would know by now that the noose was tightening and he'd have to escape with Khumalo. So, in all probability, the search was on for just the two of them.

If the airport, harbour, and main roads were all blocked, the only alternative route would be via the mountains. But how would they escape from the mountains?

Mountain climbing is treacherous at the best of times. It would be folly to depart from the well- known tracks. This would narrow the routes down. Furthermore, mountain climbing would have to be undertaken in daylight, as there were ravines and snakes on the mountains. They'd have to have their wits about them, to say nothing of avoiding contact with other hikers.

A submarine escape would be feasible, but which country would risk a diplomatic rupture resulting from such an action. It could only be Russia, who already openly supported the UAC. Maybe Russia had her eyes on the bigger picture: our minerals. But why risk having her sub being blown apart by blatantly entering another country's territorial waters. Unless, of course, they had no intention of violating our waters and were waiting outside the limits. That would be a lot safer, but our territorial limits are fifteen nautical miles out—a long, long way from land.

The main question remains unanswered: even if they were to avoid all obstacles, how would they get off the mountain undetected and rendezvous accurately with a sub in the middle of the ocean? How indeed? This was the key. It would have to be an aircraft of some sort, but there were no runways on the mountains. A glider or hang-glider would require no runway, but gliders have to be towed by other aircraft to take off and hang-gliders have no propulsion. They depend entirely on thermals. That would rule them out, especially as accurate instrumentation would be a necessity. Perplexed, he phoned his secretary and asked her to resume his calls.

By 2:00 p.m., he had the sinking feeling that time was running out. On the spur of the moment, he decided to phone home. His fifteen-year-old son would be back from school.

"Dean," he said, "you're always studying books on trains and planes, so I have a hypothetical question for you. If you were on top of a mountain and needed to rendezvous with a vessel out at sea, how would you do it? Remember there are no runways on top of this mountain."

"I would use a microlight, dad," answered Dean. "It's a relatively new concept in flying. I've seen a few around, and one or two have already taken off from Table Mountain."

"Really? Tell me more about these microlites."

"Well," he said, "I've just been reading up about them in the latest edition of *National Mechanix*, and they're extremely lightweight and can carry one or two passengers."

"What's the method of propulsion?"

"They have a two-stroke engine, are manoeuvrable, and have fairly sophisticated instruments, so much so that they're able to lock into a beam signal sent out by a vessel at sea and make a perfect rendezvous. They're also fitted with an altimeter to gauge heights above land and water."

"Is that so? Who imports these planes?"

"I don't know who actually imports them," said Dean, "but I believe they have a club at Zeekoevlei."

"Thanks, my boy. You have been most helpful."

Well, I'll be, he thought, *out of the mouths of babes . . .* That *must* be the answer! They're using a microlight. We'll have to move fast, as my sixth sense tells me that the breakout is imminent.

He phoned his secretary and asked her to get the Zeekoevlei Microlight Club on the line. A few moments later, she phoned and said that the secretary of the microlight club was on the line.

Posing as a potential club member, he said, "Mr. Arnold, I am interested in microlight flying. Are these craft equipped to fly in any kind of weather, particularly in our strong winds?"

"Yes, but we strongly recommend early morning or late afternoon flying because there is very little turbulence at that time of day. These planes are lightweight and easily buffeted by high winds."

"Do they need lengthy runways like other planes?"

"No, they can take off from the proverbial postage stamp."

"Thank you for the information," said the brigadier. "I will be in touch with you again."

He buzzed his secretary and said, "Please contact Constable De Beer. I believe he left his phone number with you. I need to speak to him urgently."

The secretary rang him through. "Constable De Beer, Brigadier Meiring here. I believe I have cracked the case. Please proceed immediately to Ysterplaats Air Force Base and link up with 16th Squadron. It is my contention that the fugitives intend to fly out using a microlight aircraft, which will be hidden and waiting for them somewhere in the southern mountains. From there, they intend flying out to a rendezvous with a waiting submarine, probably Russian.

"What we don't know is where exactly the submarine will be. It could be anywhere off the tip of Cape Point, but probably not near our naval base at Simon's Town. That would be extremely foolish. Therefore, I'm ordering 16th Squadron to send up five helicopters to cover all known mountain routes. You'll have good light until 8:30 this evening. We've been informed that microlight club members are fond of taking off from the mountains and flying back to base at Zeekoevlei. Consequently, your presence is vital, as you are the only person on our team who can identify Watermeyer positively. We must not, under any circumstances, harm innocent microlight enthusiasts, who may be using the mountains at this time. The opposition press would crucify us.

"Major Grobler will be expecting you at the air force base. He'll be your pilot. You'll be accompanied by a flight engineer and two police officers, who will make the arrest. Your unit's orders are to identify and bring the fugitives back, dead or alive.

"We need a positive identification of the submarine so we can establish the country of origin. Also, we need to know if they have invaded our territorial waters. Chopper One will cover the East Fort/Constantia Berg/Silvermine route. Chopper Two will cover Silvermine South, and Chopper Three will cover the Silvermine Panorama route.

"In case I am wrong about the escape route, I'm sending out two more helicopters, Choppers Four and Five, to cover Table Mountain and environs. Please keep in close contact with me and the other helicopters. I won't be leaving the office tonight. If, by dark, you have drawn a blank, return to base, spend the night there, and take off again at first light.

"My feeling is that the breakout will take place late this afternoon or early tomorrow morning. If they resist arrest, your orders are to shoot them down. They must not get away.

All evidence indicates that they will be heading for a Russian submarine at a position just beyond our territorial limits, which is fifteen nautical miles out to sea. That could be anywhere. Find the microlight, and they will lead you to the submarine.

"Your unit is to do everything to prevent the escape, which means attacking the submarine if you have to. They will be no match for you, as their torpedoes and missiles are not designed to attack aircraft. The moment you spot them, contact Choppers Two and Three for backup and let me know immediately, so that I can alert coastal patrol."

Rushing to Ysterplaats Air Force Base in his bright yellow VW Beetle, Jannie De Beer could not believe his luck. Through no fault of his own, he had befriended a terrorist these past few years. He felt a sense of shame. However, what was important was that he found himself in a key position in a moment of great crisis for his country.

And there was the one million rand reward, which must surely be awarded to him for identifying the traitor Watermeyer. Let's see, he would buy himself a new car with the money, perhaps a Porsche. That would really enhance his image on the campus. His girlfriend, Christine, too, would be most impressed.

Wednesday, February 13, 1980 at 4:00 p.m. Ysterplaats Air Force Base

Jannie was still on cloud nine as his yellow Volkswagen reached the gates of the air force base on the northern outskirts of Cape Town. He brought his car to a halt and was asked to produce his pass.

A tall, thin man stepped forward and said to security, "It's okay. We're expecting this person." Turning to Jannie, he offered his hand and said, "You must be the reservist Jannie De Beer.

I'm Major Grobler. Please park your car. Our Alouette is on the runway ready for take-off."

The flight engineer and the two police officers were already seated as the pilot and Jannie stepped aboard. At 4:15 p.m., five Alouettes took off in the late afternoon sun with orders to reconnoitre specific mountain routes around the southern metropolitan area.

"I have these for you," said Major Grobler, handing Jannie a powerful set of binoculars. "However, trying to identify hikers from the air is like trying to find the proverbial needle in a haystack. I believe our best bet is to concentrate on finding the getaway aircraft. Microlight flying is a relatively new sport, so there can't be too many around. Besides they should be easy to spot with their large, delta-shaped wings."

Chopper One headed south across Table Bay toward Table Mountain, and then turned right over the coastline to follow the coastal road to Hout Bay. Flying over Little Lions Head, Jannie could clearly see Villa Castello.

"See that large house down there?" he shouted to Major Grobler over the headphones. "We caught some foreigners there flouting the Immorality Act. It was quite a scene, I can tell you."

The pilot laughed inwardly, imagining the humiliation it must have caused the victims. They flew over East Fort and over Constantiaberg. After a two-hour fruitless search, they found nothing. The four other crews, likewise, reported negatively.

"Return to base and take off at first light," instructed Brigadier Meiring.

At base, they were joined by the other crews, who also were going to spend the night there.

"Feel like a drink?" asked Major Grobler, as they walked toward the canteen. They sat down and ordered two beers.

"Tell me, Constable," said the major taking a sip, "how did you get mixed up in all this?"

"The person who has masterminded Khumalo's escape, a chap called Philip Watermeyer, used to be a close friend of mine at Stellenbosch University," answered De Beer. "I'm the one who has identified him. I had absolutely no idea he was a terrorist. Brigadier Meiring is of the opinion that the fugitives are hiding in a safe house either in Llandudno or Hout Bay and are just waiting for the right moment to escape.

"So far the location of the safe house has eluded everyone."

"Well, when we catch them, these criminals will get what's coming to them," answered the major.

CHAPTER 34

THE LOITERING POSITION

February 9, 1980

After a long and uneventful transit, the *Admiral Federov* finally arrived at its loitering position 360 kilometres due west of Cape Point, the pre-determined position at which the captain was to check for any messages and, in particular, receive the vital information regarding the rendezvous. The broadcast would be repeated every four hours to ensure that the message was received by the sub. The message was not to be acknowledged to avoid interception.

"Prepare to come to periscope depth," he ordered.

On reaching a safe depth of eighty metres where even a vessel with the deepest draught could safely pass overhead, the officer of the watch began the laid down procedure for proceeding to periscope depth, where the surface picture is visible through the periscope lens. The surface picture was clear.

"Twenty metres," ordered the captain. The submarine surged upwards.

"Up periscope," he ordered as they passed through thirty metres.

The periscope broke surface, then dipped again as the plainsman momentarily struggled to keep the heavy submarine at twenty metres.

"Periscope clear." A quick all-around sweep to check for surface contacts revealed all was clear.

"All clear on the surface," the captain called out. "Raise the navigation mast. Check our position by GPS."

This was done and a fix taken. They were now in the loitering position, ready to receive messages. Their navigation system had not let them down.

The captain silently marvelled at its accuracy. The four hours broadcast was about to come through.

"Read the broadcast," he ordered.

"No messages, sir," replied the senior communications rating.

"Dive to 200 metres," ordered the captain. "Officer of the watch, remain at 200 metres depth and within fifteen kilometres of our loitering position."

"Aye, aye, sir," came the acknowledgement.

The submarine settled down at 200 metres to await final instructions, returning to safe depth every four hours to read the broadcast. To do so at this depth, it was necessary to reduce speed and trail the floating aerial.

The captain was fully aware that this contained an element of risk, due to the remote possibility of the aerial being detected. But it had advantages over coming to periscope depth. On each occasion that the mast was raised, there was no news. The pattern was becoming repetitive with frustration setting in.

Uncharacteristically the captain became agitated and short-tempered. There was nothing he could do but sit morosely in his cabin. Two days had already been wasted in the loitering position, waiting for the expected broadcast. He was in an irritable mood. There was a tentative knock on the door. It was the chief engineer.

"I'm sorry to disturb you, sir, but I am afraid I bring some bad news," he said with a fair amount of trepidation, being all too aware of the captain's mood.

The captain looked at him apprehensively.

"I have to report a major defect on number one air conditioning unit, sir. A hull cooling valve has jammed in the closed position and put the system out of action."

"What does that mean?" the captain demanded, although he already knew the answer.

"I'm afraid we will be limited to two thirds of our normal top speed, because of the excessive heat generated inside the submarine," came the reply.

"And action stations?" queried the captain, his brain racing to consider all options and permutations

"We'll be limited to action stations for only a short period of time, sir. Having everything switched on will give off so much heat, that some equipment may suffer permanent damage," the chief replied.

"Damn! How long will it take to repair?"

"About six hours, sir, if no further snags are encountered. The valve will have to be removed and repaired. In the interest of safety, I would strongly recommend that we remain stopped or at best move slowly through the water while the job is being done."

The captain remained silent for a few moments, considering his options. The next broadcast was due in little more than half an hour. "Before I let you tackle the work, I need to see if there are any messages for us," he said tersely.

The chief left, thankful at not having received the full force of the captain's wrath.

No sooner had he left, when the captain hurried to the operations room and ordered the officer of the watch to prepare to come to periscope depth. The submarine moved first to safe depth, followed by the standard procedure to come to periscope depth. Speed was reduced to five knots, sufficient to maintain depth using the planes, but slow enough for optimal listening conditions. All round sonar sweeps were ordered. On completion, the blind stern area was cleared by altering course by forty degrees and the all-round sweeps carried out again. This procedure was necessary to ensure that other vessels were not being masked by the submarine's own propeller.

Within twenty minutes the surface was confirmed clear. The loitering position had been carefully chosen, well clear of normal shipping activity.

"Twenty metres," ordered the captain. "Up periscope. Periscope clear. Clear on the surface," he sang out. "Raise the communication mast. Read the broadcast."

"One message received," the senior communicator called out.

"Down all masts two-hundred metres," ordered the captain, retiring expectantly to his cabin to receive the message. This is what he had been anxiously waiting for.

Within minutes there was a knock on his door. It was the senior communicator.

"Immediate top secret for you, sir."

The captain reached for the signal board and rapidly scanned the pink signal paper.

R V 140900 B 270 DEGREES SLANGKOP LIGHT 15. ONE FRIENDLY MICROLIGHT. TWO PASSENGERS, was all it said.

"Tomorrow morning at 8:50 local time, fifteen kilometres due west of the Slangkop Lighthouse," he murmured to himself. And they will be coming by microlight. How bizarre. In just over twelve hours. Under normal conditions, no problem, but there was a jammed hull-valve to consider. It would take at least six hours to repair, which left six hours to get into position. At maximum speed of thirty knots, we will just make it. But if there are any snags or further holdups, the South African VIPs in the microlight could run out of fuel and almost certainly face a grim death. That would be disastrous, considering the risks that had been taken to get them out. It would be a humiliating, strategic blow to the Motherland, to say nothing of the damage to his personal reputation. What a way to end his career, he thought.

The burden of command had never rested more heavily on his shoulders. He agonized for a few moments longer. Then, his mind made up, he addressed the waiting communicator. "Call the chief engineer."

The chief appeared in seconds.

"Carry out repairs on the hull valve. You have five hours," the captain ordered.

The chief departed on the run. The submarine slowed. Work began. Four and a half hours later there was a knock on the door. It was the chief again, his face smeared with grease, his once-white overall dirty and drenched with sweat. It was obvious that he had got stuck in with the rest of the black gang.

"Yes?" the captain enquired expectantly.

"Another hour I'm afraid," the chief answered.

The captain felt like exploding, but he knew the chief was pulling out all the stops.

"Okay," he said," but no longer."

The chief disappeared. The captain was left to brood alone. He felt helpless. Precious time had been wasted. The fate of a nation hinged on the next few hours. Sixty minutes passed. There was a knock on the door. It was the chief.

"Repair successfully carried out," he said wearily.

"Well done chief," blurted the captain, hurrying to the operations room. "Steer course zero-nine-zero degrees. Full steam ahead."

CHAPTER 35

THE BREAK-OUT

Thursday, February 14, 1980. Hout Bay. D-DAY + 3

Truman and Philip arose at four in the morning. Wiping the remnants of sleep from their eyes, they gulped down the strong coffee provided by their host. Outside the stars twinkled in the clear night sky, presaging the onset of a perfect summer's day. A gentle south-westerly breeze rustled through the trees at Little Lions Head, as the village below lie asleep. Apart from the occasional dog bark, all was quiet.

D-DAY Plus Three had dawned, and both Truman and Philip were acutely aware of its significance. What would the day bring: escape and a new beginning or capture and more repression? Ahead lay the most daunting task of all: the strenuous mountain climb up the Constantiaberg and the risky microlight flight to the waiting submarine out at sea. Even if they were to evade their pursuers, Philip thought, this would still be no picnic. He had had only a rudimentary course in microlight flying and that was in peaceful conditions. How would Truman cope with the potentially strenuous mountain climb? The ultimate prize, freedom, was worth all the risks, however. He kept these thoughts to himself, as he drained the last remnants of coffee from his mug.

They donned their mountaineering outfits and the Wuppertal tyre-sole boots, which had arrived in the parcel a few days earlier.

"Hell, these are comfortable," commented Truman. "The one thing I really missed on the island was a nice pair of boots."

Otto had filled a rucksack with refreshments.

"Climbing makes one hungry," he said supportively, as he left the house to bring the car to the front door. "I'll meet you in the courtyard."

"I see you have a suitcase on your back seat, Otto," noted Philip.

"Yes, after I drop you guys off, I am going straight to the airport to catch the first available flight out of here. I will say goodbye to you now," he said, as Truman and Philip climbed into the boot of the car. "God speed, good luck, and please let me know how things turn out."

"We certainly will," replied Truman "and thanks for everything. We could not have got this far without you."

In the still of the morning, Otto drove his passengers away from Villa Castello, the safe house that had been their refuge for the past few days. At the main gates, he turned right and headed for the village. In the village, he took a left off Victoria Road and a right into quiet Empire Avenue before stopping the car at the bottom of the avenue, where the road met the beach. It was still dark when he opened the boot to let his passengers out. With a wave and a silent good-bye, Truman and Philip stumbled onto the beach. They would make their way toward Chapman's Peak Hotel on Chapman's Peak Drive, the start of the world-famous scenic route. The indigenous melkhout trees, coastal vegetation, and sand dunes would provide adequate cover on the beach until they reached Chapman's Peak Drive. Mindful of the roadblock, they looked left and right before scurrying across the road. The noisy clatter of police manning the road block lower down filtered up to them.

So far so good, thought Philip. First objective achieved. It was still dark as they reached East Fort, 1.5 kilometres from the hotel. Philip glanced at his watch. It was 5:00 a.m.

The lights of Hout Bay sparkled against a smooth indigo sea. The sky was just beginning to lighten. Dawn was approaching. The two men turned their attention to the slope ahead. In the early morning gloom, the path ahead appeared extremely steep. It was hard to imagine an easy route through the forbidding buttresses of the Constantiaberg. In the distance, they could see the low neck at the top of Blackburn Ravine, their next objective. It looked daunting. Philip wondered how his companion would cope.

They followed the zigzag dust road behind East Fort for about twenty-five minutes. The air was crisp and fresh with the aroma of mountain fynbos. At the end of the forestry road, they continued along the well-worn path. Sections were coloured with a purplish stone.

"This is manganese," commented Philip, pointing to the coloured stone. "On the crest of that buttress over there are old manganese mines, some of which penetrated all of eighty-four metres into the mountain side. Those columns down there in the bay are the remains of the pier where the ore was loaded into waiting boats. As the manganese was found rather high up in the mountain, they built a crude chute, about 750 metres long, shoved the ore down the chute, and simply let gravity do its work. It must have been quite an awesome sight in full cry. The mine closed down in 1911 after only two years operation."

Slowly, the two men zig-zagged up the ravine. Dawn had broken, lightening the sky with delicate pastel colours. The noise from below had increased. A rooster announced the start of a new day; dogs began barking; and motor cars were making their presence known. Tiny armadas of fishing vessels were preparing for the day's harvest. Factories in the confines of the harbour sent up plumes of steam to waft lazily in the soft morning light. The Cape was awakening.

Thursday, January, 14, 1980 at 5:00 a.m. Ysterplaats Air Force Base.

Jannie was lying on his make-shift bed. He hadn't slept much. He had been dreaming about that elusive safe house. It had been bothering him. At 5:30 a.m., he was dressed and shaved. Turning to Major Grobler, he said, "You know, major, Brigadier Meiring was saying that the people sheltering the fugitives would either have to be sympathizers, fellow communists, or maybe someone with a grudge against the government. Remember yesterday I pointed out a large house to you from the air called Villa Castello? I said I was on duty the night we caught some foreigners . . . *in the act*. Well, the owner of the property, a German guy called Otto Schtiller, was very upset, as his guests were in the country for the first time. These foreigners don't always respect our laws, you know. He could well have been harbouring a grudge against the government. They come here for a holiday, enjoy our hospitality, and then think nothing of collusion with the blacks. The house is along the suspected escape route and is conveniently secluded. It's a long shot, but worth investigating."

"Well, why don't you phone Brigadier Meiring and pass on your suspicions," commented Major Grobler. "It may save us a fruitless search. There's a phone in the lobby."

He phoned the brigadier, who instantly put a call through to Warrant Officer Pretorius.

"Sorry to phone you so early," he said, "but I have information that the house called Villa Castello on Little Lions Head could be the fugitive's hiding place. Please assemble a squad and go there immediately. If the information is correct, we may catch them asleep."

"We've been there already," replied the warrant officer, "but we'll go again and be in touch presently."

6:00 a.m.

Having received no orders to the contrary, the five Alouettes took off from the air force base heading for the southern mountains. The bay sparkling in the early morning sun looked serene and calm, giving no hint of the events to come. Across the bay, Table Mountain gazed protectively down on the mother city. It was another perfect day in the Cape.

6:40 a.m. Villa Castello

"Brigadier," said Warrant Officer Pretorius, "I'm speaking to you from Villa Castello. We've unearthed a motorbike hidden in a store."

"What make is it?" asked the brigadier.

"It is a twelve-hundred CC Harley Davidson Sportster. What's more, a thorough search has uncovered a secret underground bar, which eluded us on our previous visit here. That bar could have afforded the perfect shelter for the fugitives. The house is deserted except for two guards at the gate and a cook. The cook has admitted, under interrogation, that Truman Khumalo and another person were here."

"Well done, warrant officer," said the brigadier elatedly. "That confirms my hypothesis. They are probably somewhere in the southern mountains right now on the last leg of their escape. If so, our choppers will find them. I hope to make an arrest within hours."

It was 7:00 a.m. by the time Truman and Philip reached the neck. Three kilometres still to go. Exhausted, they collapsed on a flat rock to catch their breath. Looking back, the view in all directions was tremendous. Toward the north, lush fynbos could be seen covering the slopes of the Constantiaberg. To the south, were the precipitous buttresses of Noordhoek Peak. Below, the omnipresent blue sea.

"This mountain is like a cathedral devoid of all politics," remarked Truman. "Just look how puny Hout Bay looks from here."

"Actually I don't know if you are aware of it, but Hout Bay has had a particularly colourful history," explained Philip, while opening the hamper provided by Otto.

"The first White men to see Hout Bay in October 1652 were an armed party under a chap called Pieter van den Helm. They came expecting to find an armed Portuguese stronghold, but instead found a sheltered bay with a thick forest of trees. This was to provide the Cape settlement with wood for a long time to come. It was Van Riebeeck, who, as you know, came from Holland to be the first governor of the Cape, who named it Hout Bay—*hout* meaning wood.

"I've read somewhere that the Dutch Government capitulated in 1795 after ruling for 150 years. The British took over under Captain Bridges and bolstered the Cape's defences. They installed a battery of eighteen pounders at opposite ends of the bay and called them East Fort and West Fort. We passed the ruins of East Fort early this morning."

"Well, that is interesting," commented Truman. "I always wondered how Hout Bay got its name."

Their reverie was interrupted by the thudding sound of an approaching helicopter.

"Quickly, dive for cover!" shouted Philip, the contents of their hamper spilling in all directions. "That's a police helicopter, and they could be on our trail. This is not good news. They seem to be looking for something."

"And have you noticed those hikers down there? They appear to be gaining on us," said Truman, casting his gaze downwards.

"We had better move on. They could be cops," said Philip.

The helicopter, meanwhile, completed a wide circle to the east.

"He's coming to have a second look," observed Philip, wiping the perspiration off his face. They dived for cover again. The helicopter passed over them and disappeared over the ridge. After dusting themselves off, they moved off at a brisk pace in a southerly direction. The Silvermine Nature Reserve loomed ahead, from which point it was mercifully all downhill. They had made fairly good progress and still had a little time left before their pre-arranged contact with the microlight pilots.

In the morning sunlight, they followed the easy track to the Silvermine circular road, which was used for firefighting purposes only. A different panorama unfolded. From this position they could see Muizenberg to the east and the mountains of the South Peninsula curving all the way down to Cape Point.

"This is spectacular," commented Truman. "Now I know why mountaineering is so popular in the Cape."

In the middle distance, other helicopters could be seen hovering like wasps, obviously searching for them. Continuing down the zigzag road, they came to the Silvermine Reservoir, which was in a cool pine plantation. They were sweating and it looked irresistible.

"Feel like a quick swim to cool off?" asked Philip. "I think we still have a twenty-five minute lead on those hikers in Blackburne Ravine, and we will be shielded by the trees."

Truman nodded and, under the security of the vegetation, they stripped for a quick swim. Though it was summer, the mountain water was icy.

"Let's do the route again," said Major Grobler, as the helicopter flew over Blackburn Ravine for the second time. Jannie De Beer had his binoculars firmly focused on the well-worn zigzag path.

"There's a party of five down there at the base of the path, but it can't be them. They wouldn't be travelling in a group," declared De Beer.

In the near distance, they could see the other two helicopters covering the eastern escarpment.

"Let's move over to the coast," instructed the pilot.

Invigorated by the swim, Truman and Philip continued through the pines to the head of the tarred road in the reserve, for the vital pre-arranged meeting with the microlites. It was 7:55 a.m. when they arrived at the top of the road. No microlites and no evidence of anybody. The hikers behind them were closing the gap, and the searching helicopters kept up their menacing presence. Fear began to set in. From behind, there was an explosion of a diesel engine.

Panicking, they dived into the bushes at the side of the road as a red fire truck came thundering past. A thick-set man was at the wheel and two children were his passengers. Truman and Philip realized that it was the ranger taking his children to school.

"Let's hope the microlites arrive before the ranger returns and those hikers following catch up with us," Philip remarked anxiously. "They could be cops."

At 8:00 a.m. on the dot, five colourful microlites appeared like giant butterflies over the Steenberg Ridge, landing one by one down the small road into the south-westerly. At the bottom of the road, they turned and taxied to meet Truman and Philip.

CHAPTER 36

THE RENDEZVOUS (RV)

The team in the operations room looked at each other. The big moment must be arriving. The submarine gathered speed and rushed blindly through the dark water; its ears, the sonar, rendered helpless by the vast ambient noise generated by the high speed.

The transit had to be deep to minimize leaving a heat trail in the sea, which could be picked up by infra-red imaging on other subs. The captain carefully watched the soundings below the keel, frequently consulting his chart. The plainsman on the one-man console, keeping both depth and speed, restricted the movement of his control column to a minimum. One false move and they would strike bottom or rocket to the surface.

The captain kept the safety separation below the keel at 100 metres, decreasing depth as the water shallowed. With only two hours to go, they were still fifty kilometres from the RV, and, once there, would still need to go through the time-consuming procedure of coming from safe depth to periscope depth. In the shipping lanes they were about to enter, that would take at least twenty minutes at much lower speeds. *Would they make it?* he wondered, beads of perspiration appearing on his brow.

"Action stations," he barked. He needed the best people closed up. The harsh sound of the claxon rent the air. Men scurried around him. Reports came through.

"Control centre closed up at action stations. Propulsion compartment closed up at action stations. Missile space closed up at action stations." The reports kept coming. Bleary eyed men having just awoken were suddenly alert and moving through their drills with practiced ease. The operations and control room were bathed in the soft glow of the red night lighting. The whole submarine throbbed with life and expectancy. There was adrenaline in the air. This was what the captain lived for.

The depth shallowed remorselessly. Soon they were at safe depth, but still thirty kilometres from the RV. At this speed, the safety separation below the keel had to be maintained. They must come to periscope depth.

"Speed fifteen. Prepare to come to periscope depth," he ordered. "Sonar checks all round. Check the stern areas."

As expected, there were numerous contacts on sonar. Each was briefly assessed; his mind in high gear. None too close, he concluded. It had only taken a few precious minutes.

"Twenty metres," he ordered. "Up periscope. Periscope clear."

The sun was already up. In the pale morning light, during his safety sweep, he saw a number of ships of various sizes, all some distance away.

"Clear on the surface. Check our position by GPS. Eight kilometres to RV. On course zero-nine-zero degrees, sir," the second in command reported.

The captain looked at his watch. It was 8:35 a.m.—twenty minutes to RV at maximum speed. Travelling at maximum speed at periscope depth, would leave a huge wake on the surface. Too bad, he thought, he had no other option.

"Speed thirty knots," he called out, his eyes glued to the periscope, watching for any sign that the wake boiling behind them had been noticed. The force of the water causes the periscope to vibrate. He was all too aware that it was not designed to be used at this speed, but it was essential for him to continue to monitor the surface picture.

The depth below the keel continued to decrease at an alarming rate. The depth would soon be less than 100 metres, and still four kilometres to the RV. The plainsman deftly held the submarine at twenty metres. It was a risky business. All aboard knew the dangers in moving at such high speed in shallow waters. The captain wiped his brow as he maintained watch on the periscope.

CHAPTER 37

FINAL LEAP TO FREEDOM

In the 1960s and 1970s, it was increasingly difficult for the average South African to oppose Apartheid. The government propaganda machine had very cleverly exploited the UAC's alliance with the South African Communist party so that all who supported them were branded communist or anti-South African.

Although the official opposition, the Progressive Federal Party, representing mainly English- speaking voters, were vocal in their opposition to the government's racial policies, they were too weakly represented in parliament to make much of an impression.

Besides, living standards for the average, white-South African were high, perhaps among the highest in the western world. Apart from some half-hearted international sanctions, the country, on the surface at any rate, was thriving. The military was strong and loyal to the government. It was thus easy for White South Africans of either language group who opposed Apartheid, to simply shrug in the face of overwhelming odds and do nothing.

There were, of course, notable exceptions. Peter Marshall was one. He and a small group of students at the University of Cape Town actively opposed Apartheid at every opportunity, often at great personal risk to themselves.

When the call came to assist in the Khumalo escape, Marshall immediately mobilized his group into action. No one knew why he and his group suddenly became interested in microlight flying or how they managed to get their hands on five of these aircraft, nor was there any reason why, the day before the mountain rendezvous, five expensive microlites mysteriously disappeared from the runway of the Zeekoevlei Microlight Club.

Peter Marshall was at the head of the flight of microlites as they taxied to a stop. His was the two-seater with blue wings, complete with the pendulum light attachment and yellow life jackets. Behind him were another two-seater and three single-seaters, all with brightly coloured delta-shaped wings. On coming to a halt, Marshall hastily alighted and, keeping the engine on, picked up a restraining stone to place in front of the wheel.

Giving both Truman and Philip a high-five hand shake, he wished them God speed. Putting on their helmets, life jackets, and goggles, they mounted the plane, with Truman in the front seat and Philip in the rear. This modified arrangement would allow Truman easier evacuation at the RV point. Marshall kicked away the stone from in front of the wheel and, at full throttle, they took off into the brisk south-easterly. The headsets in the helmet would allow them to communicate above the noise of the engine.

Within thirty metres, they were airborne. Surrounded by nothing but fresh air and with only their seat buckles to restrain them, it was both a hair-raising and an exhilarating experience. The wind whistled between their legs, as their little aircraft reached a cruising speed of eighty kilometres an hour.

Just then, the group of hikers who had been shadowing Truman and Philip up the neck, emerged from the shadows of the forest. On sighting the planes at a distance, they ran toward them, gesticulating and firing their rifles in the air. Peter Marshall waited a few seconds to see his wards take off safely, and then he too took off with the pilot in the second aircraft, the yellow one with the two seats.

They were closely followed by the red, the green, and the purple microlites. Having reached their pre-determined altitude of fifty metres, the four microlites peeled off in different directions: one heading for Fish Hoek; another heading for Noordhoek just south of Hout Bay; a third for Zeekoevlei; and a fourth for Muizenberg on the East Coast. It was impossible to tell from this manoeuvre who was on a clandestine mission or who was an innocent enthusiast enjoying an early morning flight.

As briefed, Philip locked his radio into the submarine's frequency, which would lead him directly to it. His immediate task was to head in a south-westerly direction toward Slangkop Lighthouse, the well-known landmark on the West Coast, at latitude 34 degrees, 8 minutes, 35 seconds south, and longitude 15 degrees, 19 minutes, 17 seconds east. At the lighthouse, he was to alter direction and fly due west over the Atlantic Ocean.

He looked at his watch. It was 8:15 a.m. The distance to the lighthouse would be thirteen kilometres, to which must be added another twenty-five kilometres for the ocean flight, making a total flight distance of thirty-eight kilometres. He calculated that flying at his cruising speed of eighty kilometres an hour, he would reach the RV position by 8:50 a.m. Flying at such a low altitude over the trees gave an eerie sensation of traveling must faster than they actually were.

***

Chopper One did a wide arc and returned to the Silvermine area.

"There's something down there!" De Beer shouted excitedly, pointing to the Nature Reserve below. "Yes, that's definitely a microlight taking off! It has blue wings. And look there are more—a yellow, a red, a green, and a purple one! I see five in all.

"It seems to me," said the major, "if the fugitives are in that group, they could be trying to confuse us by creating a diversion. It's over to you now, Constable. We have to rely entirely on your powers of identification. Only you know what the ringleader Watermeyer looks like. It won't be easy as their faces will be covered by helmets and goggles. Remember, we're under strict instructions not to harm innocent flyers."

Focusing intently on each microlight with his powerful binoculars, De Beer reported, "Major, there are two double-seaters and three single-seaters."

Which are the double-seaters?" inquired the major.

"The blue and yellow ones, but they have gone off in different directions," replied De Beer. "It's my opinion that our target is the yellow one, the one heading off to the east coast."

"They're travelling at an altitude of about fifty metres," said the major. "I'll catch up to them and swoop down ahead, so that you can give me a positive identification."

Chopper One increased its speed and did a low swoop in front of the yellow microlight.

"It's not easy to tell," said De Beer. "They're both wearing goggles, but judging by their builds, I'm sure it's not them. Watermeyer and Khumalo are both tall and slim."

"Damn, then we're following the wrong one!" screamed the major irritably. "It's my conviction that the fugitives should be heading for the west coast. No country in its right mind would arrange an illegal RV anywhere near our Simon's Town Naval

Base. It doesn't make sense. That narrows it down to the blue one. We've lost precious time. Can you spot them?"

"Yes," said De Beer, scanning the horizon furiously with his binoculars. "They're at a very low altitude heading in the direction of the Slangkop Lighthouse."

Philip and Truman had already reached the lighthouse on the west coast and were over the small beach when they noticed a helicopter on their tail. Philip released his pendulum light, the device by which he could gauge his altitude over the sea.

"It must be them," said the major. "Who else would be heading out to sea? It's a damn clever manoeuvre skimming the surface of the waves. Also, from a distance, their blue colour is almost indistinguishable from the sea. I'm going to try a low sweep in front of them. We have to be 100 percent sure."

The pilot flew out to sea and turned ahead of the microlight as low as he could. The manoeuvre kicked up a huge spray, causing the microlight to shudder violently with its wings almost hitting the water.

"It's him!" shouted De Beer excitedly. "I'd recognize him anywhere!"

"I'm going to notify the police control room and the other helicopters. We'll need backup," said the major.

"They're trying to force us down!" shouted Watermeyer, straining to keep control of his light-weight craft. "I'm going to try a zigzag course. As they come down, I'll move sideways."

Every time the helicopter tried to force them down, he zig-zagged out of the way, losing precious time.

"How much farther?" Truman asked wearily, drenched from the spray.

"About five kilometres," Philip replied nervously, "and our fuel level has to be watched.

"They're ignoring us," said Major Grobler. "Flight sergeant, bring the target down."

Using his R1 rifle, the flight sergeant fired a volley of tracer bullets out the open door of the helicopter.

"My God," declared the flight sergeant, "I have set their wings alight, and they are still flying! But where are they flying to? I see no sign of a submarine."

Captain Yakutin's eyes were trained on the periscope. The critical moment had arrived. Suddenly, in the distance he spotted a small blue object, heading directly toward the submarine. It appeared to be about four kilometres away apparently unruffled by the south-easterly, notorious at this time of the year. Both the microlight and the submarine were converging on the same spot, reducing the distance between them.

But wait! They have a helicopter on their tail, and the microlight is in trouble. Their wing is ablaze and appears to hang momentarily over the glassy surface of the sea. The submarine was in the RV position, but the precious cargo was still inside forbidden territory. They are not going to make it.

"Our wing is on fire, and our pendulum light has hit water!" Philip desperately called out. "I don't see the submarine, but we are going down! Unclip your seat belt! I am switching the engine off! We have to jump the remaining two metres! Do it now!"

They held their noses and jumped into the open sea. There was a splash as both bodies and aircraft hit the water simultaneously, the buoyancy of the life jackets keeping them afloat. They had gone down inside South African territorial waters, and it was cold.

The captain saw the pursuing helicopter heading straight for the wreckage, now clearly visible, with two heads bobbing in the water nearby. In the far distance, he could see other helicopters closing in.

By now the submarine had passed through the outer edge of an invisible line beyond which they had been ordered not to go. He was in a quandary. In a flash he made up his mind. To save his VIPs, he would have to disobey orders and enter South African territorial waters.

"Standby to surface!" he ordered. "Speed fifteen knots! Raise the S.L.A.M.! Target the helicopter bearing zero-eight-nine degrees, range 1,500 metres! Inform me when the target has been acquired."

"S.L.A.M. on target sir," said the weapons officer in a matter-of-fact voice.

The captain kept the cross-hairs of the periscope squarely on the helicopter, which loomed large up ahead and which must surely have seen their wake now, not to mention their periscope and S.L.A.M. mast. He noticed someone leaning out of the open door of the helicopter. The person had a rifle and was aiming at the helpless figures in the water, spurts of water appeared near the bobbing heads. His precious cargo was being shot at.

The S.L.A.M. system was slaved to his periscope. He pushed the red button at his right hand and a trail of smoke shot upward toward the helicopter, its police markings clearly visible. There was a huge explosion as the helicopter disappeared in a ball of flame and fell into the sea.

"Target destroyed," he said in a calm voice.

"Surface! Blow all round!" the captain shouted as he headed for the bridge via the conning tower. "Casing party stand by on deck with rubber boat to recover two persons on board! Fire at any helicopter that comes close!"

The submarine boiled to the surface like some black monster from the deep, frothing and glistening in the morning sunshine.

The captain was first on the bridge and manoeuvred the cumbersome submarine as close as he dared to the two figures in the water.

"Launch the rubber boat!" he ordered. The casing party launched the boat off the casing with two crew members aboard. The motor spluttered to life on the second pull by the coxswain, and it curved off gracefully to recover the first person.

Gently, the captain murmured to himself, as he saw the grey-headed, tall figure being hauled into the boat. The second person was recovered more quickly and both brought on board within minutes to dry off and warm up in the ward room. There was no time to linger on the surface.

"Do not recover the rubber boat!" he commanded. "Sink it by stabbing holes in the pontoons!"

The officer in charge of the casings party ordered the two crewmen out of the boat and, leaning over the ballast tank, stabbed the boat repeatedly with his seaman's knife.

"Hurry up!" shouted the captain. The officer gave a last hurried stab and then ordered everyone below.

"Prepare to dive!" the captain ordered and turned the submarine seaward away from the sinking boat. "Dive! Dive! Dive!" he commanded, as he clambered down the ladder, pulling the upper hatch closed behind him. He glanced at his watch. They had been on surface for only twelve minutes. The submarine sank to twenty metres. At the periscope once again, he checked the surface contacts, who seemed unaware of the drama unfolding around them. But he could not be sure.

He trained the periscope one last time on the wreckage behind him. He stared in disbelief. The rubber boat, now nearly awash, had not sunk. It had drifted toward the wreckage of the helicopter. As he stared fascinated, a blackened, oil-smeared arm rose from the water, and a wretched figure rolled over the half-deflated pontoon into the comparative safety of the damaged boat. Unbeknown to him, it was Jannie De Beer.

So, one survived. Too bad, he mused, wrenching his gaze from the horror scene behind him. By now, the coast guard must have been alerted to their presence, and they were at their most vulnerable. He must use cunning and stealth to get to deeper water and safety and as quickly as possible.

"Speed five knots!" he ordered. Speed at first was barely enough to maintain periscope depth, but it was important to avoid leaving a tell-tale wake. He switched to the slender attack periscope and raised it intermittently, just managing to clear the surface for a few seconds to enable him to carry out a rapid all-round sweep. He noticed with satisfaction that the south-easterly was still blowing. *Good,* he thought, *this will create sea horses on the surface to help mask our presence.*

"Increase speed to twelve knots!" he ordered. It was time for another periscope sweep. He raised it surreptitiously. He noticed that other helicopters were closing in and a heavily armed, navy strike craft was heading their way. The missiles on the after-deck of the naval strike craft with its 56-mm semi-automatic guns forward and aft were clearly visible, potent weapons against a surface target. There was no margin for error. He needed all his experience. The strike craft may be heavily armed, but it carried no sonar. Therefore, they would have to rely solely on visual detection.

The naval craft headed for the wreckage of the helicopter and microlight-parts which still floated on the choppy surface. This would give the submarine just enough time to angle for deeper water and a safe depth.

"Depth eighty metres, speed eighteen knots!" the captain ordered. The submarine increased speed and glided to safety.

"Assume cruising watch. Navigator, plot a course for our first way point of the passage to Dar es Salaam."

He had been awake for thirty six hours. Wearily he left the operations room to meet his new passengers.

CHAPTER 38

THE BULL IS IN THE KRAAL

Immediately on coming aboard, Philip and Truman were taken below to the officer's ward room, where they were given towels to dry themselves and hot mugs of coffee. They were well-looked after by the staff. Presently they were joined by the captain.

"Good morning," he said. "I am Anatoly Yakutin, commander of this vessel, and this is Comrade Boris Mamakov, our *zampolit* or political officer. My apologies for not being with you sooner, but I was directing our withdrawal from the operations room. Now that we are at a safe depth, I can relax for the first time. You are most welcome aboard our vessel, and please let me know if there is anything you may need."

"Well," said Truman with a chuckle, "other than these large towels, we have nothing to wear."

"That has been taken care of," explained the captain. "Sorry we don't have any civvies, but we have provided you with officer's uniforms. I hope they fit."

"You must have had quite a harrowing experience," said Boris Mamakov, gazing at the bedraggled figures in front of him.

"Yes, we are lucky to be alive, and I have a lot to thank this gentleman for," replied Truman, pointing at Philip. "He and his team have been amazing."

"You both look utterly exhausted," said the captain. "Let me show you to your cabin, which is in the officer's section. I expect you will want to have a good rest. I will see to it that you are not disturbed for the rest of the day"

What the captain omitted to mention was that in order to accommodate them, two luckless junior officers had been moved to the torpedo room to rough it out on mattresses for the rest of the voyage.

"After you have had your rest, I would be honoured if you would join me and Comrade Boris for dinner tonight in my suite. I'll have a rating call for you at, say, 1830."

At precisely 6:30 p.m., they were called for and escorted to the captain's quarters. On seeing them, the captain remarked, "You are looking much better now, and may I say how splendid you both look in your black officer's uniforms, as if to the manner born. Maybe we can interest you in a career in the Russian navy," he said, to much laughter all round. "Allow me to propose a toast to our two great countries and to our continued mutual cooperation."

Without asking, the captain poured vodka into four small tumblers and he, the *zampolit*, and Philip swallowed it down in the time-honoured manner. Truman sipped gingerly—he had not had alcohol in sixteen years.

Soon the main course was served. It was *Taranka*, a dried fish delicacy, the captain's favourite, and it was delicious—the chef had excelled himself. The *Taranka* was followed by dessert.

The captain addressed Truman. "Do you have a family?" he asked.

"Yes, I have a son and two daughters."

"And you, comrade Philip?"

"I am not married, but hope to marry a Russian girl."

"A Russian girl?" chorused the captain and the *zampolit* simultaneously.

"Yes, I met her in Moscow, during my recent training for this mission. I was attached to the Institute of Strategic Studies, and she was my liaison officer. She is the most beautiful girl I have ever seen. Her name is Valeriya Checkov. Now that my mission is over, I hope to further our relationship."

"Well," replied the captain, "if ever you are in Vladivostok, please look me up.

"Our passage to Dar es Salaam will take eight days. I am pleased that neither of you appear to be claustrophobic, but eight days is a long time to be cooped up in a submarine. To relieve the boredom for those off watch, we have organized quizzes, talks, and concerts. Please feel free to attend any of these activities."

"And I hold daily classes on the history of our glorious country and the benefits of communism. You are most welcome to attend. I am sure you will find them interesting," said the *zampolit*, always on the look-out for converts to communism.

"Now that we are securely away from the South African coast," said the captain, "I have to send a message to naval command in Russia letting them know that you are both safely aboard and that all is well."

"How do you do that?" asked Philip.

"We encrypt the message into a virtually unbreakable code and then send it by burst transmission using our floating aerial. It is a safety measure."

"I, too, need to get a message out that we are safe," said Truman. "My message will not be able to have a burst transmission capability like yours, but I do have a code that will indicate that we have been safely picked up and are on our way to Dar es Salaam. Simply say, 'The bull is in the kraal'. The receiver will understand."

"That will be done," said the captain.

"I must say that this is a very modern submarine," commented Philip.

"Yes, it is the very latest Victor Class, our fastest and most advanced submarine. This is her maiden voyage. It has sonar, radar, and torpedo capabilities. This particular vessel also has a S.L.A.M. capability fitted to our mast. We used it this morning to bring down the helicopter that was firing on you. If you are interested, perhaps tomorrow you might like to accompany me on a tour of the vessel."

"I would like that very much. I am studying mechanical engineer at university," said Philip.

"There is one thing I would like," said Truman.

"And what is that, comrade Truman?"

"A pen and paper," he answered, "I intend to start writing my memoirs straight away, while the memories are still fresh in my mind."

"I am sure that can be arranged," said the captain.

CHAPTER 39

DELIVERANCE

Friday, February 22, 1980

After the excitement off the Cape Peninsula Coast, the passage was uneventful. The captain had carefully chosen a route well clear of shipping lanes and taken advantage of a favourable current. Ten kilometres south of the island of Zanzibar, he brought the submarine to periscope depth. To the west, he could just make out the faint glow of the lights of Dar es Salaam. He decided to surface and cross the shipping lanes at right angles. This manoeuvre would minimize the time he would have to spend there and use the cover of darkness to disguise his identity.

Dawn found him safely off the harbour approach to Dar es Salaam. He was due alongside at 0830 local time, but he had to be careful to avoid the coral reefs lurking below the clear waters.

"Hands to harbour stations," he ordered prudently. The forward and after casing parties clambered onto the casing deck. Mooring lines were retrieved from their lockers in the casing. Recessed bollards were pulled out and clipped into position. Key personnel took over positions inside the huge pressure hull and on the bridge.

"We have been allocated A berth, the VIP berth normally reserved for visiting liners," the navigator informed the captain.

The captain smiled to himself. This was unusual; there must be something going on. *Could it be that I have underestimated my guests?* The submarine glided silently down the well-marked channel. The captain took over the con.

"Slow ahead," he ordered. Their berth came into view, as did the huge crowd of well-wishers. *It was tempting to show off,* he thought wryly, but he was well aware of the incredible momentum of their massive vessel. The slightest error, and he would ram the quay and damage the fragile bow containing the sophisticated sonar equipment. The submarine sidled up to its berthing position, slowing to a stop.

"Pass the heaving lines," ordered the first officer. The heaving lines with their heavy monkeys' fists sailed through the air and landed on the quay where they were snatched up and hauled in to be secured over the heavy bollards. The first officer secured the submarine in position. The gangplank was lifted onto the forward casing with the help of a crane. The coming ashore had been flawless.

The captain left the bridge to accompany his distinguished guests ashore and face the already cheering, frantic crowd. Philip and Truman were wearing their mountain clothes, which had been delivered to them cleaned and pressed. In their pockets were the wallets containing the dollars given to them by Otto Schtiller, which had miraculously survived the dunking.

It was obvious that this was no ordinary reception. A brass band struck up on the first sight of the disembarking party. A small group of dignitaries had formed up at the base of the gangplank. A person wearing a smart sash around his chest stepped forward.

"I am Justin Kutani, the president of our country. May I introduce Patrice Charamba, the mayor of our city, members of our Cabinet, and the chief of police."

Truman, Philip, and Captain Jakutin walked down the line shaking hands with the assembled dignitaries. At the end of the line, Truman spied Alexander Thembo, the caretaker president of the UAC. He had shouldered the burden of running the organization during the leader's long absence in prison. They had endured the struggle together. It was obvious that there was a strong bond between them. Khumalo rushed up to him, and without speaking, they embraced. This was an important moment in the history of the UAC. They had tears in their eyes; they were united again.

Members of the international press clamoured for statements. TV crews took up their positions. A mayoral reception had been planned for 1:00 p.m. A presidential spokesman informed the media that Khumalo would not speak at the quay but would instead give a press conference at 3:00 p.m. They dispersed.

The captain headed back to the submarine. He had some final matters to attend to. The crew were smartly lined up on deck in single file. They were to be given three days shore leave. It was hot, but there was a slight breeze, just enough to rustle the coconut trees and relieve the heat.

Philip and the official party had just started moving off the jetty, when above the din, a female voice called out his name. He turned. "Good heavens!" he exclaimed. "Valeriya, what are you doing here?"

"Colonel Leonov informed me of your success. Congratulations! I am so pleased you are safe."

"How did you get here?" he asked, still reeling from the surprise of seeing her.

"The colonel has given me a few days leave and organized a lift for me on one of our air transporters bound for Angola. I arrived yesterday and booked into the Central Hotel in Acacia

Avenue. Before I go any further, let me tell you the news," she said coyly, "you are going to be a father."

Philip recoiled, but quickly recovered. "That's wonderful," he replied, swallowing hard. Then spontaneously he asked, "Will you marry me?"

"Yes," she said excitedly, "but where and when?"

"Tomorrow! Right here in Dar es Salaam. This afternoon I have to attend an official reception in the city hall in Truman's honour. I am sure they won't mind my bringing you along. This morning, I need to buy some clothes, and after lunch, we can go hunting for a preacher and a wedding ring. Presently I have no funds, so it won't be a grand ring, but as soon as I am settled, I will replace it with a better one."

"That's great," she replied, "but I need to pop into my hotel to change into something more appropriate for the occasion."

At the luncheon, Philip noticed that Truman had been shopping also. He looked natty in his new colourful shirt and slacks. It was obvious that he preferred comfort over formality. Philip removed his tie.

Philip and Truman were placed at the centre of the main table, flanked by President Kutani, Mayor Charamba, Alexander Thembo, Captain Yakutin, and various wives.

After the main course, Truman was called on to address the assembled guests. It was the first of many speeches he would be called upon to make in the coming years.

The theme of his address was reconciliation. He said he would be entering immediately into negotiations with the South African regime, with a view to abolishing Apartheid and holding democratic and free elections. To do so, it was necessary to immediately unban all anti-apartheid organizations without further delay. Unless there was progress in this direction, the armed struggle and international sanctions would continue. He advised that he would be addressing the United Nations on the subject shortly.

He held out an olive branch by saying that he hoped a climate conducive to a negotiated settlement could soon be achieved. It was his firm belief that the people of South Africa were tired of the oppressive system of Apartheid and ready for the changes to come. "Whites are fellow South Africans," he said, and he wanted them to know that their contribution to the development of the country was appreciated.

However, he warned that the far right parties in South Africa were not in a mood to surrender power to a Black-dominated government. As such, the *struggle* was far from over. As for himself, he was ready to play any role that the UAC had envisaged for him.

He now wanted to pay a special tribute to a young man, Philip Watermeyer, sitting beside him. He and his team—Arthur Norman, Vincent Malopa, Sipho Nkosi, and Faizil Khan—all had risked their lives to free him. There was no doubt that each of these men had a bright future in the new South Africa. The commander and crew of the *Admiral Federov* were also deserving of the highest praise for their bravery and gallantry in delivering him to his colleagues in Dar es Salaam.

Finally, he said that he wished to reserve his warmest praise for his old friend and colleague, Alexander Thembo and the UAC high command for holding the cause together, even during the darkest days. He would be going into greater detail at the press conference scheduled for later that afternoon.

Khumalo sat down to spontaneous and prolonged applause. He was handed a mountain of telegrams and messages of congratulations from well-wishers all over the world.

At 2:00 p.m., Philip sought out Valeriya, who was seated in the body of the hall. It was obvious that the function would continue well into the afternoon, and there were important matters which needed his attention. After all, he was getting married the following day. Before he could leave though, he needed to speak to Truman and at the same time, introduce Valeriya to him.

"Truman," he said, "guess who's here. My fiancé, Valeriya. To my surprise, she arrived yesterday. May I introduce her to you?"

"Pleased to meet you," Truman said with his disarming smile. "I've heard so much about you."

"We have decided to tie the knot tomorrow. Would you do us the honour of giving the bride away."

"It would be my pleasure," said Truman. "Congratulations. And where is the ceremony to be held?"

"I'll phone you later with the details," answered Philip.

That evening Philip phoned Truman to tell him that the ceremony was to be held at 3:00 p.m. at the Lutheran Church in Azania Front. He asked Truman to extend an invitation to Alexander and Evelyn Thembo, as well as his colleagues at the UAC office.

"Just a second," said Truman, "I need to speak to Alexander."

After a few minutes, he returned to the phone. "Alexander and Evelyn would be delighted to come. In fact, Evelyn says she would like to send the bride off from her house. Also, I believe I can get the UAC to foot the bill for a small reception at our offices after the ceremony."

"That would be wonderful!" exclaimed Philip.

"By the way, Philip, I have been meaning to ask you, what are your plans for the immediate future?"

"Well, I certainly can't go back to South Africa right now," he said. "Perhaps I could continue my engineering studies somewhere else. My long-term goal though, is to buy a small farm outside Stellenbosch and become a wine grower."

"I have been talking to Alexander. The UAC has a temporary vacancy in our London office. What about it? We can think of something more permanent later on."

"That would be perfect. Valeriya is well-acquainted with London, having spent some time there as an *au pair*."

"Then it's settled. You leave for London in two days' time. Please report to our office in the morning for your briefing. See you tomorrow at the church."

February 23, 1980 at 3:00 p.m. Lutheran Church, Acacia Front

Philip and his best man, Captain Jakutin, were at the altar. Organ music was playing lightly in the background. This was more nerve-wracking, Philip thought, than the assault on Robben Island. There were about seventeen guests present. The *Admiral Federov* was represented by Captain Yakutin and five of his top-ranking officers, and the UAC by Truman, Alexander, and four other colleagues and their wives.

There was a pause as everyone waited for the bride. At last she came, tall and statuesque with long, flowing auburn hair. Evelyn had scouted around for a white lace dress for her. Truman guided her slowly down the aisle, her face half hidden by a white veil. Someone had placed a few bouquets of flowers on the aisles and on the altar.

As they progressed, Philip turned to glance at her. His heart skipped a beat—she was so young, so beautiful, so graceful. He had no doubt he had made the right choice. In fifteen minutes' time, he would be married to her.

They pledged their love and troth and promised to be faithful. The minister pronounced them man and wife. Philip kissed her for a long, long time. They hurried down the aisle hand in hand. Their honeymoon would be spent in London. He could not have imagined this scenario in his wildest dreams.

CHAPTER 40

THE FINAL CHAPTER

In 1980, the South African Government was undergoing international pressure, as nations across the globe began to impose economic sanctions. The military wing of the UAC had stepped up sabotage on power stations, military bases, and police stations. Prime Minister Bothma warned White citizens that they must either adapt or die. Foreign investors and banks were insisting on political reform as the only way of stabilizing the economy. Although important changes were occurring, Blacks considered the new version of Apartheid not much different from the old.

The government was trying to walk a fine line. On one hand, it had to convince the country that it would not be turned over to Black rule, and on the other hand it had to assure Blacks and foreign investors that genuine change was being made.

Of the 25 million South Africans, there were only 5 million Whites. Besides, the Black population was growing five times faster than the White population. Whites were becoming more and more a minority.

In the intervening years, Prime Minister Bothma, whose title had meanwhile changed to president, was forced to resign due to ill health. He was succeeded by K.R. De Witt. Ever the pragmatist, De Witt realized that Apartheid could no longer be sustained. In addition, the economy was slipping and unrest was reaching new heights. The British government issued a report wherein it warned that serious steps needed to be taken if South Africa was not to become the scene of the worst blood bath since World War II. Americans were shocked at the violence they were seeing on television and in their newspapers. It was time for a change. Apartheid had reached its end.

The South African government sent out signals to Khumalo that they were prepared to talk. Both sides promised to work together. However, the struggle was far from over. Khumalo's desire to form a single democratic government that would represent all the people, i.e., a government of national unity, attracted much opposition, not only from the White-controlled NP Government, but also from other Black political parties and tribes.

In particular, the Inkatha Freedom Party (IFP) representing mainly the Zulus from Natal, were proving a major stumbling block. Then there also were the expectations of other ethnic groups such as the Coloureds and the Asians.

Violence had broken out in the townships again. The situation called for great statesmanship on all sides.

Since his escape from Robben Island, Khumalo carried the tale of South Africa's freedom struggle to more than twenty countries around the world. The more recognition and support he earned from the world community, the more powerful he became in his negotiations with the South African Government. However, violence, strikes, and demonstrations were the order of the day.

"Our country is passing through the most important phase in its history," he said. "The passing of the old order of Apartheid rule, and the birth of a new era will be marked by trials, tribulations, and immense sacrifice."

Meaningful talks between Khumalo and De Witt began.

Eventually, after more than a year and a half of talks about talks, the real talks, called CODESA (Convention for a Democratic South Africa) began. This took place at the World Trade Centre, a modern exhibition centre near Jan Smuts Airport, Johannesburg. CODESA was comprised of delegations from the whole gamut of South African politics, plus observers from the United Nations and the Organization of African Unity. The parties committed themselves to an undivided South Africa. Even the I.F.P. [Zulus] participated, albeit at the last moment.

In one of the most remarkable events of modern times, all parties sat down to map out a future for their country. The talks were a triumph of common-sense over adversity. It was a shining example to the entire world of how people drawn from different racial groups with a common love and loyalty to a country could sit down at a table and solve their problems.

At the conclusion of the talks, Khumalo approached De Witt and said, "We are going to face the problems of our country together. I am proud to hold your hand for us to go forward together."

For their efforts in masterminding this remarkable event, De Witt and Khumalo were jointly awarded the Nobel Peace Prize.

A year later, general elections were held. These elections were held in a calm and peaceful atmosphere. South Africans were ready for change. The UAC polled 62.6 percent of the vote. De Witt made a gracious concession speech. Apartheid had truly been consigned to the past.

A few months later, Truman Khumalo was elected president of the Republic of South Africa. K.R. De Witt became the second executive deputy president. History will record that Truman Khumalo went on to become a great president, feted and respected by all the nations of the world.

CHAPTER 41

FINÁLE

February 11, 2008 at 12:15 p.m. The Dining Room of the Houses of Parliament, Cape Town.

"Well, Mr. Henderson, I have tried my best to recreate the story in the few hours we had at our disposal before lunch. I hope I haven't bored you."

"On the contrary, I was absolutely enthralled," replied Henderson.

"You know so much has happened in the past few years," said Khumalo. "Who would have thought they would have found a cure for the AIDS pandemic right here in the good old Eastern Cape. I mean no one gave the old prickly pear a thought. What a fillip it has been for the economy.

"The Africa Recovery Plan instituted by my successor, Thabo Mbeki, is coming along very nicely too, especially as the Zimbabwe and Democratic Republic of the Congo problems are a thing of the past. It is good to see our country taking a leading part in shaping world affairs for a change, especially here on the African continent."

"You must also take some credit for that, sir."

"Thank you, but Thabo has done very nicely. He deserved to serve two terms as president. I chose him myself, you know.

And who would have imagined that tourism would have taken off as it did. Awarding us the 2010 World Soccer Cup was such a coup for our country. Just look at the magnificent stadiums they are busy planning. You know, Mr. Henderson, so much has changed. It is quite bewildering. But there is one thing that never changes," said Truman pointing out of the window.

"What is that, sir?"

"Table Mountain," he replied.

THE END

AFTERWORD

1. Truman Khumalo and K.R. De Witt were jointly awarded the Nobel Peace Prize in December 1993, making them the third and fourth South Africans, after Chief Luthuli and Bishop Tutu, to achieve this prestigious award. A remarkable achievement for such a small country.

2. Philip Watermeyer sold his story to a London tabloid for an undisclosed sum. With the proceeds, he fulfilled his long-cherished dream of buying a wine farm on the outskirts of Stellenbosch where he settled down with his Russian wife and two children. He tried his hand at planting Sauvignon Blanc.

3. Hendrik and Hendrina Watermeyer, Philip's father and mother sold their cattle farm in Vryburg and moved to Stellenbosch, to be near their grandchildren.

4. Jannie De Beer recovered from his injuries suffered in the helicopter crash. He duly qualified as an attorney at Stellenbosch University and then returned to his hometown of Bloemfontein, where he joined his father's law practice. He later became a member of an extreme right-wing political party and fought vainly for a separate Afrikaner homeland.

5. General Boris Chernenko who had taken the credit for the rescue operation, was awarded one of the Soviet Union's

highest awards, "The Order of Victory," in the mistaken belief that South Africa had been secured as a client state.

6. Colonel Aleksandr Leonov turned his considerable talents to the threat and encroachment of N.A.T.O. He was eventually to become a major general.

7. Lieutenant Nikolai Petrovich Ivanov continued to work for the Institute of Strategic Studies.

8. Captain Anatoly Yakutin retired from active submarine service and was elevated to the post of Commander Operational Authority, based in his home town of Vladivostok.

9. Vincent Malapo, Sipho Nkosi, Faizil Khan, and Peter Marshall were all given senior positions in the new government of national unity as a reward for their services.

10. Arthur Norman became the South African Ambassador to the Soviet Union.

11. Otto Schtiller resigned from B.A.S.E. Pharmaceuticals and retired to live in Villa Castello, Hout Bay. He later married a Coloured South African girl.

12. South Africa was readmitted to the Commonwealth of Nations.

REFERENCES

———. *Long Walk to Freedom: The Autobiography of Nelson Mandela*. Little, Brown and Company: New York, 1994.

Review Requested:

If you loved this book, would you please provide a review at Amazon.com?

Lightning Source UK Ltd.
Milton Keynes UK
UKOW04f1202260215

246901UK00001BA/22/P